SHUNT

FriesenPress

Suite 300 - 990 Fort St
Victoria, BC, V8V 3K2
Canada

www.friesenpress.com

ISBN
978-1-5255-7510-5 (Hardcover)
978-1-5255-7511-2 (Paperback)
978-1-5255-7512-9 (eBook)

1. FICTION, SCIENCE FICTION, HIGH TECH

Distributed to the trade by The Ingram Book Company

SHUNT

a novel by

Jason Arsenault

CHAPTER 1

—

Post-op, I felt fantastic. The PrimaCore spinal implants were guaranteed to provide moderate to satisfactory relief for all types of suffering. The problem was, they shouldn't feel as good as this one did.

Weeks after the ordeal, and with no signs of appeasement, I finally opted to receive a pain surrogate shunt. The following day I felt little or no grief at all. It seemed surprisingly too effective, but the company wouldn't question such a positive prognosis.

We had all seen the commercials. PrimaCore Industries supplied these on demand and as prescribed, with already more than a billion users worldwide. Anyone who wanted to feel a little less grief, worry, or stress or who needed a little more love, pride, and tranquility would uplink those disturbing emotions, which were then released inside diametrically opposite neuro-idents. Almost all subscriptions were anonymous—for good reason. But I was about to discover my surrogate's identity.

Years ago, the industry permitted people to exchange online messages with their pain surrogates, so each could benefit the most from the other's vices like a masochist to their sadist. But ethical concerns arose when those relationships proceeded beyond the superficial. Users readily accepted the illusion that they were meant for each other as their grooves fit easily into the other's longings—and the voids they desperately needed to fill. But after the first surrogate-associated homicide, the anonymity clause was added to all membership agreements. I had ratified mine only weeks ago. At that point, I couldn't have cared less about my pain surrogate's identity.

But I did now.

I started having vivid memories of my little brother, memories that could only have come from the murderer's perspective. The images I saw weren't through my eyes; they couldn't have been. With the help of police-confiscated security footage, I discovered that my highly detailed dreams coincided with the horrendous crime. A man had been watching Bill when he went to school every morning, waiting in his car on the edge of the mall parking lot, chain-smoking throughout the schoolchildren's routine. I saw my little Bill walking past, kicking pebbles as he trotted to school. Mantis Monk t-shirt; it was the morning of his death. I hadn't been with him that morning—I could have been, but I wasn't.

The dreams disturbed me, not because they brought more pain but because I could hardly feel anything anymore. It was too inhuman. I should have felt something terrible. And apart from the shunt's efficacy, I thought I had received a little more from the service, something personal between my surrogate and me, which should not have been possible.

Could my surrogate actually be my brother's murderer? The first time I inquired about that, the customer service representative assured me that it was nothing to worry about, that my mind was connecting events that weren't associated, events that couldn't be associated. She concluded by saying they would look into the matter and modulate my signal feed accordingly—whatever that entailed. When things normalized, and I felt some palpable grief, I thought the surrogate issue had been handled. But later I began to feel robbed once more. And when that alien neutrality turned into pleasure—actual pleasure from the absence of my little brother—I couldn't accept it any longer. Another counseling session with different reps concluded with the mutual understanding that I wanted to feel some degree of grief.

"I don't want to be an automaton," I said.

"To be frank, Miss Hilt, we rarely encounter such levels of appeasement," the rep said. "Oh, don't get me wrong, our customers are satisfied, but almost never to the degree you report— let alone complaining they wish to feel more pain."

I wondered whether I was making too big a deal out of the situation. Perhaps I should have been content to find such tranquility following the incident. But I felt too unlike myself. I got a flash of when I was dragged, kicking and screaming, through the psychiatric ward. No one who had gone through what I had would have come out unscathed no matter what they jammed into their central nervous system.

The rep sighed. "Customer satisfaction is our primary goal, so I'll schedule a rendezvous for you at one of our clinics. We can lower the signal gain, so you can feel slightly more of your . . . natural emotions."

"I always wondered how you match up everyone so effortlessly," I said as I got up to leave. "I mean, there are certainly more of some types of people than their neuro-ident opposites. There must be more depressed individuals than, like, megalomaniacs seeking your aid."

The rep laughed. "It's not effortless. That analogy is used far too often to make people understand. Personally, I prefer the sexual explanation. The fact is, the algorithms are far more complex than most people believe. They don't disclose the minutia of the process, not even to us—proprietary protection and all—but it works. And it's more than just matchmaking peeves. Not so grandiose as to equilibrate psychological disorders, although that does occur sometimes."

"But you switched mine without much effort last time," I said, rather surprised by her answer.

The customer representative frowned. "We never said we did that. Anonymity aside, we can at least tell you it's the same." I felt uneasy about that. "The algorithms don't make those kinds of mistakes," she continued. "Your neuro-ident surrogate is the best match for you. Then we tweak the parameters to each person's satisfaction." She paused as a thought struck her. "Why? Did you have a prejudice in the matter?" She opened her tablet-clipboard and, after reading my previously catalogued complaints, answered her own question. "I see. And these dreams have returned?"

"Not exactly, but the texture, the memory; they were more than dreams."

The rep shook her head confidently. "The shunt connections can transfer emotional waves, subtle feelings crawling over your cognitive processes, but they aren't capable of transmitting thoughts and ideas. No technology in the world can do that. Someday maybe, but not today."

I forced a smile. "It just feels . . . off somehow."

"You're sure you want your signal reduced?" she asked. It seemed like I didn't know what I wanted. She thought I needed my signal gain elevated. But customer fulfillment was paramount, so she acquiesced. Through the mandatory checklist on her tablet, I saw her note that she thought I was a potentially difficult member to please.

That avenue being a dead end, I contacted one of my high school acquaintances to ask about ident hacking. He was the RAM-geek type who had been attracted to me. But I didn't feel the same, and things ended there. Sifting through the contact information of people I hadn't talked to in years, I finally found who I was looking for. I inquired via private message whether his skills had improved. Apparently, they had, and he could.

"How much?" I asked, my face too close to the webcam, like a noob. I prepared for the blow. Hacking surrogate idents was a booming black-market industry.

"For you, it's gonna be fifty," he said.

"For me. Is that more or less than what you would charge someone else?"

"Go on a date with me, and I'll cut it in half."

"Fuck. I'm not a whore, France."

He laughed. "No one calls me France anymore. Feels nostalgic." After seeing my glare, he changed his tone. "I won't hit on you, Jade. I promise. Just keep me company for a few hours and talk about old times—who got fat, who got rich, and shit. Nice place, no rundown low-district joint. I promise."

"Alright," I replied reluctantly. He would at least bring what he promised—if he could actually get it. Then I cringed. On some level, I felt I shouldn't delve into it. But now I was committed.

A few days later, he announced he had gotten what I asked for. The name and neuro identity of my PrimaCore pain surrogate.

Prior to our date—I flinched thinking about it—I cursed my complex emotions, as subtle as they were now. I felt exhilarated to finally go out again, though I was uncomfortable about the situation in which I had placed myself. Getting someone to hack into PrimaCore's registries had serious legal consequences. Hopefully, he wouldn't get into trouble. I also thought I might have misled Francis, given him false hope. Therefore, I dressed nicely but not too nice. He would get the hint to keep it friendly, or I would leave, with or without my ident.

Arriving at the table, where he was waiting for me, I relaxed with sips of champagne. Laser lights illuminated a stream of fast-moving steam, creating the illusion of walls between the black leather dining booths. The tables were finely polished and rested on marble tiles and underground aquariums filled with neon-colored fish. The restaurant was more luxurious than I expected, and I hoped he would pick up the tab given that I had promised him $25,000. But he was courteous, kind, and looked much better than he had back in high school, or at least he'd learned to dress better.

I could see he still found me beautiful. His gaze drank in my lustrous silver hair and piercing blue eyes. "So, how have you been holding up since . . . since the . . . you know?" he asked after awkward moments of polite greetings.

"I've been doing okay," I said. *Certainly fucking better than okay.*

"They'll catch the guy eventually." He stared at me, apparently seeing no discernible reaction on my face. "The spine shunt's helping?"

"It's adequate." I reddened and downed the rest of my drink.

"But you feel different?"

"I say fuck a lot."

He laughed. "You're joking." Then he refilled my glass.

"No." I didn't want to go into too many details.

"Mind if I have a look?" I hesitated, then swung my hair to the left. "Ah, these newer models look smoother," he said, looking at the protrusion just below my skull. "Fuses to the skin nicely. Following the whole 'Be who you want to be' campaign, they really polished their hardware."

"Looks like a mini-USB port with an antenna," I said. "Cheesy as hell, but I hardly feel it anymore. Kind of like piercings. You sort of forget about 'em."

"Then why all this?" he asked, pointing at the envelope he clutched under his plate, afraid I would sprint the second I laid my hands on it.

Despite everything, I thought he deserved at least some explanation. I sighed "I've felt strange since getting it. Can't really say for sure, but I've seen things in my dreams. Extremely detailed things, things that I couldn't possibly have imagined—about Bill's murder." It felt good to confess.

"And you think this guy . . . you think he's involved with your brother's death somehow?" He thought for a moment, then shrugged. "I think you're going to be disappointed. If I had known that was why you wanted it, I wouldn't have asked for so much. I thought you wanted to swindle and extort the guy like other sly surrogates. Or God forbid, marry him, like that couple in Dallas."

After biding my patience like a saint, I pulled at the envelope. His reflex was to stop me, but he let it go.

"You know, I really can't accept your money for this." I realized he thought this person's ident would be of little use to me. Getting paid was good, but now he felt like he was exploiting my recent loss. I could see he didn't want to do that.

I stopped opening the file and looked at him. "This was a risk to you?"

"Minimal."

"Look, France . . ." I wished I hadn't used his familiar nickname again. "I really don't want to owe you any favors, and you could've gotten in serious trouble if caught."

"Five will cover my expenses," he said all too quickly.

I counted the spare currency I had withdrawn. Barely $10,000. Unable to afford his full fee, I had hoped to barter, hopefully without my body. I thanked him and continued to struggle with the plastic-fiber envelop. Expenses, I thought absently. He might be buying from someone else too, a long list of hacker buddies trickling down specialties.

He handed me his steak knife. I felt a little ridiculous trying to tear open the sturdy paper simulacrum. The sheet was lustrous and peppered with a very curious-looking font. My eyes darted over the words, but my excitement quickly abated. I let the document fall onto my bread plate.

"Korea," I said flatly, thinking he had made a mistake.

"I doubt he has anything to do with it," he said. "In Waymount."

"You can't know that," I replied, suddenly more determined than ever to investigate this myself, despite the distance and the borders.

"I checked his background, Jade. I didn't want to give you the contact information of some potentially disturbed individual." France and many others thought PrimaCore members were all deviants to some extent. "It could have gotten you into a bad situation."

I smiled with some disbelief. "Thanks, but I can take care of myself." I took another large gulp of liquid bravery. "And what did you find?"

He bobbed his head, meaning not too much. "He hasn't traveled through the security zones of the Western Commonwealth—ever." Game over, he seemed to think.

"Fuck, maybe this really is a wild goose chase," I said. But somehow, I didn't think so. Something about my situation was unique; I just couldn't quite nail it down yet. Maybe I could get my security credentials renewed to meet this Korean for myself. But what kind of opposite neuro-ident would fit a grieving girl? And who, for whatever reason, would possibly want such atrocious feelings?

"Look, Jade, I'm holding a party, mostly punks, next Friday. Come by. It'll change your ideas."

Punks. He meant RAM-geeks: introverted software geniuses living in a fabricated cosplay universe, fitting the last century's ideal of cyberpunks. "Sounds like a sausage fest to me."

"All the better for you then," he said. Then he bit his lip, undeterred. "There'll be women too; don't worry. Brent's bringing his BFF, and she always comes with her own entourage. It'll be grand."

"Well, it might be better than staring into an empty corner toiling at the particulars of my existential suffering—or lack thereof."

He nodded.

My salmon was much tastier than I would have predicted and our date much less awkward than I had imagined. Overall, the night wasn't unpleasant, and I was glad I had come out of my hermit shell. For the first time in a long while, it felt a little like how my life had been before Bill died. But that was all an illusion, of course.

CHAPTER 2

—

Private James Heggard emptied his automatic, recoilless rifle with a smile, laughing as he saw the fear in the Easterner's eyes. But that wasn't enough. James shot another clip into the soldier's torso, sending it sprawling in a different direction than its lower half. Killing had never been so easy.

"Flinch, we ought to call you Trigger Man," Cal said, kneeling in the trench and laughing with glee as the spent casings rained on him.

"Works like a charm," James said, keeping his sight over the bridge. The military, with its free MedAid for active servicemen, had prescribed and paid for his implant. His spine shunt, as requested, removed the stubborn and crippling compassion he held for the enemy, which had so hindered his career—until now. It wasn't practical for him to feel deep shame and regret every time he pulled the trigger. Freedom had to be defended, but he simply couldn't shake those nasty feelings, his natural disinclination to take human life. Today was D2 of his return from convalescence. The spine-shunt operation had been a breeze. He felt like he had been wounded his entire life without ever realizing it.

"They aren't human," his sergeant had said many years earlier when James failed to execute a prisoner in his care. "They're the enemy." But James simply couldn't, in good conscience, pull the trigger that would blow the unarmed man's brains across the interrogation room floor. His commander had then shot the man. Hesitation in the field was tantamount to being KIA, but that had been murder, killing, homicide in the verbatim.

Freedom was more important than his feelings, James knew, and he was the first to admit he had a problem. So, he was sent on a temporary medical leave overseas to get the surgery. A day of recuperation later, he was on his feet and felt like a newborn killing machine. In fact, he was particularly enthusiastic to get back to his job. PTSD was completely absent, and he was discharged a week later with flying marks on the social integration index. A model success story, the doctor had said.

The military was quick to jump on PrimaCore's bandwagon after a closed-door licensing agreement with the company. PrimaCore, with their trillion-dollar contract, was to become the military's first and only supplier of auxiliary healthcare devices.

James felt like a new man, a man who could do his job without hesitation, without clouded judgment, able to selflessly protect his fellow soldiers and the constitution of the Western Commonwealth.

Another enemy vehicle drove toward the bridge from the north. "Check this out," James said. With a barbaric war cry, he sent two volleys of shrapnel bombs. The vehicle was thrown into the air, the concussed enemy bodies eviscerated like pulled pork. The burning jeep fell into the Oskil River under a cloud of black smoke.

"Shit, Flinch, you're gonna make us grunts look bad with a kill score like that," Cal said, laughing nervously. "Take it easy."

"I'd recommend it for everyone," James said, ignoring his friend's jovial comment.

"Sure they didn't implant you with some reckless, hell-bent surrogate?" Cal asked.

James laughed as he continued to scan the horizon. "It was never for fear of my own person that I wasn't the best soldier. It was that I felt . . . reluctant to kill, even enemies. I feared for them, not for me." He thought a moment. "Today it wasn't lack of fear that got me to ambush them. It's that I don't feel Easterners deserve to live. They're shit to me, vermin needing to be put down for their own sake as much as ours."

"Amen, bro," Cal said amidst sporadic bursts of gunfire. "But doesn't it bother you that your mind thinks differently now? That you aren't the same person you were before? Besides, what kind of surrogate would channel urges to kill?"

James looked at Cal like he was the weakling now. He always thought Cal was as grunt as they came, but this soul searching was unbecoming of a soldier. "Yes, sir," aim, and fire were all they needed to know. This introverted bullshit, this "how do you feel" crap, had to stop. He told Cal to shut up.

"Okay, okay, just curious," Cal said, then pointed over the ridge. James raised his rifle once again. After the napalm flares, the enemy quieted down a little too much for his enjoyment.

* * *

Later at the barracks, Cal dropped his rifle and loosened his camo. He grabbed a spare piece of lead pipe and banged it on the metal bedframe. "Listen here, you grunts."

Someone who had been sleeping told him to piss off, then turned on his side. The others waited dejectedly. Cal was a no-nonsense guy; people respected and listened to him. "My man Flinch here got one hundred and twenty-nine kills today. As far as I know, that's a platoon record."

"Yeah, Flinch!" his compatriots yelled, raising cups of moon-shine. Cheering the useless maggot felt a little awkward, but Flinch had, apparently, been cured. "De-pussified," his commanding officer had said the day after his return to active duty, while "de-pacified" was ostentatiously quoted in the official government record.

"Now, here's the thing," Cal said, pretending to ponder. "Can't have a guy named Flinch hold the platoon's highest kill score, can we?"

Most cheers agreed.

"Then what can we call this guy?" he asked.

"Faggot," someone said, getting a chorus of guffaws.

"Princess Faggot," another yelled.

"Seriously, you fuckin' monkeys."

"Headshot," someone said. Cal seemed to like that one.

"Samurai," another volunteered, but James didn't think it would go over too well racially. They had to stay politically correct, after all. These days it seemed that race was about the only thing people still got riled up about.

James chuckled and crashed in his bunk. He lay on his back in stoic contemplation, glad to finally be receiving some respect from his peers after all these years.

"Cobalt."

"What was that?" Cal asked a quiet guy wearing glasses and reading in a corner.

"Cobalt," the soldier replied. "As dirty as our bombs. Kills more than the fallout."

Cal nodded, then leaned over James in his bed. "What do you say, Flinch?" Cal's pockmarked face was intimately close, grinning like an excited child. James knew how trivial these names were, but since his current nickname had been received in condemnation, he wasn't particularly keen on keeping it. Brought back memories he would rather forget.

"If you can't fire a gun, why the fuck did you join the military?" a sergeant had asked him once after strapping him naked to the yard post, buttocks covered in bruises, and leaving him out during a monsoon in Madagascar. James had feebly tried to tell them it wasn't inability; he had to do his part to preserve the commonwealth. Freedom was worth defending.

Raised in a lower-class family, James never really had many life opportunities, unlike Cal. Cal could have gone to school, become a doctor or a politician, but he had selflessly opted to protect the constitution, which had made James envy him. Cal had done it by choice. James had tried to tell himself it was *his* choice, but it didn't feel right killing people as easily as they did. But things had changed. Now it was as easy as taking candy from a baby. No, it was more than that. He enjoyed depriving those babies of their delicious candy.

"Sure," he said.

"Let's hear it for Cobalt," Cal yelled, swinging the Western flag that had been hung above the door. The others cheered.

James was finally earning respect. After all those hard years, all it took was a simple surgical procedure. He should have gotten it years earlier. But lying there, smugly content, he understood how insignificant their opinions really were. He would watch their backs, and he was confident they would watch his. But like the enemy, these people had become unimportant to him. All he cared about was where his rifle pointed. And tomorrow he would get the chance to kill a great deal more of those pathetic Easterners. The Oskil River would be stained red with their blood.

His heart raced as he tried to calm this excitement, telling himself that tomorrow would come soon enough. Objectively, he realized these new sentiments weren't his own, and he wondered how his old self would feel about them. Probably awful, but that didn't matter anymore. It was a question for sensitive sissies, which is what he now perceived Cal to be. James simply felt fantastic. *Thank you, anonymous surrogate.*

God, it felt glorious.

* * *

Father Frederick Thompson looked overly comfortable on Dr. Bennings' sofa. His spine shunt was uplinked via satellite to the PrimaCore mega-computer, where his signal was sent to another anonymous ident somewhere on the globe. Inside the vast religious commune near Kansas, the priest seemed relaxed and restful, which was quite a change from his previous sessions.

"Despite my initial misgivings about the implant, I've seen enough progress to say that, in my best judgment, you no longer require therapy," his psychiatrist said.

"You're saying I'm cured, doc?"

"I'm saying that you, yourself, are feeling genuine love toward your fellow parishioner. And your violent urges have been, in the past months, greatly alleviated from what you first reported. Isn't that correct?"

"Oh, of course, doctor," the priest said, smiling.

"You've been coming to me for more than a year now, since you were caught by your convent sister performing self-flagellation serious enough to injure yourself."

"It was the best way to expiate the demons."

"Indeed," Dr. Bennings said. She wasn't faithful; she just worked here. But she had learned long ago that it was easier to interpret these religious implications using introspective allegory. Psychiatrically speaking, he did have demons. She always liked that analogy.

"Those were more difficult times."

"And now?"

"Mostly serenity," he said, his smile showing polished teeth. "They've had to change my surrogate four times, but I wouldn't have known if they hadn't said so. Minor irregularities, I was told."

That didn't surprise her in the least, but he was not within her jurisdiction anymore. He had signed off his mental health to PrimaCore. So, she adjourned the session. "As simple as that, I release you from my care." *And don't ever come back,* she had the urge to say.

He stood. "Thank you very much, doctor." His smile did look sincere.

Dr. Bennings escorted him out. Having a few minutes before her next patient, she calmed her shaking hands and thought how relieved she was not to have to see him any longer. PrimaCore had really changed him for the better, but whoever received his sufferings was in for a wallop.

When he had mentioned the idea, she had been reticent. Not for his sake; she wondered if it was ethical to diffuse those highly destructive impulses into someone else. She understood the science behind the principles, but she never could accept the idea that the spine shunts were the magic bullets everyone proclaimed them to be. It didn't inspire her to think that anyone could benefit from receiving even a fraction of this priest's feelings.

* * *

Walking down the street, Father Thompson remembered the dark days of his mind with a new appreciation. Like Jesus and his cousin Muhammad, he had endured the hard path to emerge pious. It was so easy to be sincere now. So many years of arduous faking. Smiles and praises and best wishes and blessings. He had secretly cursed them all. They had seemed so disgusting then, so full of germs and cum, frolicking in their own excrement and grinding on Satan's leg like bitches in heat. He laughed, knowing they still did all that, but now he also cared about them. Each individual as precious and as worthy of God's love as he was. He didn't actually believe that, of course. He considered the wide range of commandments that these average hedonists broke daily and thought nothing kind about them, but he felt like he cared, and that was good enough.

A member of the parish was out walking his dog with a remote-controlled drone. Barely past the laziness to hold the leash himself, the man saw him and waved. Father Thompson smiled and returned the gesture, relieved he didn't have the recurring urge to stab the worthless mutt in the eyes, then smear the owner's scrawny head into the piles of shit he never picked up. He did think about it but not in anger, simply as a memory of how things had been. That dog had defecated on church grounds and would need to be punished someday. But now he even held some degree of love for the creature. For all he knew, that was as much as anyone really cared about dogs, and he felt good about that too.

For the first time in many years, he walked without those demonic urges. Father Thompson wouldn't normally have laid his faith in the hands of atheistic medical scientists unless he, others, and the big man upstairs thought it necessary. But even with faith in the Lord his mind could still stray. So he thanked the Lord for the blessing of this holy spine shunt.

The sun was shining, and he felt truly happy. He leaped in the air and clapped his shoes together like he had seen in those musicals from the early twentieth century.

The man smiled. "Good day, Father Thompson."

"Yes, quite a nice day," he said, walking toward him. "I just returned from hearing Dr. Bennings' confession."

"She must be a troubled soul for the number of visits you've granted her."

"Oh, it's but my duty," he said. Then he leaned forward. "As she is in my confidence, I would ask that you don't speak of it." The man nodded enthusiastically, happy to oblige.

Farther down the grassy trail, Father Thompson glimpsed the panoramic view of the Fellowship of the Ardent Faith, the largest and most expensive religious commune in North America. Containing only rural towns, the sector was tantamount to a state within the commonwealth, with its own laws and com-mandments—Thompson himself being a fervent advocate of the Old Testament ways. There were no skyscrapers, highways, advertisements, or flagrant vices, and the bustle of life was more akin to the pace of the previous century than the hedonic chaos of the metropolis. Wide acres of trees had been planted decades earlier, like a swath of green embedded amidst the graying corn-fields. But what he liked best was that the population density was maintained. Admittance was dutifully controlled.

He saw the brown roof of the limestone cathedral, beside which stood the convent and his presbytery, all linked by open arched hallways. His church was fortunate to receive hefty donations on a weekly basis, money diverted from big-city businesses and turned to ascetic pursuits. He never questioned where it came from, sent off the surplus as requested from the higher echelons of the organization, but the money never stopped flowing. His superiors were adamant that God was certainly appeased by such copious amounts of currency.

Things were ideal but not perfect—the daily sugar quotas were sometimes difficult to stomach—but those who managed the convent told him they had good reasons for it. So, he accepted that as part of their duty while he had his own to focus on. At least now he could do his work with a clearer conscience.

As he entered the convent, the bright sunlight and sudden motion of the door sent a nun into a panic. When she saw his face, she clamped her nails tightly on the old wooden desk. He used to ignore Sister Bernadette, storming off to his own chambers on the top level. But now he smiled and genuinely wished her a good day. She looked like she couldn't decide which was worse.

He knew she'd noticed the change in his demeanor since his operation in Topeka Central. She had been understanding of his reluctance to venture into the provincial capital, and she knew he had done it, despite his own misgivings, for them. He had never been easy to deal with—that was obvious. Before, his face would have twisted into a snarl at the sight of her, but since the operation, he had been nice, even to the sisters. They knew what he was like away from the crowd, that the face he showed the public wasn't the real face of Father Frederick Thompson. They had witnessed the maniacal switch, like Jekyll and Hide, numerous times before. The crowd adored his grin and loved his public persona, but it wasn't the real monster he was inside. Now all that had changed.

He jogged up the stairs in rapid bounds—he had always been fit—but then paused. "Sister, would you like some tea?"

He could see she was about to protest. Perhaps she wondered if it was a trap that would invite a harsh lesson to the soles of her feet. Then she uncharacteristically agreed. "Yes, that would be nice."

Returning a moment later, he poured the aromatic brew into tiny antique cups adorned with flags of countries that no longer held any sovereignty. He sighed contently. The sun shone through the large kitchen window, highlighting the ancient woodwork dating back over a century.

As Father Thompson smiled at her, he remembered his violent mood swings and the manipulative ways in which he would get others to hurt themselves for his own amusement. The nun sipped her tea cautiously, as if his evil could have made the liquid vile. But he had steeped it carefully, and the drop of lemon made it just right. The situation seemed unreal to her.

"My psychiatrist released me today," he said to ease the tension. "She said I'm cured." He raised his cup like a victory pub cheer. Sister Bernadette smiled, her lips clamped shut.

"That's good," she said timidly, then looked down into the swirling bits of leaves in her tea.

"I know—" he started, then paused. "I know I haven't been the best priest that you've ever served with. As you know, I've had to fight my own demons a great deal throughout the course of my life. They've always been there. They were always my burden. But that's changed now." He beamed.

"Of course. No reason to dwell on the past, Father," she said politely.

Indeed, he hadn't been the pleasantest of fathers: invasion of privacy, denigration, starvation, humiliation, intimidation, bondage, and physical violence, such as lacerations, cuts, and punches. Worst of all was his harassment, the vehement flow of putrid bitterness that spewed from his cursed mouth, attacking any weaknesses he perceived in others. If there was one thing he could do, it was to find anyone's fragile center, the insecurities and fears that everyone hid, and rattle them until they shattered. He had purposely made Sister Bernadette's life—all their lives—a living nightmare, day in and day out, since he took the appointment eight years earlier. He had managed to scare them into subservience so badly that no one ever dared to confess his sins to the legal or religious authorities.

Her hand trembled. She lost hold on the cup, and it shattered on the stone-tiled floor.

Stupid fucking bitch! *Oh, you poor sweet girl, you must be so frightened,* his mind generated concomitantly. He should have slapped her for her clumsiness, but instead he reached for a cloth and sponged the mess by her feet. I'll be damned, he thought, chuckling with pride. He was showing honest humility.

She sat rigidly, watching him with the eyes of a spooked animal.

"There, there, don't worry. It's just a cup." Some tea had fallen on her open sandals. He noticed the shapely legs from her devout lifestyle, then caught a glimpse of a gun in his mind. Something carnal was working below. He felt the wave coming and prepared for the impact, the onrush that would send his demons flowing, but it never came.

* * *

James "Cobalt" Heggard's anger turned into violent spasms as he cried with inexhaustible rage. The area would become a demilitarized zone if the enemy kept retreating. He had to advance, or he would see no action. His orders were to hold his position for minimal disturbance to the economies of both commonwealths. The directive was to maintain the war zone at his location until deemed otherwise. But he got an idea, a major idea, and his dick was in full support.

Cobalt went AWOL.

* * *

"Fantastic," General McStevens declared after seeing the territorial activity report. "Arms expenditures were maximized, and he didn't lose an inch of territory. But why did so many enemies gather to this location? We—and they—thought it non-strategic."

"Um, yeah, sir. It's a little difficult to explain," Corporal Mathews said. The general raised his eyebrow and waited. "Sir, Private Heggard infiltrated enemy territory under no one's directive and found the daughter of General Natchev—she's Eastern military." The general whistled in astonishment. What audacity. "He killed the guards," Mathews continued, "captured Natchev's daughter, and bled her a little with his knife, leaving a trail to a puddle where he scrawled the name of the bridge. There, he stripped her naked and tied her on our end. The soldiers who followed him knew it was a trap. They weren't about to just walk out and get shot. So, he raped her."

"He raped her," General McStevens repeated, slack-jawed.

"Yes, sir, in ways that would make her cry out most."

"Jesus."

"They didn't want to use bombs because they wouldn't risk her safety. Cobalt knew that, although she ordered them to do so herself. Then they stormed the bridge. But Private Heggard was ready to move. His pants were off, but his boots were laced. Had a prototype submachine gun planted behind the outcropping. Tore them to shreds. Then he continued to . . . intimidate the enemy, until General Natchev himself arrived. He walked out, unarmed, and said, 'I don't have any authority to surrender or to ask for yours, but this soulless warfare demeans us all. It has to stop.' Heggard simply took him out and then strolled back while the adversaries were too dumbfounded by the sudden change in their chain of command to decide what to do. Then he shot the girl like a discarded object, hardly having any interest in her once Natchev was eliminated. He laid a snare and waited like a trapdoor spider. He said he had to hold ground, had to make the enemy come to him. That those were your orders, sir."

General McStevens shook his head slowly. "Incredible."

"Sir, don't you find it somewhat immoral?"

"Ethics aren't my department, son."

Corporal Mathews sighed without much surprise. "We had to evacuate the area. Private Heggard ordered it himself, knowing the enemy would send directed bombardment to their location in retribution."

"He was the commanding officer? What happened to his superior?"

"He, um, stepped down, sir," Mathews said.

"Can't have insubordination in our troops. That's completely unacceptable."

"Heggard just told his CO to write it up. That no matter what, his position in fifty-fifth wing delta platoon was about to change. Not risking his own skin to exact corporeal punishment, the platoon sergeant simply bowed him into acting command." The general frowned. "He sent the platoon to advance," Mathews continued, perusing his reports. "Later, when things cooled down, they retreated to the west side of the bridge with a skeleton crew to reestablish the border. That location was hit badly the next day."

"Was Private Heggard a casualty?"

"No, sir."

"Oh, thank God."

"He ventured north, so we tentatively reassigned him as a rogue tactical unit. Special ops."

CHAPTER 3

—

Officer Stacey McGee walked the long staircase leading to the PrimaCore central hospital in Boston. The business headquarters, which was also their biomedical research institute, functioned like an independent city. Unfamiliar with this sector, she walked slower than her short stature would have permitted, craning her neck to look up at the tallest building in the metropolis. It hadn't always been so magnanimous. During her childhood, the mismanaged startup had struggled to stay afloat.

Once approved for the spine shunt, she had requested to go there directly. She was uncertain why, but the PrimaCore satellite facilities, such as at the cinema megaplex, didn't inspire the most confidence. Something being stuck inside one's brain should require a more pristine setting than a back room wedged between a shoe store and a vitamin supplement shop. But confidence—in others and especially in herself—was her biggest difficulty.

Farther away on the elevated parking lot she saw a small group of protesters with signs proclaiming various religious condemnations: that putting one's faith in the hands of technology was tantamount to sacrilege, that PrimaCore was toiling with things only God could fathom and would bring about the end of days through their unholy pursuits. Stacey didn't think it possible to objectively weigh these concepts, but she knew quite well that fanaticism rarely helped anyone. They must have been crowd controlled already because they maintained their slow, circular march in the designated protest zone, far enough to make it impossible for them to disturb the institute's normal routine in any way whatsoever. Today she was off duty—no lump or ticket quotas to fill—so she ignored them and continued.

Her thick ham thighs—as the instructor at the gym had called them—forced her to walk awkwardly, almost waddle as she climbed the stairs. She felt winded but getting closer to the atrium made her feel like she was taking her first steps into a better life, finally taking control. If the NetV commercials were correct, the spine shunts would help her manage her adversity, improve her self-confidence, and control her anxiety-induced eating binges—the vicious cycles that made her cry with self-loathing. Perhaps then she would be able to find a boyfriend, to have a real relationship, to have sex more frequently than that pity fuck from three years past. "It's not that you're ugly," the last boy she dated had said. "A little overweight is all." She had tried to look unfazed by his absentminded comment, but she had cried herself to sleep that night wondering why she—unlike everyone else—had to bear such difficulties. Despite it all, she tried to remind herself that she was a good person, as deserving and as capable as anyone else. But those lies and self-denial wouldn't matter anymore if today went as advertised.

Once inside, she marveled at the unrelenting luxury of the place. The lobby held the water fountain of all water fountains, which towered, in comparison to the building itself, almost as high as the eye could see. The open-concept design was interspersed with marble columns of Roman inspiration. Everything fooled her vision with its cyclopean audacity. In addition to its amazing height, the facility also spread horizontally farther than she could discern. Moving walkways, forking in multiple directions, took staff and patients to wherever they needed to go. She felt small there, but she had always felt insignificant.

Had she been endowed with a body that was tall and fat or short and slim, she wouldn't have it so bad. But short and fat made her feel even more trivial—except to someone sitting next to her in the metro, she thought painfully.

The receptionist, seemingly occupied, turned to her with a smile. She wore professional-quality makeup, and her straight blond hair looked as pristine as a Photoshopped model. Stacey felt there were chauvinistic overtones to her attire, but if she looked that good, Stacey didn't think she would mind a little friendly harassment at work. She told the woman her name and, after a quick scan on the computer, the lady kindly told her to follow the green path. *Courteous but dismissive, like most people.*

Daydreaming her way through the maze of glass and mirrors, she lost track of time riding the walkway. To her left, large 3D screens showed a scientist interviewed by the West-Times. The scientist, named Dorothy Lundquist, looked much like the receptionist—as naturally blond as they came. "What psychiatrists realized years ago was that, on multifactorial scales, individuals fit on a spectrum of profiles, each requiring their own types of psychological fulfillments to be happy," she said. "Some require love and attention while others prefer to be left to explore their own internal worlds. Well, these contrasting individuals, for example, could be matched to expunge excess trauma that the other finds pleasant or beneficial."

The voice trailed off, then came into sync with the next giant screen. The interview, which was part of an educational documentary that Stacey thought she had seen on NetV a couple of years earlier, played on every monitor the entire length of the extended walkway. Next came the owner of PrimaCore himself, Keneth Mansfield, advertising their newest campaign. "In fact, the more members we get, the better our matrix becomes. Each neuro-ident enhances the system, makes the profile matches slightly better every time." The sturdy man, who looked to be of Indian descent, seemed like the friendliest person in the world. Always smiling, he looked as trustworthy as anyone could. Being a police officer, she thought she was a fairly decent judge of character. "The highest demographics we cater to are techophili-acs," he said. "Then depressives, and thirdly, those with general-ized anxiety . . ."

Stacey leaned her elbows onto the railing of the moving walkway, watching as the interviewer posed the next question. "When you give a person the ability to cope with their daily lives using someone else's profile, both users feel better from the exchange, each ultimately happier with the feelings coming from the other's mind. Then why don't these people simply exchange lives instead of brainwaves? Wouldn't they get the same benefit from living in the other person's shoes rather than being plugged in to the other person's head?"

Keneth laughed at the question. "I get that one a lot. And the reason is simple: because we have free will, my dear. Each of us can follow the lives we want, we now can be who we want to be. Here at the institute, we make that possible. We make it bearable for them, whereas their previous state of mind was highly prob-lematic—whatever that was. We address the difficulties they live through day in and day out. We allow them to do their jobs, take care of their families, and we alleviate all kinds of disorders these people have." He leaned back in his chair, dressed in gorgeous purple velvet. "Besides, if you picture some of our neuro-ident profile matches within their surrogate's shoes—as you put it—you'd realize the exchange would be quite preposterous." Both laughed in a very friendly tone.

Stacey almost tripped at the end of the walkway while trying, after the presentation looped, to count how many internal levels there were. Their main research department was some-where above, she remembered from the documentary. Dorothy Lundquist and the charismatic owner were probably up there right now.

Directly ahead she saw the clinic with half a dozen patients waiting within. She approached the receptionist, who, curiously, looked much like the first. Stacey told the woman she had an appointment. Stacey thought the receptionist was honestly compassionate, but when the lady turned, Stacey saw a little nob protruding from her neck and sighed. Maybe it did take brain surgery to make someone genuinely like her, she thought dismally. Then she took a seat.

A few short minutes later—about as lengthy as the walkway ride to bring her there—another blond-haired staff member asked Stacey to follow her. Stacey wanted to ask why she had been given priority over the other people in the waiting area, but instead she merely smiled nervously.

"Is this your first visit here?" the woman asked.

Stacey nodded.

"It can be a bit difficult to find your way through this fortress. I hope it wasn't an inconvenience to you."

"I was told to follow the green line," Stacey said timidly.

The woman laughed. "Yes, I suppose they've simplified the choices a great deal since I started here. Security was increased these last few days—impending VIP visit, I was told. But most of the lower levels are public access."

Stacey shook her head. She hadn't seen any security in uniform, but the place was rumored to have extraordinary security—both biological and digital. "I didn't notice."

"Manne likes it that way," the woman said offhandedly.

"Main?" Had she heard correctly?

"Well, better pronounced *may-na*. M-a-n-n-e. Dutch, I guess. Our head of security."

"Oh," Stacey said.

"We must do it differently than the police," she said after looking at Stacey's personal file.

"Different in that we want to be seen," Stacey said, but she meant it was within their prerogative to be visible to the populace. She didn't like to be seen. In uniform, she was barely more than a laughingstock.

The woman shook her head free of trivialities, then caught Stacey's eyes. "Miss McGee," she paused and rechecked the information on her pad. "May I call you Stacey?"

"Yes," she replied after a long pause.

"I'm Customer Representative Goldman, but you can call me Elizabeth." She looked at Stacey for a moment. "You can relax. Everything, absolutely everything here, will remain confidential. These walls: soundproof." She paused before continuing. "You don't look very comfortable. But the procedure is extremely safe; I assure you." Safety wasn't a concern. Shunts were reported to have fewer side effects than Viagra.

"I'm sorry, Miss . . . Elizabeth. It's just that . . . it's because, I've kind of, over the years, learned to distrust beautiful people."

Elizabeth giggled, then waved a hand to cool her blushing face. "You really think so? Oh, you're too kind. But really, your best interest has always been our leading concern here at PrimaCore."

Stacey wondered why gorgeous women always felt insecure about their looks. It made no sense. Couldn't they see they were better endowed with pleasing bodily proportions, clear skin, and bilateral symmetry? What could be the problem: getting too much flirtatious attention? It almost made her laugh.

"We always prefer a little more information prior to implantation than the questionnaires can reveal. As I'm sure you can imagine, people aren't always completely forthcoming about their reasons for requesting the implant."

Stacey nodded.

"It's in their best interest, but most people don't want to admit their faults, let alone that they aren't in control. Worse yet is when someone coerces them into getting the operation. At PrimaCore, user satisfaction is our primary end point. Others around you might get vicarious benefits through your curative process, but *your* willingness to become a member is a necessary part of the treatment."

"I understand," Stacey replied.

Elizabeth smiled slightly. "You want this procedure for yourself?"

"Yes," Stacey said, squeezing her hands between her thighs. "Very much so."

"Good," Elizabeth replied with what looked like a genuine smile, but Stacey hadn't seen the back of her neck yet. Would it still be honest if the emotions came from someone else? She didn't think so, and she had trouble imagining how it would feel, post-op. If it helped her confidence and controlled her eating habits though, then why would it matter if it was natural or not? Everything from dieting and life coaches to medication and exercise had been a dismal failure, and those weren't natural either. It was all simply too difficult to maintain. Then she would give up and binge until the tears flowed.

"You've stated that your unhappiness stems from a lack of confidence and an eating disorder, each condition exacerbating the symptoms of the other. Unable to identify any triggers, you reported that your cravings come spontaneously, and no identifiable endocrine disorder was ever diagnosed."

"That's correct," Stacey replied, her voice barely audible. Her eyes watered as Elizabeth read Stacey her own questionnaire.

The rep pushed a box of tissues toward Stacey like it was the next bullet point on the interview checklist. "Psychological associations are important to identify, but our cognitive mapping will pinpoint the pathological synaptic connections." She looked lower on the pad. "And you report that your condition seriously affects your ability to work? As a peace officer?"

"That's correct," Stacey said after blowing her nose, wastebasket ready by her feet.

"Can you elaborate?"

She would have preferred not to, but she took a deep breath. "Co-workers are always trying to be nice, to help out. They speak to me quietly, but that's the worst. It's like they know I'm less able than they are. Like I'm a goddamned cripple or something."

Elizabeth amended the information on her pad without judgment as Stacey continued, "The real problems started when I tried to apprehend a perp by myself. No one wants to listen to a short, fat, squeaky-voiced cop. Sometimes—" She fell into another bout of crying. "Sometimes they just run away. There's little I can do." Elizabeth nodded slightly but didn't look up. "That was when my CO paired me with Officer Jeffries. They said it was protocol, but it wasn't. They just thought I was completely useless. He's nice to my face, yeah, but I know what he thinks, what he says behind my back."

Elizabeth finished with a few other clicks to her pad, then smiled. "I think we can help you."

* * *

Stacey was prepped for surgery by another representative with blond hair. Her nice legs reached up to perfectly shaped buttocks that any het man would kill for. I don't need an implant, I need this girl's body, Stacey thought. Despite her envy, she sensed a pleasant anxiety, a hopefulness that things would turn out for the best after this ordeal. With a courteous smile, the nurse left momentarily. Stacey wondered whether she was a member too but couldn't tell due to the way she wore her hair.

Stacey lay naked in a sterile-looking, alcohol-smelling, smooth-textured white room. The gown they gave her barely wrapped around her hips, the strap uncomfortably tugged around her ass. Behind her a highly complicated and malevolent-looking device, with a drill-bit-like protrusion encased inside a protective plastic hood, had been turned on. A control center and a brain imager were on the opposite side.

The nurse returned with an electric razor and a facecloth. They had to shave her neck. She grew apprehensive about someone seeing the thick hairs that grew back there. But the rep neither commented nor hesitated. The rest of Stacey's far-darker-than-blond hair was tied aside to keep her neck exposed.

The nurse asked Stacey to lie on her stomach on another immaculately clean bed that looked like a massage chair. She used another hospital gown to cover Stacey's exposed backside before the doctor arrived, almost on cue.

He, on the other hand, gave little pretense to cordiality. He had a dark complexion and looked exhausted. "Gave her local?" he asked the nurse while washing his hands. She confirmed. He went to Stacey and pushed something against the back of her neck. She felt a distant pressure but no pain. "That hurt?" he asked, not seeming to care either way.

"No."

"Kay, bring her," he told the nurse, who for the first time showed signs of irritation. They moved her bed until it sank into the floor groves, resting in a precise position relative to the shunt injector. The bed was mechanically adjusted while the doctor rapidly keyed the instrument from the other side. A domed shell below the protrusion was lowered to surround her head, reaching over and around her skull.

"Okay Miss," the doctor said while looking at the real-time functional brain mapping that appeared overhead. "I want you to think of your most troubled thoughts."

"Just like that?"

"Don't move," he said. "Just think about it, the more painful the better. Come on, I don't have all day."

"I . . . I'm not sure how," she said.

He sighed and rubbed the bridge of his nose. "Fifty million new implants already this year alone, and FDA still requires an MD to supervise this process. It's all automated, for God's sake. Miss, uh, Miss . . ."

"McGee," the nurse finished, having familiarized herself with Stacey's file.

"Miss MacGree," he said, not even bothering to pronounce her name correctly, "we need to identify the regions of your brain that cause you the most difficulty, but you need to relive some of those emotions to configure the shunt properly. If you're not suffering, then we don't have much to work with here, do we? Just put your mind in a state that makes you feel unhappy—whatever that may be." He spoke in a tone that indicated he did have an idea what that could be.

She tried to remember several incidents that had been uncomfortable, but it seemed that after talking with the rep Elizabeth, she already felt much better. Not as sad as usual. Maybe she should just get up and go home—no harm done, good day, ciao, bye.

"Resolution is still too low," the doctor grumbled. "Assistance might be required here."

The nurse leaned down beside Stacey. "I'm sorry for this," she whispered. Then she stepped back and took a deep breath. "You fat fucking bitch. Even now, you're still useless. You should be ashamed of your fat fucking self."

"Wh-what . . . why would you—"

"Don't move," the doctor said. "Talking is moving. Just think about it. It's all true, I guess . . . or whatever." As the tears came to her eyes, he smiled. "Bingo."

"You did great," the nurse said, then walked over to the display. She and the doctor both commented on certain brain locations, which Stacey hardly understood. Something about connections to an arcuate nucleus—wherever that was—more coordinates and the hypothalamus, connections to other coordinates, and something about her cerebellar peduncle.

The doctor looked at the nurse. "Does this seem okay to you?"

"Oh, definitely. We have a high convergence with known connectivity and sigma value highly congruent to her pathos."

"Of course it's okay," he said, his arms raised. "I'm completely superfluous here."

The nurse turned to Stacey. "Now you'll have to stay still even though the helmet holds your head. The nanowire growths are guided by the computer sensors into your brainstem to modulate the regions we identified. Don't worry; the electrodes don't penetrate very far. But it's better we don't have to start again. Now take a deep breath, and slowly exhale to the count of ten. Deep inhale, and ten, nine . . ."

As she listened to the count, Stacey felt another pressure on the back of her neck. There was no pain, but she felt a warm tingle in her toes and fingers. Her anxiety increased as she was certain that this wasn't normal; the procedure was surely going astray. She urged herself not to move and felt shame knowing that the doctor was probably seeing the brainwave equivalence of her fright in real time as the electrical cables crawled deeper into her central nervous system. What if she became lobotomized? Then she would be fat, short, and retarded. Oh, jeez.

". . . two, and one," the nurse finished. "All done."

The doctor pointed to something on the imager. "There's a slight micro deviation of one of the channels," he said to the nurse, "but it isn't significant. The end contacts touch exactly where they're supposed to." The nurse verbalized her agreement. "Okay, thank you, and you're welcome," the doctor said to Stacey. He was out of the room before she could find her voice again.

The nurse gave her some topical cream. "Apply this around the edges twice a day. Try to avoid the circuit parts, but don't worry about that either; we always degrease before plug in. The implant contains a scaffold for your skin to grow into, heals much better than any jewelry would. But try to leave it alone for a few days. The cream takes care of the itch too."

"Can I shower?"

"Oh, they're completely waterproof, one thousand meters."

Stacey wondered why anyone would test that. The person would be crushed by the pressure long before the shunt failed.

"Those things you said," she asked after sitting up.

The nurse rubbed Stacey's shoulder kindly. "I didn't mean any of it. I promise. Sometimes patients need a little push. I'm here to do that too. Legally, we require an MD for the procedure, but most nurses here have more skills, expertise, and even education than doctors. Very stringent employment policy here at PrimaCore."

Stringent indeed, Stacey thought. Everyone except the doctor looked eerily identical. "So, he was being an asshole for my benefit," she said.

The nurse laughed. "No, he's just like that. Might need a shunt himself. I think he's afraid to lose his job, so he pretends he hates it. Besides, he's external. MedAid, not officially with PrimaCore. Manne wouldn't permit that either way."

* * *

"We're almost finished," Elizabeth said. Stacey was now an official pain surrogate member. "Brain mapping was good with very little signal ambiguity, I'm told. That data is being processed now, and you'll be paired to the best-possible match. Soon, your profile'll be uploaded into our system."

"And I can't ever know who the surrogate is?"

"I'm afraid that's against company policy. But it hardly matters. You'll have changes to your everyday emotional processes, the way you feel will differ slightly, and from that you might adopt different attitudes and behaviors. But the effects are subtle, shaded. You'll always be yourself—with your own thoughts and memories. We describe it as a type of crutch, like living with a precise type of medication that never fades."

"I see," Stacey said, but she didn't really. It all seemed like an overly subjective way to describe something that could redesign a person's mind, which designed the very fabric of their reality. It should be much more than brain regions and connectivity coordinates, she thought. Where was the individual? Where was the soul and the psyche?

Elizabeth's tablet chimed. She nodded, reviewing the results. Then she guided Stacy toward a much friendlier-looking apparatus in her office.

Stacey sat like she would in any chair and waited for Elizabeth to do whatever she did. She simply unfurled a cable from the machine, moved Stacey's hair aside, swabbed off the orifice with some acetone, and plugged her in. Stacey had been told that the shunts functioned wirelessly, but installation, activation, and fine-tuning were much easier to accomplish at this data flow rate.

"Some might assume that brain-to-brain interphase needs an astronomical number of bits, but it's rather simple electrical pulses, precisely timed, and frequency personalized, which hardly requires petabyte carrier capacities." The rep giggled—an inside joke. "Here's a picture of your surrogate."

"But those are only squiggly lines," Stacey said, incredulous. The screen showed exactly that: moving sinusoidal patterns of different colors, speeds, and intensities. A rapid sequence of numbers of a significance she could hardly fathom flickered at the bottom.

"Those brainwaves are all that surrogates need," Elizabeth said. "This individual was matched previously, but your neuro-ident is even more compatible than who he was paired with before."

"So, you just switch him?"

"The surrogate will be notified, of course. That's protocol. If there are any issues—there rarely ever are—the surrogate can have his signal, the one he receives from you, changed slightly, if needed. This computer lets me modulate the settings a little, so you can feel optimal. But from what I see here, you two have an almost perfect diametrical compensation. Meaning, you're as good a match as we can get."

"And if you couldn't find a good match?"

"Rarely happens, but like anything, it works better for some than others. Sometimes, eccentric neuro-idents need to wait a little, post-implantation, to find a good match, but with so many users these days, that's extremely unlikely. Less than one tenth of one percent of members have incompatible pairing after profiling. The surrogate selection algorithms are really impeccable."

She keyed in more information on her computer, which sent information to the shunt programming apparatus. "Ready?" she asked.

Stacey felt more reluctance than ever. Without much hesitation, Elizabeth decided for her.

Then it came, and she felt the rush.

Like a crazy-eyed, cocaine-junkie perp, she stood, almost ejected from her seat, feeling like she had just climbed Mount Everest. Stacey was on top of the world. "Oh, fantastic," she said, her voice ten decibels higher than before.

"And?"

Her heart was pumping, her mind racing, and she had an almost irresistible urge to do squats and pushups right there and then. "Oh," she said, then thought a little more. "I'm much taller than I was."

"No, it just seems that way," Elizabeth said enthusiastically, then noted a few things on her pad. "I've started you on a normal signal gain. I recommend you schedule a meeting in about two weeks with one of our reps to see how you're doing. Any PrimaCore clinic's fine. You don't need to come all the way here."

"I'm going to conquer the world," Stacey said with wide licentious eyes.

"I'm glad you think so," Elizabeth said, smiling with pride.

* * *

Karl brushed the dirt and cigarette butts off the corner of the desk, then started his ritual. Spoon, lighter, tourniquet, a glass of water, syringe, and crushed-up Dilaudid, which he kept in an old plastic bag. He placed them in a precise order, as he had done more times than he could count. His friend—if one could call him that—Moustaffa, with his tribal-tattooed face, watched Karl's polished gestures with blank apathy. Already as high as could be, he didn't seem to care that Karl had told him he had required medical help.

"Lighter," Karl said, extending his hand without looking up. Moustaffa, who had pocketed Karl's lighter earlier—by mistake, he often fibbed—languidly searched his pockets with palpable annoyance. Lighters flowed between junkies like an endless baton pass where everyone raced to outrun the crash. No one in a group ever seemed to be able to keep possession of them. Or they would suddenly discover, after a long binge, that their lighter was a wholly different color than what they had started with the day before. But Karl was still lucid and knew quite well that "Moose" had tried to pilfer it, again.

"Here," Moose said after a long exhale. He looked annoyed at such a disturbance, but it didn't matter anymore as he lay back into his void and onto the couch, which enveloped him with warm love. Karl's blue cat, Plasma, chasing some random insect, landed on Moose's stomach. He groaned but didn't move, his skinny arms dangling beside his chest.

"Scram," Karl said. Still short tempered—but much less so than before his operation—he plunged the liquid joy into his overwrought veins. Then he leaned back with a pleasant exhale, resting on Moose like a pillow. They stared at the crumbling plaster, which had, through constant vibrations from the highway resting atop the building, congealed onto the damp floor like rock-hard mashed potatoes. Beside it the wastebasket overflowed into a mountain of garbage that Plasma climbed onto, resting on an old pizza box like he was the king of the hill.

"Didn't you say you got it to stop?" Moustaffa asked after a long silence.

"No," Karl said more than a minute later. "I just wanted to stop feeling bad. Remember when I owed Eye that grand?"

Moose nodded but didn't seem to care or remember.

"Had to do some pretty vile shit to get it. Brought it to him before he came to me. You don't want Eye to come to you."

"God no. That guy's a maniac. That's why I never get credit from him."

Karl knew Moose was lying. "No, you get credit from me and everyone else," he said, suddenly looking disgusted.

Moose shrugged.

"That's when I knew I needed help," Karl continued. "Real help, not that counseling shit. 'Cause I was willing to do anything to get my fix. Didn't matter who I fucked over. Couldn't be like that anymore."

"Ya got them to remove your cravings?"

"Told them I didn't want to feel the crash anymore, that I didn't want to have to smoke weed to stomach anything."

They heard loud banging coming from outside his studio apartment, then a woman screamed. Shortly thereafter, she began to giggle hysterically until the laughter faded down the hallway. Karl didn't like these sudden jolts, but most of his neighbors were rotten incurables who couldn't be helped. Came with the low rental price, which still managed to consume most of his monthly government stipend.

"Didn't work?"

"No, it works. Works real good. In an hour you'll be cramped and sweaty, but I'll be just fine."

"Took the withdrawal."

"Eh—most of it."

"But you still use."

"'Cause it feels fucking great," he said, looking at Moose like he was an idiot. "And see this?" He raised his tattered black t-shirt and slapped his skinny belly. "Gained twenty pounds since last month."

When Moose regained some of his voluntary motility, he reached for an unopened envelope that had fallen from the cluttered pile on Karl's ridiculously small desk. "PrimaCore," he read from the letterhead after unzipping the flap without permission. The plastic paper sprang open and unfolded as he shook it. "Didn't pay your bills, man. They're gonna come get your brains—by force."

"Not my problem. All paid for by MedAid. Addicts are considered disabled, remember? They paid the fees directly. I pay nada."

"Shit, man, that's sweet."

"Yeah, go register yourself as an opioid addict. Then, when you get this special red card, you can use it to sign up with PrimaCore."

"I can just get the feelings I want, get rid those I don't?"

"Yeah, kind of. You can get the personality you want but keep your job and everything else. That's the whole point. They don't say it directly on NetV, but you can stop trying to become a better person, and you don't need to do shit. Just plug in, get fixed remotely, and as easy as that, you start to feel better about it all. So, you can keep droning on through your boring day-to-day life, pressing all the buttons that the man tells you to." After a moment of seeing Moose reading his mail, he tore it from his hands and gleaned it. "Just an advisory to let me know they've changed my surrogate," he said. "I'm to contact them if there's a problem." He chucked the document toward the garbage pile. Plasma jumped on it like it was prey. "I got no complaints," Karl said and smiled smugly.

After a few minutes of muted conversation, Moose scratched his needle-scarred arms. "You got anymore I can bum off ya?"

Karl suddenly didn't want him there anymore. "Fuck off," he replied without looking. "Don't forget, you still owe me for the last batch." Reminding junkies of past debts was a great way to get them to split.

"In good time, my friend, in good time." He pressed his nauseating belly over the armrest. "Alright, alright, I'll go see what Smith's up to."

"Yeah, you do that."

Moose stood but then paused. "You did look mellow earlier. Ain't got your usual screaming tantrums. Maybe it's worth filling out all those MedAid forms."

"You might get some pharmaceutical-buying government money of your own," Karl said as Moose walked out the door. But without a fixed address, he knew Moose's application would likely be disqualified. He sighed, then looked over the table. "Motherfucker," he whispered.

Suddenly, he ran to the door and called out to the dickhead. "My fucking lighter," Karl said with a disbelieving grin.

"Why you freakin', bro?" Moose asked, still walking down the hall. "It's jus' a light. Come on, how else can I burn my smokes?"

"By using your busking change and buying 'jus' a light' of your own."

"Alright, alright, don't be flipping," Moose said. He took out a crumbled cigarette pack, straightened a lone, rumpled Marlboro, and lit it. Then he tossed the empty pack and the lighter back to Karl as if he were a spoiled child and relished his fresh air as he walked down the decrepit hallway.

CHAPTER 4

—

France's residence was a warehouse. I had no idea how he managed to afford such a place, but I thought it might be from some zoning misappropriation, squatter rights, or that he had hacked himself into ownership of the place.

When I arrived in the sector, I thought I was lost—easy prey for night lurkers—but seeing the eclectic bunch of costumed gamer geeks, I knew I was close and followed them. The address was as he had explained, and remembering his curt directions, I realized what his weird instructions meant. Behind what looked like a bum's den with insalubrious couches, a high security gate surveyed by two cameras barred the random riffraff from access. I was to input the key code (24666), walk inside, and take the third elevator on the left. That elevator alone, among the other seven, was the only passenger lift that went to his flat. The colorful bunch of overzealous cosplayers of mixed genders I couldn't readily classify punched in the code ahead of me. Clad in dim gray pants and a dark-caped frock overcoat, I looked like the vestigial remnants of the Victorian era in comparison. Seeing them go directly to the proposed elevator like they owned the place, I snuck in behind them.

Ambiguous about needing to initiate small talk, I stepped inside and hoped to be ignored, but the taller cosplayer turned to me. "You here for the event?" He was tall, wore extra layers of eyeshadow, and was highly effeminate, but his stubbled, shaved-against-the-grain skin betrayed his masculinity. With long mascara, he winked at me like an old movie projection shutter.

"Yeah," I said, "I guess you could say that." He simply looked at me. "I'm an old friend of France—Francis," I explained.

"XP opens to everyone, and we love it that way," he said, though I didn't know what he meant. Was "XP" France's geek name? Sure sounded like one. But he also insinuated, albeit politely, that I was an outsider. Two of his friends giggled. I blushed but realized they were preoccupied with their poly-techs and not me. "I'm super flipped for tonight," the tall guy said, his arms shaking with excitement, which made me cringe. "You as well?"

"Yeah, sure," I said, feeling more reticence than excitement about it now. Was I becoming a misanthropist? I'd barely had any desire to socialize since the implant. Was that part of losing my grief, becoming dispassionate about any friendly human contact, as apathetic about that as losing my brother?

I gulped, hoping these people would be the eccentrics rather than the norm. But when the doors opened to fog machines and laser lights under techno-trance beats of aggressive nostalgia, my jaw dropped. To call the flat large was an understatement; it could have been a department store. The partygoers, who numbered over fifty, were as diverse as could be. It seemed like the only consistency was going out of one's way to be inconsistent. Polka-dot makeup, fluffy pink frills, chainmail fishnets, demon costumes, and full-frontal nudity were just as free to be as the t-shirt-and-denim Harvard frat boys.

A liquor-and-amphetamine bar, stocked and manned like a downtown nightclub, was illuminated on the far side. Opposite that, floor-to-ceiling windows across the southeastern face showed a clear view of the metropolis—PrimaCore research headquarters across the bay highlighted with spotlights as bright as the metropolis between.

In the middle, the densest cluster of "flipping" friends cheered what must have been the official reason for the party. A cluster of networked computers had been fitted—although I wondered whether this was part of France's normal arrangement—and half a dozen RAM-geeks, exhausted with sweat, fingered the keypads like their lives depended on it.

Then a roaring cheer acknowledged the victor of whatever this was. A scrawny kid, no more than thirteen, jumped with exuberance. The other code crackers slunk back with cries of lamentation. The tall effeminate guy I had met in the elevator lifted the boy onto his shoulders and paraded him around, then went off toward the bar. One of them wanted more buzz.

Curious, I approached before the next round of this obviously very important contest was to begin. Another group of geeks took seats seconds before lines of HTTP-like code peppered the screens.

"I'm glad you came," Francis said, surprising me from behind.

"You live here?" I asked, still incredulous.

He nodded, then shrugged. "Exchange of services has benefits," he said cryptically.

"Prime real estate," I said. "Must cost a fortune."

"It would," he replied.

I didn't think he would be more forthcoming, so I left it at that. "What're they playing?"

He laughed and passed me a drink that he manifested like a magic trick. I raised an eyebrow. "Only alcohol," he said. "No spike. You can get more if you ask the guy with green hair." He nodded toward he bar. "But I wouldn't accept anyone else's if I were you."

"If you were me?" I asked, a little insulted.

"Well, if you want spike, you can get that too."

"No, no, this'll be fine, thanks," I said, then became distracted by a trio fucking athletically on the floor beside a giant blue teddy bear. Two muscular men were doing a woman they held in midair; must be hired sex artists, I thought. A few people watched, but most were preoccupied with the RAM contest.

"They're cracking PrimaCore proxies," he said.

"What?"

"It's not a game," he said. "Well, I mean, it's more serious than that."

"They're hacking idents?" I asked, surprised.

"Not exactly," he replied. "Proxies are decoys, but these kids work where the money flows. Nobody cares about state secrets anymore, and with so many celebs remote-scanned nude, the fans aren't much excited about that anymore either. Idents, real internal deviancies, those are the last remnants of privacy that still exist in this world. Since the online surrogate program was launched, it's the newest thrill."

"More than to simply identify the surrogates?"

"People want to know what their friends and enemies want to change about themselves. Of course, big business has a huge interest in this black market—knowing how people are compelled or persuaded, how they feel or how they wish to feel. The values that drive consumerism is their priority. Not officially, of course, but they definitely want to know."

"And why proxies? Why not the real deal?" The woman who was being shafted from both sides toweled off, tied the cloth around her waist, then walked casually to watch the next round of code breaking. I noticed a shunt behind her half-shaved head and wondered how many people there were active users. Francis wasn't, but the more I looked around, the more I realized how widespread the trend was. Many I would have thought completely balanced and normal were, in fact, unable to cope with life on some level.

"We know they're decoys, but the *ice* is just as thick. They can't do much better than their best, so the proxies are just as solid. They have a few more tricks, sure, but nothing's impenetrable." He cleared his throat.

"I'm surprised you let so many people in on this," I said. "It would be a field day for the feds to find you all here."

He laughed. "I can vouch for most people here—not to their integrity but their lack thereof—so, as long as the payout is bigger than any bounty, I know where their loyalties lie."

"You're really not worried?"

"Oh, I'm just a little guy, a middleman with some talent maybe, but some of these punks are true phenoms. I wouldn't be more than a footnote in the legal files, if I were mentioned at all, and I'm appreciated here—or so I hope—for having parties like this."

I nodded, then took another sip of my drink. Vodka with fruit juice. Not too bad, not too diluted. Gave me an immediate glacial kick.

"But it surprises me," he said after a moment. "I thought you knew about this. You contacted me for exactly that."

I shook my head, suddenly expecting to be asked to leave, right when I was starting to enjoy myself. "No, I just thought since, in high school, you were always everyone's IT guy, that maybe you'd know."

He looked at me like I was an extraterrestrial or an eastern spy. "A coincidence," he said.

"I guess so," I replied, receiving a curious look from him.

He shrugged. "Well, I'm glad you're here nonetheless."

I wondered whether I had alienated myself from him, but he remained friendly, barely ever sneaking a peek below my collar. After a few minutes, he excused himself to join the spectacle as another race was drawing neck and neck.

One of the well-built male models—now wearing a thong— came up to me. "You want to have the next go?"

I blushed. "No, no, that's okay," I said a little too quickly. "But thanks for asking." He smiled, and his male companion, wearing nothing but a white mask, joined him to look for their next exercise partner. *Too bad.* They looked quite capable, and well endowed. Later, when I might be in a more permissive mood—albeit I would have preferred a more private venue—they probably would be spent.

I clasped my drink and, looking at it, wondered whether I should have stayed home. These people were okay, but these days I barely felt comfortable around so much exuberance. I gave myself a few minutes to think before vanishing and sat on a large donut-shaped sofa near the floor-to-ceiling windows. I swirled the liquid around, feigning independent comfort though I had little, and took another large gulp.

When I lowered my glass, I noticed a tall, archaically aristocratic woman walking toward me. She wore a tight-fitting blue dress, a long shawl, and held a classical ballroom mask in her drink-free hand. She smiled, sat next to me, and threw her gaze back toward the party, like she was excluding us from the rest—a time-out zone from all the craziness.

"Couldn't do this every night," she said after a lengthy pause.

I raised an eyebrow.

"The party," she replied. "I see you desire some attention, but you try to hide it. You want to be with others, but you'd rather they think you want to be left alone." She smiled and leaned back. "Why else come here?"

I didn't know what to say, but I didn't really know why I had come either. I felt like I had accomplished something by going out. I told myself that, but was that it? "Francis is . . . an old friend," I said and told her my name.

"A pretty tail like you, I'm sure XP's glad you came."

I laughed. "Look around," I said, noting another younger girl, pants at her ankles, being given the next ride while all around many other women, fully covered or not, were just as nice or better looking.

She shook her head. "Those aren't the same. Groupies and whores. Geeks put out. XP doesn't want what he can get. He lusts for what he can't. Like everyone."

The topic was making me even more uncomfortable, but I did feel a certain zeal knowing I had been classified as unattainable. Indeed, for Francis, I was. As for the two performers, after a few more drinks, I wondered . . . But at the moment, I didn't want to become the spectacle. God forbid if I were to attract more attention than the central event. No, it wasn't the night for such things.

Either way, after we spoke, I didn't feel Francis was so glad to see me. Something about my apparently complete ignorance had spooked him.

"And you?" I asked to avoid looking like a total snob. "What brings you here? You don't seem to be of the regular demographic—whatever that is."

She returned a smile. She had lovely lips, a wide mouth, and perfect teeth. Could have been a model or a movie star. "I came with Brent. I'm Sam."

A vague recollection came to mind. "You're Brent's BFF?"

She raised an eyebrow. "Francis told you that?"

I nodded but regretted asking.

"I would hope we're a little better than fuck friends," she said, pretending to be more shocked than she was. Labels meant little to her, it seemed.

"I just assumed."

"Don't worry. We've been a couple—no matter what anyone else calls it—for eight years."

"Fuck, wow," I whispered. I couldn't recall the last relationship I had that lasted more than a few weeks. Maybe Jack or Mink, but I could never see a future with either of them. There was always a palpable uncertainty to my relationships. They were nice while they lasted, but they were always in a continual process of collapsing, whether I forced them to or not. Too many romantic betrayals in childhood, I suppose. I had lost the comfortable prospect of becoming a mother and having a family. Back then it had seemed like the only thing to do. Now it was anything but. Hadn't I always felt this way? Or had it changed since the implant? "Longer than most marriages. Are you two going to?"

She cocked her head and laughed exuberantly. "Why? We're not homo."

It reminded me about another function of the shunts. Many people used them to switch orientations. Those who wished to become het or, more frequently, hets with too many broken hearts, decided to opt for the rainbow party life instead, believing that a new sexual preference would solve their insecurities. But broken egos transcended all genders and orientations.

"Relationships that require contracts aren't relationships that are meant to last," Sam said. "Brent and I, we comfort each other when necessary, satisfy each other when needed, and give each other as much freedom as required. It works out."

My parents had only been together for a total of six years, two of those before I was born, up until I was about four. Then they had hooked up again—for a grand total of ten days—exactly nine months before Bill joined us. Brent and Samantha seemed like a fairy tale nowadays.

"Don't you ever have the urge to bed other people?" I asked. None of my boyfriends were ever open to anything like that.

"Sure, sometimes we do," she said, rolling her wrists. "We discuss it beforehand, of course. It's no big deal. It's just sex."

"Yeah, sure, but guys get jealous."

"Not Brent. Besides, he's preoccupied with other things." She scanned the crowd around the computer hub. "And," she pointed at the girl being professionally manhandled in an orgasmic swoon. "See her?"

"Yeah," I said, enjoying the sexual spectacle more than the RAM orgy.

"She's mine. But Brent can have her if I'm not in the mood. Same with the one in the pink frilly skirt and the girl with the blood-red hair over there."

"They're yours?" I asked, surprised and genuinely interested now.

"In a way," she said, smiling. "I'm a facilitator. They pledge themselves to me, do as I ask, and in return I grant them whatever their hearts desire."

The girl being double-teamed was placed on the floor, where she lay sweating and panting for a moment. The guys toweled off again, rubbing aseptic gel on their shaved, picture-perfect genitals. Toward the bar, Blood-Red was sniffing lines of white powder. At the center, Pink-Frills jumped wildly when the next victor was announced.

"Everyone has their vice," Sam said. "I make sure they get as much of it as they can handle."

"And them?" I asked, pointing to the two sexual performers.

Sam's lips curled as she noted what she thought I might want most, but she had also seen me finish my drink rather fast. "They're hired and worth every penny, I promise you. They'll be as nice—or as rough—as you like. They've been vaccinated for every known sexual infection and are guaranteed sterile. Normally, they're quite pricey. I'd like to see you try."

"Maybe later," I said, blushing again. "But this all seems so expensive." I looked around at the disco lights and the bar patrons, noticing more staff than I had seen earlier.

"It is," she said, leaving it at that.

Francis returned. "May I offer you ladies another drink?" Samantha nodded, and I, with little hesitation, took the other. He leaned down to kiss Sam on the lips. She reached over and slid a small USB drive into his pants.

"That should cover it," she said.

I didn't know what data could have been on that drive but thought it better not to ask. XP departed, dancing awkwardly to the music, and joined the event groupies cheering the next race.

She turned to me. "Brent's much better than XP, but no one's going to say that straight up. Brent finds the money to front the party, and, well, since he's mine, this is pretty much mine too. I do the human logistics, and XP covers the infrastructure. It's a nice little web we weave. And everyone has their place." She smiled smugly while looking at the people enjoying themselves. "Everyone . . . except you."

"Me?" I said, surprised. "I just thought it a better idea than staying home alone staring at an empty corner, pondering my existence. I'm just a designer—clothing." I didn't feel so welcome there anymore, but Samantha didn't display any signs of distress. She was pondering something.

"There are several, let's say . . . sensitive information packets here. We wouldn't want names and faces to be associated with what goes on here. Do you know what I mean?" Her expression turned more serious than before, but I could only shrug. In truth, I didn't know much about how things worked there anyways. Samantha stared at me with what looked like covetousness. "On meds?"

"No. Well, not really." I turned toward the elevators and flicked the flexible TPE antenna. Like a miniature dildo, I thought.

"Oh?"

"I was grief-stricken. My brother was . . . murdered a few months ago."

Sam straightened fast, spilling some of her drink. "That's terrible."

"No, it's fine," I said, then shook my head. "I mean, no," I added and sighed. "I don't know what I mean. It's definitely not fine. But I'm . . . coping."

"If you needed one of those, it must have been tough."

So many people were using spine shunts that her comment seemed outdated. How old was she? Barely a few years my senior, I would have guessed.

"Yes, it was."

"You know who your surrogate is?"

I nodded. "Paid Francis to get the ident."

"How much?"

I waved it off. I didn't feel like disclosing, fearing it would be ludicrously too high or too low.

"Anything exploitable?" she asked.

"It's not about that," I said, recalling the dreams. "I seem to have gotten something a little too personal."

Sam looked like she wanted to know, but instead leaned back on the sofa. "Now your pathos can be bartered online," she said with a wink.

"I never thought about that," I said, looking over the scrolling lines of code projected on the central screens. "But why would anyone want to know mine? I'm nobody."

"No one is a nobody to everybody. But some are definitely more important than others."

I frowned, but ultimately, I didn't care too much. Of course, anyone would be sad about losing their little brother, but it wasn't anything profitable, like deviant sexual urges or racism, which could be blackmailed. My dilemma was excusable.

"There's at least one person who knows." Sam craned her chin toward Francis, who returned a cumbersome smile from afar.

"He looked into mine?" I asked, more surprised than I should have been.

Sam leaned in closer and smiled. "You paid him to." Her breath smelled of strawberries, liquor, and a hint of potent alkaloids. But this was a bitter revelation. I realized Francis had to decode my ident to get info about my surrogate's. "It's a circuit. He needs to hack into the output before he can discover the input. President Alan Elsmutt Bouquets," she added, the name sounding vile coming through her mouth, "has half a dozen registered idents under his name, proxies for each, and enough non sequitur information to make the geeks chase shadows well past the next election campaign. He wants his rivals to get misinformation, if he even needs a shunt at all."

"I didn't know things were so convoluted."

"When idents are so profitable, Miss Information beds them all."

I thought about that for a moment. "Then how can Francis— XP—know he's gotten the right information?" I asked. Maybe he made a mistake.

Sam looked me over from head to toe. "In your case, I wouldn't have much doubt." Feeling a little insulted, I reminded myself that I was a nobody.

A short, dark-skinned guy wearing fancy lapels walked over and kissed Sam. He had a curious racially indiscernible appearance, looking both Ethiopian and Scandinavian, mesmerizing and elegant. "Brent, this is my lovely new friend, Jade," Sam said.

Surprised that such a short man was romantically involved with Samantha, who was so tall, I paused but then reached out.

"Enchanté mademoiselle," he said, then kissed the back of my hand.

"Such a gentleman," Sam added.

He whispered something to her in a language that wasn't English or French, then returned to the party. Sam didn't react at first, but then she frowned and bit her lip, as if thinking things over. Then she did a peculiar double take and looked me up and down again. "Jade, I'm afraid our evening might be cut short, but before we part ways, I must request that you join my entourage."

I was shocked. "But I don't need a job," I lied. "Not at the moment anyway."

Samantha didn't look like someone who would easily take no for an answer. "Circumstances might soon differ," she said. Out of her tight dress, she manifested a digital business card, the type that wirelessly connected to URLs, and gave it to me. The shimmering hologram overlay displayed a voluptuous body that I thought was hers, framed without a head, and armless like the Venus de Milo. If it were her, she had nice tits, I noted enviously. Her company had no name but that of her silhouette. Sam looked back, winked, then walked away.

Thinking things through, yet not knowing exactly what her proposal entailed—a deal with the devil if I had ever heard one—I was about to finish my drink when I heard a harmless-sounding pop, like a dislodged champagne cork but different. I was startled but thought it a normal part of the festivities, until someone screamed, and several people raced for the elevators.

Sam must have known it was going to happen, but she was nowhere to be seen. The music stopped, and the lights came on. Someone at the computers was royally pissed—bashing his fists on the keyboard—then decided to leave too. Still stunned, I looked around like a disconnected observer and saw a body toward the other end of the floor. Blood was spreading steadily from where his eye had been, everything turning tranquil as partygoers disappeared with orderly haste.

I felt curiously drawn to the corpse, like it was the most fascinating thing in the world. But this wasn't part of the evening, and everyone—those with more human compassion than me—scrambled to get away from the horrible tragedy. The person on the floor, I realized all too slowly, was the tall, effeminate man with whom I had arrived.

"Come on." Francis, who thought I was in a daze, shook me. I simply felt everything was inconsequential, comfortably apathetic like I mostly felt every day since the operation. "We have to leave—now." He grabbed me while I held on to my drink, trying to not spill it. The floor became completely empty save for the dead man.

We went into another room behind the bar, where I saw a smaller freight elevator. Like clockwork, one of the last flippant RAM-geeks walked in without so much as a word exchanged. We headed down. More intrigued than frightened by the situation, I didn't know what to say, so I only observed. Francis was freaking out and pulling at his hair. "Informant," he said.

I looked at him with wide eyes, then followed him out of the elevator. The others darted away once the door opened to the street level. Francis tugged at me. In the distance I heard emergency-response vehicles approaching, but I couldn't see them yet. He pulled me away from the building and far across the lot. Then he paused, drew his poly-tech, flipped across various functionalities, and looked up. The illuminated top floor of the building exploded. Bright shards of glass rained down like snowflakes.

Like an idiot, I smiled at the pretty, shimmering lights.

CHAPTER 5

—

Corporal Mathews entered swiftly, standing tall like he had in the Oval Office. This meeting, he was told, was as significant as a presidential visit. They required PrimaCore's cooperation. Alpha priority. As he was about to greet the CEO, he noticed the incredibly alluring legs of Mansfield's secretary, who had escorted them inside. Oddly, he hadn't noticed them earlier. His attention must be fading, he thought.

The youthful lady bowed and walked over to the dark-skinned man wearing a purple velvet suit. His eyes looked wide and energetic, and his lips curled into a smile.

"Good evening, gentlemen," Mansfield said. "Please sit down."

"Yes, Mr. President," the corporal replied, nodding to his officers to do the same.

"Keneth. Call me Keneth," Mansfield said with a laugh. "I'm *a* president, not *the* president."

"Not yet," the tall lady wearing the dark silk skirt whispered proudly.

"Eh—yeah, Keneth. My apologies. Our superiors treat you as a state dignitary." Mathews coughed and cleared his throat. Radioactive dust often destroyed the pulmonary system. "I'm Corporal Mathews. This is MedCom Specialist Beckers and Military Intelligence Specialist Petterson." They nodded in turn. "I wouldn't wish to make things more contrite," he said, then caught the woman's gaze. She was appraising him but not for his looks. He felt suddenly threatened and cornered, like in the trenches. But how, from her? The CEO and his secretary giggled at his comment—or his reaction; he wasn't sure.

Keneth waved his hand dismissively. "May I offer you refreshments?"

"Water's fine, thank you," Mathews answered for all three of them. Then he noticed what was bothering him. "You're not the same woman who escorted us from the first floor to the elevator, then to the office here."

She giggled again but more demurely.

"He's an attentive one," Keneth told her.

"That was Amanda," the woman said. "We switched."

Mathews found that very curious. He had not seen the exchange, but they were both stunningly beautiful and indistinguishably blond.

"Can't I choose candidates based on looks?" Keneth asked. "That old equity law's been repealed. Besides, I don't work well with men. They're lazy and piss me off. Women," he leaned back and locked eyes with her, "they can be excused."

"It has advantages," she said.

"Manne could be a great secretary, but she has other duties within my organization," Keneth said, introducing her.

"Such as security," she added.

"But when?"

"After you deposited your weapons in the lobby. I'd rather not say where," she replied. "You can fantasize about that on your own."

Keneth laughed for a moment, then turned serious. "I hope this isn't a problem, gentlemen."

"No, sir," Mathews replied. "We're here strictly on business. Office proclivities are a municipal HR responsibility." He paused to clear his throat. "The change came as a sudden distraction is all." From her firm muscle tone, he realized she was most likely quite capable, but there was something fervently menacing about her he couldn't quite pinpoint, like a hungry predator staring at her next meal. Her lips curled slightly as if she knew what he was thinking.

The CEO patted her back. "Manne is indeed multi-talented."

"I'm sure," Mathews said. But they had no reason to fear or be feared. Just stooges, really, he thought sardonically. Any vendetta toward the military would be aimed higher up.

"So, why come all the way to me?" Keneth asked. "I'm sure our reps can answer most of your questions regarding the collaboration we have. MedAid covers your active soldiers who qualify. You're happy, we're happy."

"Yes indeed, sir—eh, Keneth," Mathews began. "As we mentioned in our last briefing, one particular candidate, uh, Private James Heggard, has exceeded all expectations. We've seen drastic improvements in his fighting capabilities, his willingness—hell, his entire physical performance jumped three points. That's almost unheard of, even with anabolic steroids and large doses of amphetamines. And we're talking about a mental-only change here. Whatever feed he's receiving, it's . . . it's phenomenal."

"Excellent to hear. We've seen individuals receive renewed energy, which has made them more physically active."

"Indeed. But more of this feed is what we need."

"Neuro-ident surrogates are confidential," Keneth said halfheartedly.

"Well, we have ways of finding out," Mathews said, "but that's not the point. We'd like to replicate the feed into multiple fighting units, essentially commercialize that surrogate's neuro-ident profile."

Keneth cringed, then touched a panel on his desk. Mathews foresaw a trapdoor springing open below his feet. Instead, a voice came from Keneth's desk. "Yes, boss?"

"Hi, Charlene. Can you tell if Dorothy is still in her office? If so, send her up."

"Certainly, Mr. Mansfield." There was a short pause. "She isn't there now, but she often works late in the lab on Tuesdays. I'll page her to come right up."

"Only if it isn't an imposition. She's very dedicated."

"Certainly, boss."

"What you ask is not so simple," Keneth said, redirecting his attention to Corporal Mathews. "I called for someone who understands these things much better than me." He paused to think for a moment. "Apart from the doubtful feasibility of it all, I must also remind you that my public image is not at its apogee with the knowledge that we are business partners. It's difficult for me to go past supplying pharmaceutical implants to the military—at reduced rates, mind you—to alleviate psychological distress. Not just in the West. We also have over two hundred million users across your fluctuating border. They aren't in the least happy about it, I can assure you."

"The whole 'Support Your Troops' Pharmaceuticals' banner might have helped," Mathews said, "but I'm certain our financial investment will far outweigh any potential loss your company might encounter due to public outcry—from either side of the war zone. Reports today indicate that Propaganda Industries is on the rise, and our own entrance rates increased eight percent from last year. Meaning public support for the military is at a five-year high and growing."

"But not to alleviate disorders. You're talking about enhancing, weaponizing the technology," Keneth said with a clenched fist. He shook his head.

The war was sustained only to keep both sides' economies at full-steam. A war that made little headway while both governments, for decades, proclaimed victory inevitable, fighting over insignificant skirmishes, all the while, slowly devastating Eastern Europe as the national lines danced back and forth like an obliterating wave. No wonder propaganda investments were so necessary and omnipresent on both sides.

Keneth took a deep breath. "Even if we remained confidential, test cases, plausible deniability for us—it's not that. We've considered multi-channel links, double surrogates, feed-splitters, but nothing works. Only one to one. It's not the technology that's the problem; it's the human brain."

Just then, someone knocked once, and the door opened. A woman entered briskly. She looked at Manne, who was standing beside Keneth, then stopped at the other end of the table. She observed the three military officers with indifference. Curiously, she also looked like Manne: tall and slender with long blond hair. She stared at Manne while Keneth spoke.

"Dorothy, this is Corporal Mathews and company from the DOD. He was just asking me about replicating a neuro-ident for mass distribution. Might you enlighten him?"

She shook her head. "No, that's not how it works."

"You can't send a signal to more than one person?" Corporal Mathews asked.

"While the signal is transmitted wirelessly, the circuit is biological," Dorothy said. "It only works one to one."

"Why is that?"

"If you plug in only one contact prong in an electrical socket, what happens?"

He shrugged. "Nothing much."

"Electricity flows in a circuit. You need a direction for the electrons to flow. Both poles are required for something to be turned on. The mind works according to similar mechanisms. Thoughts flow in a circuit of wave patterns." She looked at Manne again, then took a deep breath. "Say you see a nice piece of ass. Your visual cortex records the curves, which are compared from memory in your hippocampus and cerebral cortex. The hippocampus analyzes the recognition, confirms it's the best you've ever seen, and triggers higher cortical functions associated with sexual procreation. It sends signals to your amygdala and hypothalamus, elevating core reproductive instincts, your stress response, blood pressure, etcetera. This elicits your nucleus accumbens and nigrostriatal regions, where you begin to anticipate potential pleasures. The signal goes back to your hippocampus till you covet what you see but can't have. It receives continued input from your visual cortex, reinforcing your previous circuit till you potentiate your own male bravura and make a move or tuck your tail and run—fight or flight—and hope she doesn't find you alone at night. 'Cause that one, oh boy, you should be happy she's out of your league."

Manne smiled. Keneth looked like he thought Dorothy's speech might have been slightly askew.

There must be some history between the two girls, Mathews speculated.

"Ladies, ladies, please behave," Keneth said.

"Thoughts are never static," Dorothy continued, looking straight at Mathews now. "They always flow. Circuits stop when you're dead. It's also the reason there's no center in the brain that's responsible for consciousness, self-awareness, what some would call a soul. The sentient entity, the person, is born out of the complexity of these networks. All we can do is modulate some of those pathways in a highly precise manner, then both brains work in conjunction with each other. One gets a slight boost of whatever socially prone behavior one wishes to have, depending on the imbalance and each other's neuro-ident profile, alleviating anything from depression to nervous ticks—"

"I think our friends understand," Keneth said, tapering her speech.

"But why couldn't you, say, link patient A to B, then patient B to C, then patient C to A?" Mathews asked. "Both B and C would be connected to A, n'est-ce pas?" He had done some homework.

Dorothy shook her head. "No, A would send to B, but A would only receive from C, meaning only one of them would receive the feed from A. It needs to be balanced." Specialist Petterson, sitting on Mathews' right, nodded in agreement.

"We've modeled tripartite surrogates in the past," Keneth said. "Maximizes the potential connections, but all pilot subjects aborted."

"The sustainability of the field never lasted more than forty-eight hours," Dorothy added.

"Then what?" Mathews asked.

Dorothy looked back at Keneth. He obviously held the final decision on confidentiality. "Very unpleasant sentiments for all involved," the CEO said.

"What if you had two identical profiles, both at half feed, going into one surrogate?" Petterson asked. Mathews was instantly curious about the answer.

"If they were perfectly matched and no imbalance occurred, the . . . twins would only get partial aid or none at all. It might be okay for the individual compensatory surrogate, but it might be suboptimal for the twins. And like all other triplicate connections, there's always someone going off on a tangent. But let's be realistic here. No two profiles are identical. Not even clones, *if* they were even legal."

"What if we don't want to use it for treatment?" Petterson asked. "Say the side effects are what we're after. Wouldn't it be possible to protect one neuro-ident but pair a couple, or a sequence of couples, that are surrogate matched onto the feed of the protected neuro-ident? Meaning A is connected to B, and it's a stable match, then you add C and D attached to A. Technically, assuming this works, you could then add matching E and F and so on. They all would receive A's boosted feed, but A wouldn't be compromised since each new pair would be normalized already. What about that?"

Dorothy and Keneth's eyes met before he raised a finger for patience. Then he said a single word: "Hydra."

Dorothy twirled her eyes. "It's an experimental project that still isn't through troubleshooting, but you are correct that, in theory, it could work." She clicked on the table's computer screen. Then the digital interphase model of the Hydra configuration appeared as a 3D hologram over the table.

"It was a way to address the martyr issue," Keneth explained, "where one person could sacrifice his or her own happiness in order to accept the wide range of negative feelings from others, linked, like you mentioned, in a hydra array. And while this martyr would be suffering quite dearly, I assure you, it would enable a group of people to be happier, on average. We realized many years ago that neuro-ident profile demographic imbalances do exist, and one way to potentially deal with that is Project Hydra. Some might choose to endure intense discomfort, if adequately recompensed, knowing they would be making the world a better place."

"So much for confidentiality agreements," Dorothy whispered.

"Don't worry, dear. Manne incapacitated their recording devices," Keneth said. "If they had any to begin with," he added quickly. "But we're still years away from instating a functional array."

"Perhaps we could help move things along," Mathews suggested. "Say, substantial government interest. Grants allocated to accelerate research projects."

Dorothy's eyebrows rose. There was no question that the project titillated her, but she had to be wondering what the military industrial complex was ready to do with such technology. Mathews knew that as long as they could maintain public support to continue the war, the tax money would keep coming their way, and his CO would remain happy. But he could see from the dark expression in her eyes that weaponizing spine shunts was not what she had signed up for.

"Anything else?" she asked defiantly.

"No. Thank you, Dorothy."

"See you later, gentlemen," Dorothy said with uncharacteristic joviality. Keneth frowned, but then he noticed something and smiled. "Well played, girls," he whispered.

When they turned, Manne was gone.

"What?" Mathews exclaimed. "Where did she . . ."

Keneth shrugged. "She has her own responsibilities. Besides, it works better when I don't know what she plans. Otherwise, she would have to take that into consideration too."

"You're sure you're not the president of the Western Commonwealth?" Petterson asked.

Keneth let out a hearty belly laugh, but Mathews was quick to set his officer straight. "Come on, no high treason on my shift. Jesus Christ."

After a few moments, Keneth sat up straight, staring at him.

Mathews cleared his throat again. "So, have we got a deal?"

"For now, you can tell your chain of command we have a deal," Keneth said.

Mathews reached out his hand, but Keneth shook his head. "This isn't the kind of deal men shake on."

Mathews nodded and withdrew. "Then good day to you, sir."

"I shall escort you out," Manne said, now standing behind them. Mathews urged himself to be vigilant regarding this woman.

"She has a cloaking field," Petterson said. "I didn't see it for certain, but it's the only way."

She put a finger to her lips and playfully shushed him.

"Can I see?" he asked, leaning toward her.

"I wouldn't try that if I were you," Keneth said. "She's more than able to take care of all three of you, I assure you."

They had hardly seen her move, but she had disappeared and returned without anyone noticing. Petterson nodded apologetically. "Oh, sorry. It's only professional curiosity." He leaned toward his commanding officer. "It must be just as good as or even better than our best models," he whispered.

"You need a special physique," she said as she ushered them, still chattering, out the door.

Midway toward the elevator, she silently switched with Amanda again, who walked them to the lobby. Only once they were there did Beckers, who hadn't found much to say prior to that, point out the switch with a hearty chuckle. Mathews, on the other hand, felt a chill run down his back. He thought he had been watching her. Also, he wondered what the two girls could have been discussing outside the office before Manne returned to escort them out.

* * *

High above, Manne walked toward Keneth, who was looking out at the bay, and kissed him warmly.

"Was that little display necessary?" he asked.

"I believe so, yes. The one named Petterson tried to sneak in weapons using two different approaches. Possibly just to test our security, but I couldn't be certain."

Mansfield did not seem bothered by that. "So, now they believe we also have cloaking technology." He sighed. "You and the girls are okay?"

"Yes, we're fine. We were worried for you, that's all."

"Dorothy seemed upset."

"She might have felt irritated that you interrupted her work," she lied, then leaned into him, at ease. "She's always eager to please you, you know. She would have come no matter what she was doing."

He reflected on that for a moment. "I'll endeavor to be more considerate of her lab time."

"I'm certain she would appreciate that."

"I could make it up to her upstairs."

Manne smiled. "She would appreciate that even more."

CHAPTER 6

—

I woke and saw myself. Eyes open like a deer in the headlights, I looked upon my startled face. Dangling above were two shiny appendages, wobbling with frantic urgency. At the end were reptilian hands with long gray nails. Some strange creature had invaded my bedroom.

The voice came out robotic, without inflection, and was distorted, like a radio broadcast from horridly antiquated TV speakers. "We have come from Uranus to gather human brains, but we see you have none," it said with added buzzing noises.

Groggy and dazed, I recoiled before I fully discerned the figure, a small shape that was my little Bill in a costume. Long flexible aluminum air ducts covered his arms like rickety tentacles, onto which he had glued gelatin-filled alien-hand gloves. His body was covered with duct-taped fiberglass car parts. A welder's mask—probably pilfered from Dad's shop—shields his face, on which he had glued his voice-modulating speakers. He had a talent for that kind of thing, I remembered proudly, but I would never admit it.

What is this? This can't be. Why am I in my old room at my mother's?

"Jesus Christ," I heard myself say as I turned and dove face first into my pillows. "I told you never to come in my room," I said, rubbing my eyes.

This isn't real. It all happened before. At least it's not the murderer again. But somehow, this feels infinitely worse.

No matter how much I urged myself to move, everything was happening exactly the same, immutable and irrevocable. If this were another dream, it was a nightmare from which I couldn't wake.

Bill made vomiting sounds and pretended he was going through a system crash. He had done that bit before. Shaking his body and trembling the long flexible arms, he went into panicked seizures, wailing the robotic voice like a siren. Then pieces fell off one by one as he twisted and turned. The robot suit fell, and the little human within, wearing only underwear, walked leisurely out of it to become the little brother that I knew. It made me smile to see him do it, but I didn't want him to know that. It would only invite more of these intrusive little shows. Prodigiously gifted for his age, he would become a great creature actor in the future, if his talents were properly stimulated.

What future? He would have been great, but that's all gone now. God, why do I have to live through this again?

"Why not, Jade?" Bill asked. "You're not porking any boys. You're too cold and bitchy."

"Shut up, you little turd," I yelled, then threw a pillow at him.

He ducked and made exaggerated ninja moves. "Mom said you have to bring me to school," he said.

"You know the way," I replied, then returned to the cool spot under my pillow.

"Mom said when you say no to tell you 'You're a lazy ass, and you can find your own apartment then.'"

I sighed long and hard. "Why can't you go by yourself?"

"Bunch of creepy fucks."

He made me laugh. "Where'd you learn to talk like that?"

"Eagle News."

I couldn't tell if he was being honest or satirical. "Stick to Mantis Monk. That Eagle shit'll rot your mind."

He knew. On some level, he already knew that fucking creep was after him. Bill must have told Mom. That's why she was worried. But I was too full of myself to notice, too full of my own insignificant worries to listen, to actually listen to him. Such a shitty sister. Such a perfect role model for this broken world—because everything I touched turns to shit.

He made more robot noises, then, like he was counting coup, ran up and slapped me on the forehead. "Jesus, you're such a turd," I said. "Why can't Mom bring you?"

"She starts downtown at six. Jeez, don't you ever listen?" Recently, our mother had accepted a new government job. She had to take public transit, which required her to leave at least two hours before work started.

"Right . . ."

"You wakin' up?"

I sighed long and hard again. "Fine. Get dressed, turd, and get your shit. And get all this crap outta my room."

Just snooze a little more till he gets back. I pulled the warm blankets over my head. The morning drowsiness took me almost immediately. Less than thirty seconds after Bill left the room, I was snoring again.

Wake up, you shit.

I tried to scream as I saw myself become a hopeless junkie to my slumber. I saw it like I was floating above my own life, detached of any responsibilities and the horrors that ensued. But that morning, I never got out of bed.

Bill arrived minutes later, his schoolbag packed, eating a Pop-Tart. Green shirt of that dreaded cartoon show that I reminded him of. *Mantis Monk and the Magnificent Mandibles.* So much cheese should never be allowed on a single shirt. He stood in my doorway, not saying anything, crumbs of blue frosting falling beside pieces of his robot costume. When he finished eating and saw I hadn't stirred, he sighed, then walked down the stairs and out.

Get up! You piece of shit sister.
I tried to yell, but no sound came.
Bill is gone. Bill is gone forever because of you.
That day, with no further interruptions, I slept till noon. Then I woke and cursed his name, pissed at seeing the mess still there. I kicked his gear out into the hallway like it was trash.

His body was about to be found behind a dumpster.

* * *

I awoke in my apartment, sweaty and shaking. My pulse was racing, anxiety just about choking me. But then it flushed away. All the pain and horror of that terrible day drained from me, downloaded to the mega-computer, then into whatever sick weirdo that needed such sorrow. My breathing became calmer, the pain a distant memory. His murder a simple fact, like the digits of my social security number, no more or less exciting than the explosion from the other night or the delectable salmon from my date with France.

You're too cold and bitchy, Bill's high-pitched voice said in my head.

I couldn't help but remember how I had treated him. How incredibly bad I had been to him. I was worse than cold and bitchy. I had been a piece of human scat. Now I hardly felt human at all.

I had seen myself in that visor. I was the alien robot now, neurochemical opiates drowning my sorrows. I tugged at the covers and flipped my pillow, finding that nice comfortable freshness underneath, and dozed off without a care in the world. No one would intrude on my sleep today, and I relished that certainty with cold comfort.

CHAPTER 7

—

Stern banging roused Karl from his puddle of saliva on the couch where he had passed out. Someone at the door? Still dazed from his last dose, he edged toward the peephole. No one there. Could someone be hiding? He checked his poly-tech and saw no expected visit. But someone definitely wanted him to open the door. He was just wondering whether the police were permitted to use covert force when, alas, someone kicked in his door, and two officers entered with weapons drawn. Plasma darted out of the flat between the fat lady cop's legs.

Shit.

They were looking for Moose, he learned once he was sprawled on the floor, cold metal pressed against the back of his head. Moose had probably given them this address, he thought.

Just keep still, he told himself on a pizza box. *Rest as unthreateningly as possible and pray I don't hear fire.*

They took his drugs and talked to him harshly until he asked to go along, to be arrested. Given Moose was wanted by the cops, it was highly likely that he had tried to pay off some big debt, then decided to sidetrack on that to buy more drugs. Moose would be wanted by the cops and the mob. Tonight, Karl thought, prison would be better.

The energetic fat lady also had an implant. She had mentioned it amiably during the arrest process when she had made him bend down to avoid banging his head while getting into the squad car—always laughable given the brutality of their other methods. The cops would keep his drugs, but he would be released the next day without charges, or so he hoped.

Karl felt as complacent as oxycodone shit, but this woman was about to jump through the roof. He wondered what she was getting fixed in her head. Eat less maybe—he hoped, for public transit's sake—but what else? The other guy didn't seem to trust her very much. He calmed noticeably when she holstered her weapon, as trigger happy as she looked.

Fat like that, it was almost magnificent to watch her in hyperactivity. She was burning calories, all right. But he was hungry, and he didn't feel like moving one unnecessary muscle. The opposite of her, it seemed.

It was like a reverse match made in heaven. Like what PrimaCore required for neuro-ident profile matching. Could she be his surrogate? Wouldn't the signal be stronger at close range? He didn't know much about their system configurations, but Karl giggled at the possibility that she could be his match.

Sitting shotgun, the female officer punched the roof with excitement. Her partner laughed nervously. Then she did it again. "Strengthening my fists," she said as he gave her a disapproving look.

The car swerved toward a woman pushing a stroller. Karl braced for impact. "Hey, fucking watch it, you dumb cops," he yelled. The female cop punched the ceiling again, ignoring him. "Driver, pay attention, please . . . sir," Karl reiterated.

"Kid, shut up. I got this," the driver said. "Crank it down a notch," he whispered to the female cop, then flinched. In this day and age, those words could be taken quite literally. He sighed.

Karl, being the neuronaut that he was, tried to concentrate upon his state of mind. A moment later, the lady cop fidgeted less as she looked outside. Then, after counting his calm breaths through what he termed "reality normalization," Karl tried to feel the vibrations around him and realized the female cop had become calmer too. Now the real test would begin.

He thought of the most hideously nauseating scenario his hedonistic mind could fathom. He wanted to elicit an unwarranted shunted circuit exchange. As he felt his nausea flush out of him, the woman—his potential surrogate—started punching the roof again, then slapped her coworker on the thigh. Karl was bewildered. He stared through his not-so-sober reality at the amazing coincidence that unfurled. Then he started releasing his mental burps, testing his fantastical hypothesis by releasing them in Morse code, the traditional ••• - - - •••. It was mentally tiresome, but lo, it worked. The female officer repeated the same sequence of uncontrollable jitters, unknowingly calling for SOS. Jesus! He was so hungry now.

The other officer looked at her curiously. Had he understood the coded message, the Freudian slip calling for help? If so, he just kept driving.

This is monumental, Karl thought, having realized the identity of his surrogate without paying a fee to some haughty hacker. It normally would have cost a few thousand creds—creds he never could have saved up. This discovery could come in handy. But how? Hopefully, he would get fed before any further testing.

At the precinct, he was treated the same as always. They took his info, matched his IDs, confirmed his retina and fingerprints, then brought him into a holding cell. He got his meal but could have eaten another six. The pills they had confiscated weren't prescribed to him, but being a registered narcotic addict, he had no—psychologically speaking—ability to control his use, or so went the legal rhetoric. He was the victim here. Karl hoped they wouldn't question the purpose of his implant, but those were so ubiquitous now that they hardly raised any questions anymore. Good ol' Officer McGee had one herself.

Too much time passed, so he worried. Were they perverted sadists who would hold a junkie just to watch him squirm? Would they notice his lack of cold sweats, the absence of nausea and stereotypical nervousness from his lack of withdrawal? Would they even care? The legal implications of his shunt situation were still ambiguous, to say the least. Would it make a difference to them that he chose to shoot instead of feeling compelled to consume? They followed the rules set out before them. It wasn't their place to question. Still, better not raise the issue at all, he thought.

In front of him, an older man—homeless by the looks of it— turned away on the bench, trying to ignore Karl. The last time he was in, six other people were also locked up, all much more intimidating than the lowly man. With an agreement passed between them through an understanding that permeated deeper than words, Karl was glad the other perp also chose apathy and indifference. Karl rolled up his overcoat and exhaled as he twisted to find the most comfortable position on the metal-mesh bench. He wondered exactly when prison cells had turned into free hostels, then dozed off.

In the morning—he assumed it was morning by his eerily accurate internal clock, for no direct sunlight entered the cell— the man was gone. A younger teenager—a real junkie, Karl thought—sat where the old man had been. The kid gave him a nod, which Karl ignored as he got up, peed, and then approached the bars.

"Jailer," Karl yelled like he would to a waiter in a restaurant.

A burly man came as slowly as humanly possible and then waited for what Karl had to say.

"I'm through here. Let me out."

The guard exhaled arduously, then fumbled with his keys. Archaic from the last century, they jingled as he unlocked the door and slid it open. The younger kid, sadly unregistered with MedAid, looked on with amazement as freedom was offered to Karl.

"Hey, hey, me too," he said, dashing for the door. The officer pulled Karl out, then swung his telescopic, stainless-steel baton in a meticulously polished gesture. This part of his job the officer took seriously, Karl thought as he watched the burly man strike the kid with his metallic phallus. The young man shrieked a few times, then shut up, having learned his place. He pushed himself, bloody and swollen, back to the bench as the guard slammed the door with aggressive enthusiasm. "Fuckin' punk," the officer said, casually shaking his head while leading the way for the registered junkie.

In the main part of the precinct, Karl looked around for his favorite police officer, but she was nowhere to be seen. All he knew, from her badge, was that her last name was McGee. He felt like he had lost a golden opportunity that could grant him some still-unfathomable advantage, but now it was gone—like all his drugs. The officers gave him a friendly farewell and reminded him to call the minute he heard anything about Moose.

His handicap ID got him inside the bus, and the bus got him back to his shitty flat. Outside, he looked around to see if there were any obvious goons spooking the location but saw no one of significance. Then he looked for Plasma, who had found his way back on many occasions, but he wasn't in the neighborhood.

His door was still unlocked. Inside, he noticed that someone had emptied the trash, and Plasma's bowl was filled with food. His face went deathly pale. *This can't be good.* He considered Moose but then quickly realized that Moose was constitutively incapable of taking out trash. His anxiety jumped another level. Someone had ordered pizza. He noticed the box from an unknown Italian restaurant sticking out of a bona fide garbage bag.

"Ah, shit," Karl said.

A man wearing a nice suit with a pistol resting on his right thigh and Plasma crooning serenely on his left was waiting for him in a chair behind the door. The man, with seriousness plastered over his face, looked like a goddamn James Bond villain.

"Close the door," he said, which Karl did. "Where's Moustaffa?" the man asked.

"I don't know," Karl said. "But if I did, I'd tell you for sure."

Plasma, that treacherous cat, stretched, then casually jumped off the goon and started hunting one of those random invisible things that only cats can see. The man looked almost disappointed as he pondered Karl's response. "I believe you," he said with a sigh. "We thought this place was a cover anyway. But I know he *was* here."

Karl looked at where the mountain of trash used to be. The goon, or his colleagues, had been thorough. Karl wouldn't argue with such a man. "Moose owes me two grand," he said.

"Stand in line, buddy," the goon replied curtly. His face was made of stone, Karl thought, yet he saw a hint of craziness behind those eyes, like the man could channel tremendous brutality if necessary. He was not someone to be fucked with, no sirree.

The man stood, then rolled up his classy suit sleeves. "Seems like a bum job to punish you for being screwed over, you know, but I have my orders."

Karl gulped. "You don't have to."

"Gotta leave a message. I'm accountable too, you know. My employer wouldn't be satisfied with only my appraisal of your honesty."

"I'm telling you the truth; I don't know where he is."

"And I told you, I believe you. I can tell these things, you know. People don't lie to me very often."

"I'm sure you can, and I bet few would dare," Karl reported adamantly.

The big man nodded curtly. "Right or left?"

Karl flinched in anticipation. "Right," he whispered. He felt the blackout blow, then felt himself trying to get off the floor but not what happened in between. Gravity had obviously taken its course. The man straightened his sleeves as Karl felt his eye swelling.

"Thanks," he groaned. "For feeding my cat."

"No problem, buddy," the man said while looking through his jacket for something. "I have a soft spot for vulnerable pussies."

He placed a card on the coffee table. "Heck, that cat might've saved your life, you know." Plasma's tail whipped from side to side like he knew he was the topic of conversation. "You see him, you call this number."

"If I see Moose, I'll kill him myself." The pain was talking for him. Karl wondered what Officer McGee would be feeling through this, glad that some of this pain and noxious stimuli was being shunted elsewhere.

"No, no need. He's worth more alive for the moment," the guy said in a perfectly reasonable business-like tone. "Just call the number if you see him and hope I don't come visit again, you know." Karl noticed the little antenna behind the man's thick shaved skull and wondered what such a man might have wanted fixed, but perhaps—and in opposition to what this man was trying to tell him—he really didn't want to know.

Karl stayed on the floor after the man left. He touched his orbital bone. Pain flared. He hoped it wasn't fractured. He sighed. What now? No money, no drugs, and essentially—as had been the case through most of his life—no real purpose.

Plasma climbed over his chest, touching his wet nose to Karl's. The purring sent a calm rumbling though him. "I still have you," Karl said. He tried to pet the cat, but Plasma deftly dodged his caress, walked back to the warm spot on the chair where the nameless goon had been sitting, and started licking his own crotch.

* * *

Later that day, after two failed attempts to find more Dilaudid, Karl was dejectedly watching television while holding an ancient, frozen, Styrofoam-wrapped T-bone that was more freezer burn than meat when someone rapped at the door. Karl rarely cooked but was glad he had invested in a decent ice pack ages ago. He groaned, dropped the slab of meat to Plasma's level, and pulled at his hair, for he knew who it would be. The card—all white but for a single phone number in the center—was still on the table. He eyed it for a while before getting up and opening the incessantly rattling door. Without the bolt that the officers had destroyed, he tried to open it just a crack, but that was enough for Moose to slide inside before Karl had anything more to say about it.

"You know how much fucking trouble you're in?" Karl asked.

"Chill, chill," Moose said, half-assed. Karl noticed his dilated pupils and knew Moose was as high as a kite. Moose saw Karl's swollen right eye but didn't acknowledge it. "Need to crash somewhere tonight till things quiet down."

"No fucking way."

Moose reached inside his bottomless pants pocket and withdrew a wad of cash. "What I owe," he said as Karl counted the bills, checking their veracity in the light.

"Almost all there," Karl whispered, then looked up. "What's the catch?"

"No catch, me comrade," Moose said. "And this." He dropped a bag of pills, uncrushed, uncut, and still adorned with the Big Pharma logo. Karl had no doubt he would have called the mob on Moose a few minutes earlier, but, seeing the large bag of pills next to the white business card, he, on some junkie level, reconsidered the entire situation to justify a new scenario. After all, the big man didn't say to call right away.

"I keep these. You leave first thing in the morning," Karl said.

Moose scratched his head, as if realizing he shouldn't have presented so large of a stash right off the bat. "Okay, okay," he said, like he was talking to a special-needs child. "So, we're good?"

"Yeah, yeah, we're good," Karl said after a long pause. He reached into the bag and started crushing a couple of pills. His gear was still on the table, unconfiscated, where he had left it. Once the liquid joy merged with his blood, he finally turned his attention back to Moose. "So, did ya rob a bank or something?"

"Nah, nah, nothing like that," Moose said as he prepped his own shot, not volunteering any further information. Moose seriously annoyed him, but Karl still felt bad for what he knew he had to do. Nevertheless, with such contentment pulsing through his veins, he felt little need to worry about cops and goons for the moment. What still permeated his mind was fat, little Officer McGee. The pudgy bag of energy that he was certain was linked, via the PrimaCore mega-computer, to his shunt's antenna. He had to play his cards right. After this little fiasco with Moose died down, he would need to learn all there was to know about how such a relationship could be exploited.

He had heard about wondrous possibilities—how one surrogate could become dependent upon the other, how manipulative sociopaths, after identifying their surrogate, coerced them into scenarios that fueled their own shunt feeds into ecstasy. One popular Dallas couple had made the news by finding each other and getting married, but what the public later learned was that the man had been compelled by the carefully released output of the other. That was why hacking idents was so popular and had such serious legal implications. PrimaCore also had the world's most advanced security systems. Maybe he was a mental case too, Karl thought. But he knew there was a treasure trove in front of him that he simply needed to uncover. Such an opportunity couldn't be ignored. A smile curled upon the lips of his half-catatonic body.

When his buzz wore down, he flipped a metaphorical coin and decided he would go to bed instead of shooting up again. He took the bag of pills to hide them but then hesitated and dropped a dozen into another baggie for Moose.

"Thanks, brother," Moose said, still dozing on the couch but auspiciously conscious, like an attuned martial artist toward encroaching enemies, of the precise location and quantity of all the drugs around him.

Plasma woke Karl at the crack of dawn with furry headbutts. His bowl was empty. Still groggy, Karl saw Moose asleep on the couch, a spit stain creased next to his mouth. So disgusting, thought Karl.

He poured some cat food, half of it falling out of the bowl. Plasma looked at him with his head cocked sideways but then ate the food from the floor first.

Karl went to the couch and slapped Moose awake while he took his poly-tech and dialed the number on the card. Blearily, his junkie brother sat up, looking at Karl with irritation.

"Yeah?" someone on the other end of the line answered.

"He's here," Karl said. Moose, in a rare instance of sobriety, understood the meaning immediately.

"Ah, shit, man," he said, looking at Karl with serious concern. "Ah, shit."

"Yes," Karl added. "Right beside me now."

Moose shook his head, meaning, "Oh hell no," then dry swallowed a couple of pills. No time to shoot them, Karl surmised. He put down his poly-tech. "Sorry. Had to. You might have a few minutes if you go now."

"Shit, man," Moose said, taking little time to get ready. "A little heads-up would have been nice."

"Run," Karl said with uncommon empathy. He hoped Moose had enough money left over—which he probably owed to the mob in any event—to get away and support himself for a while.

Then Moose was out the door. Karl followed, still holding his poly-tech.

Near the staircase where he could see down to the street below, he saw Moose dart to the right. A car slowed, passenger window down, and Karl was shocked as he saw the goon from the day before already on Moose's tail. They must have been close, he realized and cursed. The goon looked up at him, so Karl—cursing his weak backbone—yelled that Moose was heading "that a way." Obviously, they could see Moose from the street, but the man nodded to Karl, and the car sped off. "Run fast, Moose," he whispered.

Karl was relieved. Maybe that little show was good enough for the mob to think he hadn't betrayed them. He had called them, hadn't he? He had honored his part of the deal. Maybe that was enough. Then he called the cops, saying Moose was being chased. Perhaps the justice system could help Moose after all if he ran fast enough or hid well enough until the protect-and-serve served and protected. Somehow, Karl didn't think so, but after all, he hadn't asked for all these problems. Moose had screwed himself through a long string of exasperatingly fucked-up decisions. It was his own fault, Karl tried to convince himself. But he felt like shit, nonetheless. The stack of money and the bag of pills he got in return hardly made up for it. When he saw Moose again—if ever he saw Moose again—he promised he would make it up to him.

But all that mattered now was Officer McGee—his unbeknownst surrogate. There had to be something he could do to exploit this. Serendipity had called, and he had discovered his surrogate's identity through sheer happenstance. That had to be a propitious omen, he thought. So, sitting on his couch, he tried to meditate, to dwell upon the reality that was his life, and to figure out, under the circumstances, what vices such an opposite had to have. There had to be something his advanced introverted intellect—his ability to understand himself was preternatural but of little use for anything or anyone else outside of himself—could discover about how to use such a situation to his benefit. He sat on his couch, pondering.

Then Karl laughed—karma of all karmas—when he saw that Moose, in utter haste, had forgotten his lighter, still full of fuel, on the table. *My lucky day*. He smiled. Plasma looked at Karl like he was a curious creature indeed.

CHAPTER 8

—

As he surveyed the crowd, Father Thompson knew that his old adage remained true. He had classified the churchgoers into two main groups. First were those who crept along, listless, like it was a duty to attend, without really following the teachings of the Good Book. All the while they believed they would absorb the faith into their soul—through some divine osmosis perhaps—and, ultimately, be shepherded into eternal heaven without any effort on their part. The other group, he thought, seeing through his new vision of things, were perhaps even more disturbing: those who, with palms clasped tightly and eyes afire with holy light, believed in following every letter of the law and applying the Good Book's teachings to everything they encountered. They listened to every intonation in his words and thought him to be the direct extension of the Holy Messiahs. Few of his attendants fell far from those two poles. Looking at all the faces before he commenced mass, he realized—spine shunt or not—that these things never changed.

Like flicking a light switch, his emphatic smile, displaying rows of perfect, sparkling teeth, stretched over his face. "Welcome, faithful parishioners, on this wonderful Sunday morning," he said. It was indeed a nice day. It would have been nice to take a stroll, but this was his job, and they depended on him. He had to remain inside the somber cathedral.

Some clapped while others cheered at his beaming onstage presence like they felt the light of God emanating from his body.

No one else can do it like I do, he reminded himself and, taking a deep breath, continued with his animated sermon. "Today, we will discuss desires," he said, stretching the last word like Satan himself crept out through the hiss. "The temptations that overtake you are common to all men and women. But God is trustworthy, and he will shelter you from that which you cannot abstain yourself. With every desire that compels evil, God also provides a way to endure, an escape from that which tempts you." He paused to take a breath. "Each of you seek now, in your hearts, to stave those thirsts that are forbidden and ask the Lord for protection. Seek instead righteousness, and know this thirst for piety shall be eternally good, and you shall forever be bathed in His blissfulness."

* * *

Across the ocean in the woods near Kup'yans'k, Ukraine, Cobalt stood looking at the cindered body of what remained of his latest victim. He had stopped counting. Listening acutely, he surmised that every enemy combatant around was either dead or had fled. He had been doing this day in and day out and throughout most nights. Now things had quieted. Maybe the fun was over. Maybe the war was won. The thought worried him.

You're a monster, a distant voice resonated in his head, sounding like his old self. But it didn't matter what he thought. The job had to be done no matter how he felt about it to preserve the freedom of those who came before him and of those who were to be born in his patriotic commonwealth.

He sighed and then reached down and peeled off a piece of the private's burnt face. It tasted vile, he thought. The napalm grenades left a sticky, acrid residue on whatever they didn't fully burn, and this dead Easterner was nowhere near as tasty as the teenage soldiers he had eaten that morning. Having finished the last of his rations days ago—there was very little to eat in these parts—he required other sources of sustenance. The plants were bitter, radioactive, and barely palatable, and they provided little nutrition at all. Wildlife was almost unheard of. Only once in his entire service had he seen small rabbit droppings. As he looked down at those tiny pebbles of black shit, he fancied he had found a pot of gold. James had waited, but no cute rabbit—or a mangy, malignantly mutated one—had ever emerged from the bushes. But soldiers in enemy territory were plentiful and ripe for the hunt. Cobalt didn't feel like he could lower himself to their sub-human level by eating Easterner ration packs. Besides, cannibalism had advantages. Apart from granting loads of protein, their brethren in arms would find the desecrated bodies—thanks to the subdermal tracking devices implanted in all combatants—and fear of him would spread like a pestilence.

Cobalt was already achieving mythical status, his name whispered in enemy camps. They feared the monster who followed no orders but those of his throbbing gun. There were rumors that he wasn't even human; some abhorrent creation born of the mad minds of psychopathic Westerners. Well, perhaps the latter part was true. But his tactics weren't trivial; fear was the greatest weapon. As more and more learned of his deeds, some of those in the junior ranks thought he couldn't be killed. The last one he had interrogated—slow disembowelment was always effective—told him such and so much more.

His body was tired, but Cobalt knew his real task had barely begun. However, his wobbling legs decided to take a small break. He fell against a tree, then, while lying there, assessed his wounds. Been shot twice, one bullet grazing the calf and the other passing through his abdomen. A clean exit wound, missing vital organs in its path—or so he hoped. He took a moment to change his dressings. His hands were covered with blotch marks from napalm shrapnel—close range had been unrecommended, but that too was definitely effective—but his fingers were still dexterous. The stiches had held. The discoloration indicated a potential infection, but he thought it manageable. He reached over a charred body to sift through its duffle bag. The soldier's tube of antibiotic cream was partly melted, but the lower half was still intact. He applied the remainder to his wounds, then redressed them as cleanly as he could under the circumstances, carefully hiding any evidence that he had been hurt at all.

Beside him a tiny piece of rusted metal protruded through the leaf-peppered ground. He looked at it with profound interest, like he had those rabbit turds. With a groan, he leaned over and tore it loose. An antique canister of some sort, he thought, then noticed the classic bullet casings. From a war long past—or from a long string of sequential conflicts. He had found the remnants of an ancient battle. No matter how things changed, some things stayed the same.

His silent hip bone implanted transceiver began vibrating. They wanted to recall him, but he wasn't finished yet.

Cobalt took long, laborious breaths, then jabbed his own rib cage not once but twice. The pain flared, but he knew he could endure. He had much more to contribute, so he stood. Time for another round.

* * *

Leaning over his podium, Father Thompson met his parishioners' eyes. "Lust not for fulfillment of your animal desires but thirst for piety and reverence. Become that which God wills. Like Jesus and his Uncle Moses before him, search first for that pure consecration within yourself, and trust the Lord to guide you when the path becomes clouded." He remembered the words like clockwork, never missing a beat. Many of his parishioners were standing, their fanatical faces begging him to deliver them from such terrible temptation. *These wretched people are beautiful,* his multi-input mind conceived.

"Amen," they replied in disjointed assembly. The devout were on their toes, ready to respond. The lethargic members joined in mechanically, forever lagging behind. *Blessed be their tired heads.* His way of thinking surprised him once again. It was curious how his opinion about his parishioners had shifted since the operation.

"Blessed be Jesus and his cousin Mohammed," he concluded.

"Amen," they echoed. The lethargic ones were quicker with their reply this time, knowing the Mass was about to end.

As the last of the worshippers paid him their regards and then walked out into the sunny Sunday morning, he knew his task wasn't quite finished yet.

A fat man stood, hesitating and awkward; one who Thompson had canonized as listless. Without saying a word, Thompson knew the man wanted to confess—and the nauseating flavor of what his confession would be.

The man timidly requested a moment, and the priest mechanically obliged, guiding him into the confessional. The fat man didn't know how to start, so Thompson began the process for him. "In here the walls are sacred. Reveal your sins to me, and be blessed by God."

"It's a . . . it's difficult for me to talk about it, but I . . . I thought that telling you, by telling you, I could be forgiven."

Thompson had never liked this one. This wretched man was a waste of life, a burden to those around him. As pitiful as he was, Thompson knew deep down in his old self that God's love shouldn't be wasted on such a fool. He was a wretched man, but today Frederick felt empathy for him, nonetheless. The sentiment caught him off guard, and he almost said, "*I think I can actually love you for who you are,*" but he held his tongue.

Thompson looked at the fat man through the trefoil gratings as he tried to choke down tears. "I just couldn't help myself," he said.

Just say it, Thompson thought. *I don't have all goddamn day, goddamn it.* But that sentiment flushed out of him, uploaded into the central PrimaCore mega-computer, then downloaded into his surrogate, almost instantly, somewhere across the globe. Patience soon found him again, and his pulse slowed.

"It's alright, my child. God forgives all those who truly seek redemption."

Biting his lip so hard they almost bled, the man then continued. "My niece, she's such a wonderful child. She's only three. She likes me very much."

Thompson waited, but he knew where it would lead. Then the man started crying. Childish sobs from a grown man. He could hardly stand the utter pathetic nature of it all.

"She's so adorable. The sermon you gave today, it reminded me just how demonic desires can be."

Again, Thompson waited, feeling anger about to rise, but somehow it abated right away—the minutia of mind-computer transference eluding him.

* * *

"Fucking Easterners," Cobalt yelled with demonic eyes, a new wave of fury overtaking him; the frenetic joy of it all. The others had fled already, but this one wasn't dead yet. This pathetic one here by his feet would suffer. He lowered his shotgun and listened to the man's pleas. The effeminate Eastern European accent disgusted him. Like some bestial simian species that, despite all odds, had survived the harsh, unforgiving process of Darwinian selection and managed to spread its decadent seed, degenerating all of humanity in the process. But no longer, if Cobalt could help it.

The blast took away that part of the man. He writhed in pain and groaned like Cobalt imagined a wretched animal would (never having seen a wild one with his own eyes). No, they *are* animals, he reminded himself.

* * *

"Every time I see her I . . . get hard," the fat man said finally and brought his hands to his eyes. "Yesterday, she was playing a game where she would run and slam into me where I sat." He tried to show the priest how he was sitting, but Thompson wasn't looking. "We laughed, and my brother thought it was cute. But I couldn't control it. Then—oh God—her parents didn't know, but she saw the wet spot and laughed. She thought I peed myself." His sobbing increased in pitch.

Thompson felt sorry for him, truly. Not simply as a show. This man couldn't control his vile desires. Something in his mind hadn't developed properly, and, God forgive his tortured soul, he possessed an unhealthy attraction to children, attraction he should have had for adult women. It must be difficult to be him, Thompson thought, raising an eyebrow at the surprisingly genuine sentiments he felt, losing track of the man in the confessional.

* * *

The Easterner died too soon. Cobalt groaned with dismay. The soldier hadn't suffered enough. Cobalt's sadistic glee turned into rage as the pleasure was taken from him. He screamed and cursed at the world. He cranked his shotgun once again, firing into the dead man's skull. A spray of red mist covered Cobalt's face. He unloaded again and again until it clicked empty.

The mangled torso barely resembled anything human anymore. Cobalt dropped his gun, then thought for a moment. What a pity. By dying too quickly, the Easterner had taken away something Cobalt cherished. Their entire platoon was dead, but the carnage he begot could be useful in other ways.

Cobalt took his long knife and started his masterpiece. Before nightfall, the grove would become a canvas painted with the remains of these worthless Easterners—strands of flesh and organs to mount an effigy.

* * *

After the confession, Thompson found the church empty. Another alien thought came to him: should he tell the police about the man? There was little doubt in his mind that he would lust again. Thompson had told the man that God's power would protect him from such desires, but Thompson knew from experience that God could only do so much. Even so, the integrity of the confessional had to be preserved.

He should have referred the lowly man to PrimaCore. Father Frederick's success was impeccable, but that wasn't the way it should be. Extreme circumstances had warranted his implant, perhaps, but it was God's will in the end that would protect them both, or so he tried to tell himself.

After closing the doors to the cathedral, he went outside for some fresh air. Near the back of the structure he had built an impressive training area. He hadn't used it much since he received the shunt, but before that it had served to expiate some of his uncontrollable anger and disgust. When he saw such despicable characteristics in his fellow congregants, he would push his body to new limits. Calisthenics, weightlifting, gymnastics—whatever caused him the most carnal suffering and begot the endorphin highs—were some of the best ways to expiate his demons.

Today, the sun shone upon him like the very fingers of God. He felt little desire to punish his body, but like any addiction, his mind coveted what it used to have. Besides, he found that the benefits of his regular exercise routines granted him much more than peace of mind. His body could do far more than that of an average man. He had surpassed his brethren not only spiritually but physically as well.

Thompson decided to exercise not to alleviate suffering but to benefit his being. He relished that he now had such choices. It wasn't necessary; it was good for him.

He removed his robes, placing them on the wooden stool he had carved himself. His muscular chest, seemingly chiseled out of marble, gleamed in the sunlight. He stretched, then ran through the wooded path, which he had cleared years earlier. It sloped up and down, included wooden stumps and barriers that he leaped over or slid under. Ten laps of the course would be followed by a thousand push-ups—not too strenuous but a respectable number—and about as many upside-down crunches and pull-ups. He had to accomplish at least a modest fraction of what he used to do. He couldn't let the spine shunt turn him into a lethargic.

* * *

A military helicopter approached Cobalt's position. He could hear it from under the foliage, but he couldn't yet make it out. His creative endeavor unfinished, he cursed and picked up a piece of heavy artillery. Then he sneaked toward a clearing to get a good shot.

The craft passed him, then doubled back, heading directly toward him. They know my location, he realized. Perhaps he had pissed off too many generals, and his side had sold him out, given the enemy his transponder code. All they had to do was drop a few concussion bombs, and there was little he could do about it. This wasn't typical Easterner tactics.

When he saw the craft, he lowered his rifle, which was loaded with armor-piercing rounds. It was a Western 'copter. That was unusual, given he was deep inside enemy airspace. It was atypical for either side to openly transgress boundaries like that. Skirmishes in that region were typically infantry based. With so many bureaucratic restrictions to warfare these days, it was amazing anything got killed at all. But the COs on both sides had set the ground rules for sustainable warfare decades before James enlisted, so it wasn't his place to question.

They had come for a retrieval—or an execution, he speculated. Perhaps he had rattled so many cages that they were tired of him. Dejected, he sighed and headed for their apparent landing spot. Regardless of his talents, he was still a soldier, and soldiers followed the chain of command, he failed to convince himself. He'd at least hear what they had to say, packing more firepower than they could handle.

"Private Heggard," an authoritative yet familiar voice echoed through the tapering turbine engines. The general held his hat while shielding his eyes from the setting sun.

Cobalt emerged from the sunlight like a specter of doom. His rifle was raised, the general in his sights. "I'm not finished here," Cobalt said. He had met this man before, he realized. It was General McStevens, the head commandant of the entire infantry regiment, right there in the flesh. This had to be important, though it was strategically unwise for such a general to venture so far into enemy territory.

"Put your weapon down, son. I just want to talk," McStevens said. Cobalt waited, refusing to reply. No one else dared to exit the craft. "We need you," McStevens continued when he saw Cobalt was disinclined to obey. "We'll get you back in action as soon as possible; I promise you that. Eastern C. granted us a temporary ceasefire, so we could retrieve you. They think it's to bring you out of commission. Eastern DOD agreed heartily."

After a tense standstill, Cobalt lowered his weapon and approached.

"You're quite valuable to us," McStevens said. "Officially, you're AWOL. Too much fallout in the brain, and you went nuts. Unofficially, and to show you how serious we are, I came myself, unarmed."

McStevens might have been unarmed, but the 'copter sure wasn't, although Cobalt saw no indication that it was about to target him.

"We need you," McStevens said. "We need to replicate what's happened to you. But to do that, we need to *temporarily* bring you to R and D medical to fine tune the new special-forces battalion. The battalion that will be yours to command."

Cobalt didn't like the idea of babysitting other troops, but if they could do as the general said, a horde of rogue soldiers like him would be invaluable. But maybe they didn't realize how truly efficient he was. Did they know how close to death they were at that moment? The military investors, sitting comfortably far from the conflict, didn't want the war to change—everyone knew that—but Cobalt knew the Western Commonwealth was how the rest of the world should be. With a battalion of soldiers as efficient as him, he was certain he could do much more than maintain the borders. They could finally crush those pathetic Easterners once and for all. General McStevens reached out his hand, and Cobalt shook it firmly.

* * *

After wiping his sticky fingers with an aseptic tissue, the next thing McStevens noticed, apart from Heggard's generally unkempt attire, was that he reeked of death. From the bones grafted onto the standard helmet, tanned leather of obvious yet unmentionable origins strapped around them, and brown-red paint encrusted with slime congealing it all together, he didn't doubt why.

The man, codenamed Cobalt, sitting beside him in the noisy helicopter, was trying to sleep. Another soldier looked back to ensure everything was alright. But, like any good soldier, he kept his mouth shut when necessary, and this, McStevens thought, was certainly a topic to shut up about. He had never noticed James Heggard before, nor had he seen any footage of him in action, but the impressive numbers hardly did him justice. Such a man couldn't be converted into mere data. So much would have been lost to logistical analysis. Indeed, whatever PrimaCore had done to him sent chills down the general's back. Certainly, they had succeeded, but what had emerged was something fundamentally different from anything anyone had known before. It was ridiculous to believe that only months ago this man almost sloshed out of the Army for cowardly conduct unbecoming of a soldier. It took more than a simple lobotomy to sever one's compassion, but Private Heggard was fueled by something powerful and hideous, funneled into his shunt from the mega-computer in Boston.

This man, clad in improvised weaponry and painted with entrails, was something entirely new. McStevens noticed the killer instinct in his eyes, but there was more. A preternatural readiness permeated his feigned restful antipathy. Despite his closed eyes, his other senses were finely tuned, ready to call forth the killer inside. It wouldn't take much to set him off, and they weren't even Easterners. *Very dangerous*, McStevens thought, silently congratulating himself. But can he be controlled?

CHAPTER 9

—

D orothy's lab space was immaculate, which was how she liked it. Even though most of her work revolved around complex computer models, she still preferred her wet lab tools to be in order. The other lab techs, post-docs, and students knew better than to touch any of her stuff. It had been years since she had grown neural clusters in a dish, and she often dwelled on those olden times. Now she headed a lab in the world's most advanced private research facility. Working for PrimaCore gave her little time to pursue her own interests. Her lab books had been shoved into folders and forgotten with time.

Dorothy Lundquist wanted to punish them. She was angry at everyone. First, her staff. They had no ethical backbones whatsoever to question the direction that their work was headed. She was also disappointed in her boss, Dr. Mansfield, who seemed to have become a yes-man for the DOD and Propaganda Industries. Manne, as alluring as she was, didn't want to talk to Dorothy about anything other than official work. Worst of all, Dorothy was exasperated with the forever unchanging facade of her government and the military that wished, above all else, to twist PrimaCore's altruistic technology, designed to relieve pain, into a weapon.

It wasn't the first time they had approached her. Many years before the technology was ubiquitous, she was questioned by a supposed civilian scientist at the International Neurosociety meeting in Berlin. The peculiar man with a crewcut kept turning his attention to the hardware they had recently developed. He had grown annoyingly inquisitive about receiving digital blueprints and became a nuisance until Dorothy politely asked him to leave. The symposium security arrived shortly and evicted him, but during the confusion of his forced egress, he pilfered one of her 3D printed diagrams. Thankfully, it had not been one of the new prototypes.

Upon hearing this, Keneth placed additional PrimaCore security to keep an eye on Dorothy. The thief, who must have realized his prize wasn't what he had been seeking, reiterated his interest by breaking into her hotel room. She found him going through her stuff. Once discovered, he charged at her, but she was quick to run. Outside, unknown to the intruder, was one of Keneth's towering guards. The intruder ran right into his massive frame with a noticeable groan. As they fought, she retreated from the turmoil—toppled vase, torn wallpaper, tilted picture frames, and nosy spectators peering out of neighboring rooms. But her guard was unable to subdue him. The other man was skilled and, once back on his feet, had dashed across the hall to the fire escape.

"He's military," the tall black guard told her afterwards. "Those moves come straight from infantry," he said with confidence while resetting his bloody nose, never to be perfectly straight again.

When Keneth arrived to hear the report, he didn't question his guard's assessment. "They've come to me," he told her the following evening. "I told them no." She was proud of him for standing up to the DOD and knew the private sector had been a good decision after all. But things had changed. Later he told her—through connections he would rather not disclose and about which she preferred not to inquire—that they indeed had sent a covert operative to the conference. Officially, the military wouldn't confirm or deny any of this, but their financial wing made a substantial bid on PrimaCore's new patent, the same one that led to their current explosion of profit (Keneth had created the first—long outdated—emotion transfer shunt during his post-doctoral work at Stanford). Nevertheless, it was clear that they held interests, and if they didn't get their support directly, they were ready to get it otherwise. Keneth knew that as much as anyone, so Manne was hired—or hatched out of a vat, as some jested—to overview PrimaCore's security and to implement it, non-canonically. It had to be unorthodox, and it had to be effective. She got an A+ on both counts. Keneth ran the industry, but Manne ran the infrastructure—and he gave Manne all the leeway she desired.

When, a few days earlier, the military requested a private meeting with Keneth, Manne had asked Dorothy to try to identify the old assailant from within their convoy of representatives. It was a long shot, but as Manne had argued, the military's pool of competent neuroscientists couldn't be too large. There was at least some logic to that, but the Army would have been stupid— that couldn't be discounted either—to bring the same man who had tangled with PrimaCore security in the past.

"When Keneth calls you—and there's a very high probability that he will—make sure to get a good look at them," Manne had said. "I'll give you the opportunity to let me know." He wasn't there. And what would Manne have done if he were? What could she possibly gain by eliminating him? He was simply another insignificant pawn on the overly cluttered chessboard. But perhaps Manne's interest in the situation was purely retribution—that they had dared to steal from PrimaCore or that they had tried to hurt one of her chicks, calling forth the wrath of Manne's deadly talons. Dorothy didn't know, but Manne was certainly toiling with something behind the scenes.

These days, with all her supervisory duty and project overviewing, Dorothy had little time for actual wet lab work, but she still sprayed ethanol and wiped her work area clean before Keneth arrived. It was rare that they met outside his office, but after hearing how upset she sounded, he had said he would come. The rest of the lab people had already been sent home.

Rigorous to punctuality, he entered, followed by Manne.

Dorothy started before he could say anything, "So, we give them the Hydra configuration, just like that."

Keneth nodded as he loosened his tie. "A modified version of it, yes."

"Then you can expect my resignation," she said, regretting her words immediately. She didn't want to quit.

"Let's not be too hasty here," he said, approaching her. "I need you. You're invaluable."

"It's not what I signed up for," she said. "Remember years back? We had ideals then, when we had a vision of things beyond stock values."

"It's not like that."

"We make weapons for the commonwealth, then the enemy gets envious and wants the same balance of power. The next thing you know, we're installing Hydras for both sides. How does that look for PR? All in the name of money. We aren't weapons designers. Since I joined your company—"

"Which you've been a pivotal part of ever since."

"—we wanted to study and cure neurological disorders, not turn misguided fools into super soldiers."

He grabbed her by the shoulders, then brought her into his arms. He was much taller and larger than her, and she easily fell victim to his grasp. He smelled of his classic aftershave, singular to him—she wondered whether he purchased customized cologne. She preferred imagining that he was the only person on Earth who could smell so pleasant.

"That hasn't changed," he said. "But you know how they are. I'd rather have them eating out of my hand than stealing my grain."

She didn't know what to say, but being inside his arms, she already felt better. "We wanted to end all human suffering," she said.

"We still can," he replied, his tone serious.

"You know they'll eventually take it further. They might be doing so already."

"We've progressed much further than they could possibly comprehend."

"And when they realize that, they won't restrict themselves to weaponization. They'll come here and take over by force to prevent us from using it or to exploit it themselves."

"They're still a decade behind," Keneth reiterated, but she knew that if they realized the full potential of the system, the DOD would soon make it a priority to explore the shunt's so-called Pandora's boxes.

After a moment, she pushed off gently. "Yesterday I asked my staff to prepare the hardware prototypes for our new military collaboration. And you know how they reacted?"

He raised an eyebrow.

"No one even objected or procrastinated. They went onwards, doing what they had to do, burning the midnight oil in hopes of getting a good recommendation letter. Not a goddamn one objected that their hard work would be used to enhance the military's killing capacity. Not a single one."

"If soldiers become much more reliable," he started, then paused, confounded, no longer sure he had a point at all. "Then we will need fewer soldiers. That is at least desirable, for both sides."

She shook her head. If better weapons ended wars, then wars would have stopped eons ago. Tons of fools were still lining up to be killed. All better weapons did was change the nature of the game.

"Not everyone is as unpatriotic as you," he complimented. "Many of your scientists still adhere to doctrine—believe the war is necessary. They might simply accept it as doing their part." He was trying to justify her staff's lack of apparent outrage.

"Maybe," she said. "It's still wrong."

"Some would argue the ethicality of exchanging pain," he said. "And you know we can do much more than deal with discomfort. There's a whole range of ethics that don't yet exist to address what we can do now." His voice grew stern. "It's not our place to change the ways of the world." But even he had to admit they had already changed the world, changed it irrevocably.

Dorothy had little more to say about that or anything else. He sighed, kissed her forehead, and bid her goodnight. Manne, like a statue, had simply observed the exchange. She didn't exit with Mansfield, who must have noticed but ignored the fact.

He looked defeated, and Dorothy felt bad for skewering his mood, but she had to.

"You got to him," Manne confirmed casually. "He won't easily forget what was said here."

"I hope he doesn't," Dorothy said smugly, her head cocked. But inside she felt embarrassed. It had not dawned on her until she saw him so dejected. Then she remembered: today was the eve of the anniversary of his wife's tragic death. Dorothy couldn't stand idly by while the DOD violated PrimaCore's integrity, but why did she have to spring her snake in the grass today?

Manne approached and Dorothy, not knowing her intentions, stepped back. Cornered between her bench and a sturdy electron microscope, she had nowhere to flee.

"You think Bouquets' minions are going to care whether Keneth's integrity is jostled?"

Dorothy shook her head as Manne inched closer. Her scent, unlike Keneth's hearty, safe, wood-cabin aroma, had a spicy, exotic, lioness-in-heat tincture to it. Where Keneth's was comforting, Manne's was fatal. But Dorothy had difficulty deciding which one was most alluring.

"I . . . I don't know," she said, distracted.

"At this point I don't think it'll matter in the least," Manne said. "If he stops playing ball, they'll eliminate him and find a way to license the technology without us. They already have numerous contingencies for exactly that. But Keneth's not afraid for himself. He fears for us—what they could do to his people—if PrimaCore becomes a problem." She brushed aside Dorothy's hair, which had become disheveled during her agitation.

Dorothy couldn't argue. Scared and titillated, her heart hammered. "What about you?" she asked. "Have your symptoms worsened? You're pushing yourself too much."

"I'm fine."

"You should tell Keneth," she said, trying to convince her once again.

"In time but not now." Manne relaxed and leaned against the bench. "Either way, that isn't important today." She pointed toward the open computer model. "I believe everything will work out," she said cryptically. Before Manne kissed her and departed to her own proclivities, she told Dorothy something that shook her even more than the potential dangers that Manne herself represented. She had an uncanny ability to extrapolate perfectly how certain situations would unfurl. "If you really want revenge," she said, "to get back at the military for twisting our technology into an abomination, you should give them *exactly* what they're asking for."

CHAPTER 10

———

I wanted to apologize to Francis, but I didn't know why. He seemed distressed by my obvious lack of empathy. Someone had been killed, but I hardly cared. Objectively, thousands died every day in warfare, so what difference did it make if it happened here in Boston? Murders were frequent and far from unheard of. Bill's murder had barely made the newspapers, receiving only a tiny mention in the obituaries—the small-print section wedged between a mortgage company and an air-freshener ad.

That night someone had sped us away from the smoldering rubble of his no-longer-insulated warehouse residence. Jostled from side to side, I simply enjoyed the ride. It had been more enjoyable than staying at home, but it should have been much more memorable than that.

"You don't care about that, do you?" Francis yelled. "You really don't care." Agitated and sweating, he banged his fist on the dashboard, swearing repeatedly about the infiltrator.

I shrugged. "I care, if you think it matters." He simply returned my gaze, looking displeased. Well, too bad, I thought.

"It's numbing your mind more than you realize," he said. "Like a fucking junkie." Maybe it was, but my body was fine, so that didn't seem to matter either.

A few days later, still wearing pajamas in the midafternoon, I sent him a text.

Sorry about the other night. Hope there's
no hard feelings. See you. J.

He replied shortly thereafter.

Jade, there was nothing you could have
done. I doubt you realize the implications
of what I got myself into, but the gist
of it is this. I fucked up. Fucked up
with YOUR account. I can't blame you for
that. You couldn't have known either. You
even tried to warn me. I thought there was
no need for additional security for your
account because your profile was, as we
put it, non sequitur, meaning you weren't
important enough to require extra precautions. Or so we thought. We must have
pierced a membrane, and they locked in on
us. If not you then Mr. Korea is much more
valuable to someone than we realized. We
were infiltrated, and, well, that's real
bad. So, we won't see each other again
probably for a long time. Me and a few
others have to disappear. I suggest you do
the same. Get out of town, and don't tell
anyone where. You can be eavesdropped on
from afar with little effort these days.
This text will be read, easily at that,
by under-the-radar authorities much worse
than the military or the police. Odds are
they already know where I am. So, I can't
stay here either. PC and CW gov go much
deeper than people realize and do far
worse than anyone knows. Get that piece of
shit out of your brain, and get lost, for

```
your own sake, if you care at all, or bad
shit will hit the proverbial fan.
```

His message should have been worse than merely unnerving. I wondered how I would have felt without the shunt. I didn't know if my fears had been altered post-op, but I had become less preoccupied about many atrocities in the world around me.

Francis had told me to get my shunt removed. Did he say so because he cared or because he thought PrimaCore could locate me through it? Odds were they could, I guessed, knowing little about the technology myself. Thus, there was no point in running from such a ubiquitous global entity. They most certainly could grab me anywhere, if that was their intention. I couldn't fully appreciate his paranoia. How could I? I had never even been accosted by the police or found reason to hide my activities behind troves of digital security. Throughout my life, I hadn't even used incognito settings to hide my illegal downloads. Either way, everyone downloaded, and few, except for the big uploaders, got into any serious trouble. Never did I see any cloaked figures clad in black with opaque visors spying on my activities. I simply never had that borderline schizophrenic quality that Francis and his colleagues adopted about everything—Trust no one; leave no trails. But Francis was going batshit crazy about it, so there had to be something tangibly real about his dilemma, more than the nondescript "They" prowling in the dark, capturing data on everyone and everything at all times.

The more I thought about it, the more it sounded ludicrous. So, I messaged him again, asking whether he was overreacting, just a tad, and surprising myself, asked to see him again. Was it because he had made himself unavailable that I suddenly found him appealing? I didn't know, but curiosity drove me. Intertwined within this mystery, he was much more datable now than he had been during high school.

Francis never replied. The morning after I sent another query using only a wondering face emoji. I got an automated reply telling me his address was no longer valid. Well, he sure was taking this seriously.

I barely had any friends left in the city, so it annoyed me to lose another one, especially in such a manner. His party had been more enjoyable than I had assumed, and, at least superficially, I was slightly dismayed about being left out now. But a little shopping would cure me of that palatable unease soon enough, I thought.

Taking time to stop periodically and look over my shoulder, I saw no cloak-and-dagger activity homing in. No one gave me more than the usual sexual appraisal I was already accustomed to ignoring. Even a tall blond girl paused to gaze. To test it further, I remained seated in the operatic gallery and looked for spooks, or whatever these adult children called themselves. Since most guys did check me out, logically, someone tailing me might try to avoid doing that, tracking me peripherally, feigning like they weren't. But I never noticed anyone outside of the normophilic foray of weekday afternoon shoppers. After one man stopped to ask me on a date, I realized my plan was useless. I wasn't someone who could avoid visual attention. Next time wear loose sweatpants and no makeup, I thought. But really, I had little intention of adopting the RAM-geeks' paranoia. Francis was losing his mind.

Tying my hair back, I felt the small dongle at the back of my neck and sighed. No one would even need to follow me. I was hooked up, constantly transmitting and receiving data from the mega-computer. They might or might not know exactly where I was, but they certainly knew precisely how I felt.

Back in my apartment, I opened my computer, and my jaw dropped. My heart was racing. That, at least, I still could feel. Samantha had sent me an email using a ciphered address. It wasn't the usual greetings and howdy dos.

> Jade, XP is dead. We need to talk. Come to
> the office ASAP. Sam

If that were true, the guano had really hit France's fan. I remembered the pretty, sparkling glass careening down the high-rise building, the bright explosion eviscerating all the hardware and the murder scene in the process. It wasn't something someone did with irrational haste each time they got cold feet.

Come to my office ASAP, I thought, dismayed. Samantha had never told me where that was. Given what Francis had said, I didn't think replying to Samantha was a good idea. If she indeed had a registered business, then the government certainly knew where her offices were. But Samantha didn't seem even a fraction as paranoid as Francis.

I went through my cluttered purse and found her business card. Swiping it over my computer's mag-reader, the browser opened to her URL. A large statuette of what I thought was Samantha's armless, headless body filled the screen. It seemed oddly chauvinistic, but perhaps that was her intent. Two clicks later, I found a physical address in Boston and copied it into a NavCom search. No luck. The street numbers ended long before the one listed officially on the site's map. Might as well have been called 123 Fake Street. It wasn't a mistake; the listing was forged.

So much for that. I felt like a child trying to play a game for which I didn't know the rules. If Sam wanted me to come to her office, she needed to be a bit more direct. Hopeless, I lay down. I would have to contact her again and admit what a noob I was. Then my poly-tech chimed, and I realized how freakishly eerie this was all becoming.

> No sweat. Light up the card. Sam

Impossible. Was she reading my thoughts? I seriously wondered with this thing stuck in my brain. But spine shunts, hacked or not, couldn't resolve actual thought processes, just gross neural activity—or so I had been told.

"This *is* spooky," I whispered to no one. With perceptible palpitations, I felt oddly excited, like being sucked, willingly or not, into an old-school spy movie. What did she mean by lighting up the card? She couldn't possibly mean fire. That seemed bludgeoningly unlikely given Samantha's apparent masterful control of the online world. Feeling stupid, I lay down again, looking at those miniature breasts. Then it caught my eye, like an invisible signature printed on a government ID. Something else was written on the card that I couldn't quite discern under visible light. I bolted out of the apartment, then down the stairs, forgetting to lock my door.

On the street level, cars sped past well beyond the speed limit. The night sky was occluded by smog and layers of overlapping advertisements, drowning out much more than starlight. I made my way, coatless and shivering, to the Chinese convenience store, still in business due to its unregistered, underage workforce. Inside, I went to the cash register, leaned forward, and borrowed their UV lamp. The old woman behind the counter tried to grab it, but I pulled it out of reach as she screamed what sounded like profanities in a language that definitely wasn't Mandarin.

The silhouette lit up, manifesting shimmering arms. The hands pointed to a set of numbers on the lower-right side: 250 PA 441 #24666. The woman screamed again, emitting a long string of unfathomable words—it could even have been badly accented English—but I understood one word, and it convinced me enough: police.

Apologizing, I handed over the UV lamp and bowed with hands clasped, immediately realizing it was probably racially offensive. Then I left. Best to avoid this store for a while, I thought. But I got what I wanted.

Same number as France's entry code. Perhaps this was their secret RAM-geek groupie name. The rest was perhaps an address, but the data was indiscernible to a novice like me. Didn't think it would be a good idea to NavCom the code either, fearing some invasive key-logger had already bugged my hardware. Every updated virus scan I performed identified new intrusive software. Maybe one such hack was how Sam knew I had searched the fake address online.

It started raining, hard. I cursed myself for having forgotten my purse and keys inside. A professional would have plastered a hair over the doorframe to monitor for unauthorized entry. I, on the other hand, forgot to lock my door entirely. There was no way through the lobby gate. Without an awning, I stood, absorbing the mildly radioactive rainfall until someone exited the building. I reached to grasp the door, but the man, whom I had never seen before, blocked my entry.

"Can't let riffraff in. Sorry."

"I fuckin' live here." The bitterness came out, but I didn't feel angry—automated lingual reflexes disconnected from my apparent state of mind. I was almost comically amused by my lackadaisical fuck-it-all-ness.

"Then you'd have a key," he replied.

"Jesus, fuck me in the ass."

The door clasped shut, and he moved away, unfolded an umbrella, but then hesitated. I was getting soaked and noticed that my shirt revealed more than I cared to. I quickly folded my arms over my tits.

The man stopped. "I feel like dirt leaving you out here though," he said, appraising me from top to bottom, seeing I wasn't going elsewhere.

I had nothing nice to say, so I said nothing, just smirked like some twit as he unlocked the door.

"Don't tell the supe I did that, okay?"

"Not in a million years," I said, shivering. It was surprising how his compassion increased tenfold once he had a good look at me, and that seemed like less of a favor than none.

Once inside, I ran upstairs, trying not to forget the string of numbers I had discovered on the card. I hoped I got a prize for this wild goose chase.

Unwilling to type the code through search engines, I enlarged maps of the city instead. The old-style address system had public alleyways—PA perhaps. If that was the case, then it could indicate a specific alleyway. To my surprise, such a street, 250 PA, did exist. I grabbed my things, including a new set of clothes, packed my poly-tech inside my purse, and departed.

Back on street level, I hailed a cab and then looked back, somehow thinking I would never see that place again. The driver—non-talkative, like I preferred—dropped me in the vicinity where I thought Samantha's purported offices might reside. The insalubrious nature of the alleyway made me think I had wildly chased geese after all. But the 441 address was there, and beside the industrial metallic door was an alphanumeric keypad.

There was only one way to find out.

I keyed in the PIN. A lock clicked, and the door's rusty hinges squeaked as it opened through gravity alone. The bare illumination inside didn't inspire confidence, but before I dared to step in, the hallway lit up, and two men in uniform came to me.

"Miss Hilt?"

I nodded.

"This way, please."

Well, what do you know? I had some vestigial detective skills after all.

Once inside, I heard the lock reset, and another series of lights flickered on as we proceeded, simultaneously shutting off behind us. Near a bend, the hallway led as far as I could see in northern and southern directions. We stopped near a hermetically sealed door, which I assumed was an elevator. It opened without any activation. Then they led me to an antechamber, where one of the men told me to place my belongings in a lead box.

"Why?"

"Faraday cage," he said. "Blocks EM. Cojone's orders."

"Cojone?"

"Miss Burgess."

Samantha wanted to be called Cojone. My lips curled. "Either of you know what 'Cojone' means?"

"Yes, ma'am," the other answered without humor. He motioned for me to enter, where he pressed a large red button.

The doors opened to what looked like a contemporarily designed business office. Glass walls divided the floor into numerous cubicles interspersed with conference rooms. To my right two men played darts next to a bar area, which I assumed was somewhat atypical for such places of work. Beside them a younger girl who looked familiar watched us casually. Pink-Frills, I vaguely remembered.

"Glad you found it," Samantha said, walking toward us and smiling jovially despite the reason for our meeting. She wore a slender red dress, and her hair was tied back while two strangely long braided meshes fell down the front. She nodded to the guards, who retreated to the elevator.

"You didn't make it easy for me."

"But you found it, which is what matters. Please follow me." Sam led me to a much larger office. A series of computers sat facing the walls while a large desk made of marble and glass resided in the other corner. Cojone sat at the desk and keyed in some controls before a large square tile on the floor slid sideways, revealing a Faraday box, like the one in the antechamber. "You can take your purse, but leave your poly-tech there."

"So, what kind of work goes on here anyway?" I asked while doing what I had been told. I couldn't help but think about those classic detective movies. The place felt like either a secret police institution or some supervillain's lair; I couldn't decide which.

Samantha smiled. "Essentially, information distribution, non-traditional advertisements. We work for clients who seek novel types of commodification for the vices they wish to exploit and advise them on how best to enter the market. Cybersecurity is our other spectrum, but it fundamentally works the same. They, on the other hand, seek to limit access, and we make sure they have as little or as much coverage as they need. But you would be surprised how often the best way to distribute information is by attempting to hide it, while placing data right in the open is often a great way to make it invisible. We try to stay fresh, ahead of the curve."

"You wanted my gear in the Faraday box to prevent me from being located?"

She nodded. "Or eavesdropped."

"Then what about this?" I asked, turning to show Sam my spine shunt.

She frowned, then looked aside. "Megan?"

"Scanning," the girl said. It was Blood-Red from France's party. "We're good," she replied. "Resolution's about five clicks. There's at least two hundred thousand people within that radius."

Samantha smiled, indicating everything was under control.

"What happened to Francis?" I asked, getting straight to the point.

"We're not certain yet, but his body was positively ID'd earlier today. Given the circumstances, we are almost certain it's foul play."

"And you killed the man from the party?" I asked, looking straight at her.

Samantha looked at Blood-Red, then back to me. "They forced our hand. You care?"

"Only 'cause I should. But I think you already know what my shunt's designed for."

"Indeed." She looked me over more thoroughly than the man outside my apartment lobby. "The informant had a camera implanted on his retina. We identified it from his attempt to upload the images wirelessly. It didn't transmit, of course, because our boys had sealed the room. But we picked up his attempt, and point-of-view pattern recognition confirmed who it was. We couldn't let him leave since his employers would know who we were if he got the chance to upload. Couldn't leave him or the place intact."

I sighed. "I talked to Francis recently. He was paranoid as fuck, told me to get out of town."

"We know. We read the transcript."

At first I was surprised, but given her company's apparent function, I assumed it was something Sam could easily accomplish. "And you knew I looked at your site by using your business card."

"Your computer pinged our address using your search engine, so we knew you knew it was fake."

"If I hadn't?"

"Then the cabby would have told you that your address wasn't valid, but then we would have known which cab pinged it too. Otherwise, I would have sent somebody. But I hoped you would manage on your own."

I nodded, considered everything she was saying.

"Made you feel good to find the place, didn't it?"

I exhaled with surprise. "Actually, it did."

"That's what our company's all about." She held out a chair, "Please, have a seat."

Then another thought struck me. "Did you kill Francis?" I asked, equally as bluntly.

Samantha's eyebrow rose, then, after a longer-than-necessary pause, she shook her head. "No."

I nodded like it was another inconsequential bit of daily Eagle news.

"Do you believe me?"

"For now," I said. "But I'm sure someone like you could discover who did."

"In time," Samantha said, then she smiled. "Whoever we find will be professionally disconnected from those who pulled the strings. I am certain of that at least." She looked me over again, calculating, appraising. "I like you, Jade Hilt. And I would have liked to know you better before your brain got violated, but that might have precluded our knowing each other. Because, as XP told you, the cause of all this trouble started when your neuro-ident surrogate was identified."

"Francis told me he seemed unimportant."

"One of you was sequitur. You, we know. Korea . . ." That seemed to have become his established name, for they no longer believed his supposed identity was accurate. ". . . is, at the moment, out of our playing field. But there is someone—something—of the utmost importance."

I thought about those dreams again, wondering if brain-wave patterns could be translated into actual thoughts. But like Samantha had said on the night we met, what lay within the mind were the last remnants of actual privacy. No information, once released into the world, could hide from a good facilitator like her. I had told Francis about my dreams. Had he shared them with Sam, Brent, or confessed to those who killed him? Either way I could have been recorded from afar while at the restaurant with Francis.

I was pondering that when I remembered something else. "What's a membrane?"

Samantha smiled. She must have thought me a rarity indeed, refreshingly ignorant about the digital world. "Membranes are actual physical devices, nanometer-thick layers of carbon polymers that isolate hardware components within a protected network. If anyone bypasses the security walls and accesses the information within, the membrane ruptures, melts away through the heat caused by the electron flow of data. It immediately notifies the information's owner that his data packs have been violated. Protects information that should only have been accessed from within."

"And my—me and Korea's account—had one."

"Probably alerted PC or whoever was watching when XP got one of his kids to hack it."

"And this kid of his, he's safe?" I wondered if it was the same genius teen hacker who had been dominant at the party.

"XP had his own security measures outside our management. We don't yet know. Brent also had to jump ship; disappear for some time." Samantha did show actual concern about that, or perhaps it was annoyance.

"And you?"

She smiled again. "We are somewhat . . . untouchable here for now. And Brent looks after me from afar. But we have means of defense here that supersede even those of Bouquets' secret minions. They would, in essence, compromise themselves rather embarrassingly if they tried anything underhanded. A panic button, let's say."

I pondered that. It did sound impressive, if it were true. The government had a certain omniscient power that seemed godlike, unchallengeable. But perhaps that's how they wanted to be perceived. "So, what do you want from me?"

Samantha's smile widened. "Jade, you hold the key to it all."

CHAPTER 11

—

Being charged with dereliction of duty would be a small risk compared to the best sex Stacey McGee had ever had. It only got increasingly better when she slept with her new "it's complicated" boyfriend, Karl. Something unbeknownst with this guy, scrawny and borderline criminal, pushed her desires over the edge in a way she had never experienced before and made every moment with him a surge of confident sexual prowess. Having met on duty, she hadn't even realized she was attracted to him, had hardly noticed him at all—he was as unnoticeably Caucasian as one could get. Perhaps she had overlooked him due to the equilibration period the PC reps had told her about. But now she couldn't stop staring at him.

Stacey's job had improved as well. Her partner, Jeffries, had been reassigned. She knew it had been his request, but she also knew it had been granted because her CO was confident in her new abilities—or so her new ego told her. She didn't need him tying her hands, telling her to slow down, keep quiet, or stay in the car anymore. She could take down her own perps. Stacey knew no one would fuck with her now.

Except for Karl. Karl could fuck with her. He had something that no one else had, but she still couldn't pinpoint what that was. He wasn't amazingly skilled like the performer she had finally found the guts to hire the week prior. That escort had the moves, the capacities, and the expert techniques, but it hadn't stimulated her the way Karl could. It was simply, unbelievably, indescribably fantastic with him inside her. So much so that she had never believed sex could be that great.

They had met, again, the same day she had been reassigned as a lone officer. He had been waiting in the parking lot that evening beside her car—one eye painted blue—and told her he had to meet her. She had been skeptical at first, remembering him from when they had raided his home, and she was going to tell him she couldn't associate with users. But then he looked at her with those eyes, which peered through her, all-knowing and sagacious, from some secret master within. Then she felt like she was on top of the world again, like the first shunted jolt she received upon activation, but stronger—no more equilibration period. It was like a benign drug, all the rush but without poisoning her body with medication.

"Care to go for a drink?" he asked.

"Abso-fucking-lutely," she replied and opened the passenger door for him. Her car tires squealed from side to side as she accelerated out of the lot. She had registered for a class at the gym, but knowing she had already lost a good amount of weight that past week, justified missing it as well.

That night had been like a dream. They went from club to club, ushered inside enthusiastically like she was a hot seventeen-year-old. She couldn't get enough of the lights and loud music. As the driver, she only drank lightly, but she had more than enough cash to pay for his. When he got really drunk, instead of being dissuading from talking to him, she felt increasingly involved, confessing things she had never told anyone before, while he, slurring his speech, told her how she had been missing out her entire life.

Like her, he had a spine shunt too. But these days a lot of people did. To get him off the hook he had said. If it worked even half as well as it was working for her, he certainly was getting some benefits from his too.

She brought him back to his place, address and directions coming naturally seeing as he lived near her patrol route. After he said goodnight, she followed him in. He told her it wasn't necessary, but she pushed him inside. She tried to get him going, but he was, at first, reluctant. She had never been so horny. So, when he amiably pushed her off, she stripped of her own accord and began the task herself. He frowned at her, but that made her all the more excited. "Oh God," he had said, seemingly afraid. But then he submitted, and she knew she had to have this extraordinary bliss from then on, as much as physically possible.

Today, he had called her. "Skip work an hour and come to my place." She knew she wasn't supposed to do such things, but he was irresistible. His apartment, which was already getting cluttered from when she cleaned it last, was oddly absent of furniture, a fact she noted again upon entering. He was sitting on the couch, as usual, his mangy cat playing with a stringy toy in an empty corner.

She started taking off her uniform, her utility belt thumping to the floor and sending the cat darting to another corner. "I'm a bit tired today," he said apologetically while scratching his head. But the more he demurred, the more it excited her. "We had sex two days ago. I'm only human, you know."

"Quiet," she said and tugged at his pants. He closed his eyes and seemed to think deeply about something that pained him. Then he sighed, took a deep breath, and helped her get his briefs off. She put it into her mouth, then mounted him when he was ready.

After he came—she had come multiple times already—she wiped them both clean and then started putting her uniform back on. "I need more cash," he told her from his spot on the couch, where he had collapsed, naked. Stacey, wearing only her shirt, went through her purse to get him some bills. She had taken a detour to withdraw more in anticipation of his needs.

"When you have a chance, from your precinct's evidence locker, I need you to bring me some high-grade opiates."

"I . . . I can't do that," she said, dismayed.

He didn't argue, just looked at her. That dichotomy again, the unyielding force inside, all-seeing, looking not at her but seemingly contemplating her significance in the universe, split from his awkward, scrawny vulnerability. What he asked wasn't so difficult, she thought then, and someone with her capabilities could accomplish it readily. If anyone could, it was her.

She nodded perfunctorily, then yelled with unspent energy at the rush of it all. Plasma peeked past the doorframe, then darted away again.

"Bye, honey," she said as she left. He nodded without looking while she slammed the door. She could rarely control her enthusiasm now.

* * *

"It's okay," he told his nervous cat. "She's gone now."

Part of having sex with her disgusted him, but Karl could tell that got her going even more. But there was something increasingly pleasant about it, like a bad situation that became an accepted comfort. He had brought this upon himself, he constantly reminded his confused head, but his hard work and suffering was finally coming to fruition. He was becoming adept at how to fully stimulate her shunt. He had to concentrate, or it got out of hand, but knowing when and where to initiate the pulses was his magic ticket. He knew how best to manipulate her—like any normal relationship, he reminded himself, but never to such mechanistic, surgical precision. She was like a puppet, one that had to be satisfied periodically. Sex with her wasn't as unpleasant as he thought it would be, especially after she got him started.

Hours later, banging at the door jostled him into anxiety. He had been growing paranoid about the people who paid a visit to his place. With the power he had over a police officer, thoughts of secret agents and shadow government militia haunted him. There was no way he could be allowed to keep what he had. But he reminded himself repeatedly that no one knew about it; no one could possibly know. Even if they did, the only one who would get into trouble was Stacey—and serious trouble at that. So, he had to be careful, only pushing her a little further, never overstepping the limit of no return.

Through the peephole, he saw Moose. Overjoyed to know he hadn't been killed, Karl was surprised at how happy he was to see him. Karl wanted to tell him about the extraordinary opportunity he had created for himself. But when he opened the door—latch still broken from when his girlfriend-to-be had broken it down—Moose slammed into it, giving Karl a nasty headache and sending him sprawling to the floor.

Moose closed the door and tried to latch it, fumbling as he looked for the missing piece. "Fuck it," he said.

"What the hell, man?" Karl said, rubbing his eye and forehead.

Moose wore a red-stained bandage on his temple and a white shirt that read, "I masturbate thinking of you." Only then did Karl realize how angry he was. Moose ran and kicked him repeatedly in the chest and arms as Karl covered himself, blocking most of them.

"Eye took my fuckin' ear, man," he said. Despite himself, Karl thought that funnier than it should have been but held back. "You sold me out, bitch." Moose kicked him again but found Karl's knee instead of his stomach. Moose fell and grabbed his foot, groaning in pain. "You broke my fucking toe."

"My fault?" Karl yelled uncharacteristically. "You did this to yourself." He looked at Moose, who was flinching in pain. "Karma," he said. The hurt toe was only the tip of the iceberg, Karl knew, and he almost pitied Moustaffa. "You got your own ear cut off, you broke your own toe, you drew your own fucking contract, and it read, 'I will fuck myself over as badly as possible,' and you signed on the dotted line. Don't blame this on me, bitch." Karl dusted himself off, wondering what kind of input Stacey was getting from this, then went to his drug drawer. He took out some pills, then handed some to Moose.

He looked up at Karl, fear plastered on his face. But when Moose saw the drugs, he started to cry. "I'm sorry, man," he said, then popped the pills without using any gear.

"They were watching the place," Karl said. "I had to."

Moose shook his head, but Karl knew Moose would have done the same thing had the tables been turned. "Isn't even a down payment," Moose said, pointing to the bandage covering where his ear used to be, "just an extension."

"Thought you knew better than to go to Eye."

Moose didn't reply.

Then Karl told him all that had happened since he had last seen Moose sprinting for his life. He didn't know if they had caught Moose then or a while later, but the dressing on his head looked recent. Moose, now passively opiated, listened intently but didn't seem to appreciate the full significance of what Karl was sharing.

He sat upright after a moment, then smiled. "So, you've found yourself a girlfriend." Moose took that as the most amazing part of Karl's entire story. Junkies were inherently un-datable, too enamored with their internal contentment to remain in any meaningful human relationship. Only on rare instances where two people's addictions meshed were they able to have some ephemeral sense of love, but only if the drugs kept flowing. It was pretty much the same for anyone, really. Once either partner no longer got what they wanted, they went searching for it some-where else. The only difference was that junkies could weigh that on a daily to hourly basis.

"She's not my girlfriend," Karl said sternly.

"Whatever, man."

"Look," Karl said, then opened the table lining to reveal a secret drawer that Moose never knew existed. Inside, Karl had rolled a small stack of hundred-dollar bills, neatly packed next to a few pill bottles he had purchased with his new income, and a reglementary police pistol. "She gets me what I tell her to."

"Shit," Moose said, slowly grasping the full extent of what Karl had told him. Karl could see in his friend's face the exact moment when Moose realized their ambiguous friendship was suddenly something he needed to strengthen, at least for today— or the next hour. "So, ya fuck her, and she gives you what you ask for?"

"Yeah, I guess," he said as if Moose had indeed alluded to a perfectly normal relationship.

"Then give me another shot," he said, pointing to the crushed pills.

"I'll do better than that," Karl said, speculating on just how much power he really had pulling on Stacey's strings. "I'll go see Eye and sort out your debt. Can't give you the money directly, obviously."

Moose and Plasma looked at him like he was insane, head cocked sideways, no discernible sign that either of them under-stood the words Karl spoke. Evidently, such generosity was inconceivable to Moose's reality, so Karl reiterated. "I'll get them off your back."

"You would?"

"Yeah, I will, but you're going to owe me, and you have to promise you won't go back to them no matter what. Fuck, I'll even help you write up your MedAid application." Stacey could do that, he imagined.

Moose bit his lip, still incredulous. "Yeah, but shit, that's going to be in a while. I need that shit now."

Karl sighed, then scraped over half a dose using an expired credit card.

* * *

Stacey shook her head. "I can't get you that much money." She had told herself this was as far as she would go, that any more would likely get her caught. There was only so much pilfering one officer could do in the evidence locker before those who chose to look away simply couldn't anymore.

"Then get it somewhere else," he said. She could see he didn't want her to get caught either. Was he worried he would lose her and her police access, or was there another reason? "You know the security more than me. You can improvise. You can do anything."

And indeed, at that moment she felt she could. But should she? He had an odd way of dawdling her into compliance, but she enjoyed that too, didn't she? It was confusing, and if she hadn't felt like she was on top of the world when she was around him, the blood of Superwoman pulsing through her veins, she might have been more concerned.

"I know," she said with newfound maniacal fervor. Her plan would work at least once, she thought. She would make it look like she was someone with leverage, and those crooked ones would give her a wide berth, at least once. But any more than that, and they would go after her; the slightly less than very crooked cops would get her out of the picture.

The western branch of Boston's CW Bank was well fortified from external bombardments and contained state-of-the-art antipersonnel theft protections. But as she knew, it was vulnerable from the inside. This was for a good cause, she reminded herself, then blushed.

She asked the receptionist to speak to the manager about a potential security issue. The woman obliged quickly enough while Stacey sat in a lobby chair where she didn't feel squeezed or stuck inside the armrests. Banks either convened to the corpulent, or she had lost more weight around her ham thighs than she thought. Sex was the best exercise, she reminded herself, reddening once again.

The man, who she assumed the manager, shambled nervously to greet her. He didn't say any more until his office doors closed—hermetically she noted, hearing a short hiss. The room was soundproof and out of camera view. Then she told him he needed to up his protection.

"But I've paid this month already," he said, shaking his head in dismay.

She didn't know how these exchanges went, but she knew from reading between the lines and listening to the words unsaid by some fellow officers that this place was one of their best payouts. Jeffries had stopped there himself, for mumbled reasons, while she was made to wait in the car.

"We've upped the fee," she said. "I came here today to tell you, and I need to collect now. Five thousand more."

"Five thousand," he said flatly. She felt unsure whether that was exorbitantly high or insignificantly low. What amounts did the others ask for?

"You wouldn't want us to lose this address on our NavCom or be held up in traffic when you really need our help, would you?" She imagined the crooked ones saying such things.

"Okay," he said, "but tell Muncho not to send anyone else anymore, and not on weekdays. I told him that before."

"Add this to your rate. Give it to . . . Muncho, next time he comes visit."

The nervous man nodded agreeably, like he had made an important profit on the stock exchange. She took the bills he removed from an auxiliary safe in his office and placed them inside her overcoat. Then she briskly made her way out of the building.

There was no mistaking her for anyone else. When—or if—Muncho asked about the extra money, the manager would certainly describe her, and she would quickly become the only possible culprit. But given the extra five Gs, he might simply look away or take it as good faith from the bank. If they found

out, which, evidently, they could, they would see it as an ultimatum, one from which she skimmed some off the top too, but
an ultimatum they couldn't do much about, since they would
incriminate themselves in the process, however high up it went.
Although she had grabbed five Gs, it wasn't from their cut, and
it guaranteed them a bigger payout for subsequent months. The
only thing they could do was frown and hope she wouldn't push
her luck. No, it was a nicely conceived stalemate, she thought.

Back in her car, she handed the bills to Karl, who sat next to
the shotgun. "You have a different holster, don't you?" he said,
looking at her belt. "We need to get you out of that uniform."
Her cheeks reddened again, and her arms, peaking with tension,
shook with excitement. But she continued to try to rationalize
and legitimize the bad behavior in which she was engrossed.

* * *

At Karl's apartment, following another session of messy mutual
satisfaction, he told her to get dressed in civilian clothing and
hide her gun. He said he was going to pay off a friend's debt, and
if he didn't, his friend would be in big trouble.

"You can protect me, right?" Karl asked, wondering if Eye's
people would try anything funny. He hoped that paying him
something would put him in better confidence than none. But
Eye was known to be . . . shifty.

"Oh yeah," she said, then slapped his cotton-covered ass.

He groaned in pain but then laughed nervously and pocketed
three Gs. The two that Moose owed Eye and the preemptive extra
thousand that he might request as interest—although Moose's
ear had supposedly covered some of that.

Eye controlled a building of flats similar to the one where
Karl lived, and he owned most of the residents too. On every
floor, drug dealers, unlicensed-hookers, thieves, and murderers
provided a cornucopia of services highly valued and necessary for
a healthy underworld.

Karl approached the doorman, nodded in recognition, then told him he had cash for the Eyeball.

"Who's she?" The guard wore a plain black hoodie, which did little to hide his blemished face.

"My girlfriend," he said, quicker than he cared to admit. Then he leaned in close. "She's a little coked up right now." The man sized her up. Karl noticed Stacey looked nothing like a police officer. The doorman would have had to know she was a cop, or else it would have seemed completely incredulous. Short, still fat, and walking awkwardly, she looked like the least-dangerous person Karl could imagine—until she started doing cartwheels, that is. But Karl had been careful to keep his output low, at least for now, and he hoped she wouldn't be recognized.

Her frock coat was all the way to her ears, and her hair was disheveled—he had added that detail himself—and she hardly looked like she did in uniform. She seemed to have adopted the junkie look. She was a natural at undercover infiltration, or was it because she was slowly becoming like him, that he had led her into the narcotic subservience that had so enslaved him and Moose? He gulped at the thought and decided he had already crossed those ethical implications long before meeting her.

Eye's quarters were laid out like a throne room. Karl remembered the place from a previous visit when he had simply been another drunk, stoned partygoer. To serve his ego, Eye made people wait in line, so they could request a favor that was unfairly and clearly biased to his advantage, just like a king or a trickster genie.

No, he wanted to be a pirate, Karl reminded himself, seeing the eyepatch that covered the empty socket from when he had, apparently, removed the eye himself—to stop seeing the transdimensional goddess who haunted every second of his life. "Must have been some bad trip," Karl had told Moose after hearing the story.

The man on the throne, which was made of corrugated card-board and wooden shipping pallets, gave Karl a languid look. Karl told him why he had come. No funny business, just pay up, get Moose off the hook, make everyone happy, and peace out.

"Why?" Eye asked.

Karl hadn't been prepared for that. Perhaps simply because he could. "Me and Moose, we go way back," he began, knowing such bonds meant little to such a man. "I owe him for something he did for me," he added. That was true, he supposed on some disconnected, paradoxical level.

Farther back, he noticed the well-dressed goon who had paid him a visit. The man sat quietly behind the scenes, cracking his knuckles after Karl made eye contact, hoping to be used, if needed.

"Who's she?" Eye asked.

"My girlfriend," Karl said, surprising himself once again.

Eye looked her over. "Moustaffa owes me two Gs," he said while keeping his sight on Stacey.

Karl counted the bills in his jacket—out of sight—and took out two grand.

Eye snapped his fingers at a goth girl sporting tattered fish-nets. She took the bills from Karl, tallied them, nodded to Eye, then placed the money inside her zipper-covered leather jacket, flashing a pierced nipple in the process.

"So, you're gonna leave Moose alone?" Karl asked, then regret-ted it immediately. Like the path of a hurricane, Eye would do as he pleased, and that was that.

"I might," he said, chuckling.

Karl was getting nervous. He felt Stacey's hand brush his. "I'll give you an extra half G for good measure," he said. "Clear up hard feelings."

Eye waited as Karl counted five more bills. This time Eye stood and walked to him, taking the cash himself before taking another good, long look at Stacey. "So, you've found yourself a sugar mommy."

Karl's unease grew as he realized that, through his output, Stacey's shunt was receiving a little extra motivation. She darted toward Eye, pointing a rigid finger almost up his nose. "I'm no one's sugar mommy," she said in a high-pitched voice and then grabbed Karl's groin. He choked out a groan. "This here's mine, and I'll do with it as I see fit. Now, we came here to make a deal, not dick around. What's it going to be, Eye?" For once, Karl was glad she was pathetically unthreatening.

Upon hearing her tone, the hefty bodyguard sat forward on the edge of his seat, but Eye merely smiled. "Give me the rest you got, and we'll call it even."

Karl gulped, pretended that was financially unacceptable to him, then, feigning reluctance, emptied his jacket of the other five hundred, showing Eye the inner seems of his pocket.

"And you?" he asked Stacey.

"I'll give you my boot up your ass."

Eye was taken aback, and Karl's face went deadly pale. He knew she wanted to gun them down, probably get them all killed, and a wave of nausea crept over him. He couldn't control his output anymore. That wasn't good. She would jump into full throttle any second.

"My, my, Karl, you've caught yourself a feisty one," Eye said, smiling. "Well, you caught me in a bit of a crunch, and today I'm in a good mood, so okay, I'll leave Moose alone. But someone like him's going to find himself out of favor again soon enough." The smile was devious. "Will you bail him out so effortlessly next time?"

Karl took a deep breath, focused on controlling his breathing, and pulled Stacey back. "If Moose owes you even one decimal point, I'll haul his broke ass to you myself."

* * *

"You did good," he told Stacey once they were outside.

She nodded and told him she knew who Eye was, but they never had anything to pin on him. He always had fallout perps. That didn't surprise Karl. "You think he's going to keep his word?" she asked.

"Hope so. Not much I can do about it though."

"If they don't, I'll come back and shoot him in his other eye myself."

Karl laughed nervously. Crazy gazed, she lunged forward, pressing her lips to his.

CHAPTER 12

———

Cobalt felt ill at ease letting these civilian scientists toggle with his mind. There were, he had to admit, some tantalizing advantages to the system his superiors proposed. Yet, sitting there strapped to a chair while half a dozen lab coats discussed why he had been such a success, his urge to burn the world returned full force.

"We're not going to change a thing," the long-blond-haired Dr. Lundquist reassured him. He could kill her easily, snap her fragile neck, and she would fall, lifeless, to the floor. But for now he was playing along.

He had told them he didn't want anything changed, that his initial configuration was optimal. Or was it? Could he get even more than what he was receiving?

"For you, it isn't an issue about signal gain or what . . . feelings you receive," she said, "but how it's configured, where the wires touch inside your brain."

Ten more volunteer officers had been prepped and were awaiting the sacred gift that only he possessed. Cobalt wondered why he held such religious sentiments. His views had been rather agnostic before his implantation, more so because he hadn't thought it through enough to know himself. But the energy that flowed through him had changed that. It couldn't be solely due to psychological factors. This was, as he had come to describe it, jarring open the gates of hell. God help those who stood in his way.

Curiously, he had become much more introspective of late. Granted, he had always wondered why his weak heart couldn't stomach the role that he and other soldiers had to play to uphold their homeland. But more recently he had begun to wonder whether he had also become . . . transubstantiated into something greater than human. What was his true purpose? Physical ability aside, why had he been so weak before, and why had he become the way he was now? He was superior to these people, could dispatch them effortlessly whenever it pleased him. But there was a purpose to these gates of hell. A cleansing process, as he had begun to understand it, was transforming the world around him and doing so through him. Easterners lacked the backbone to question their government, but many Westerners didn't possess enough patriotism either. Most deserved to die in order to preserve the sanctity of their nation. They were weak, like he had been, and he hated them for it. Despite doing their duties to an acceptable degree, they were incapable of being true citizens of this great nation under God.

"How do you feel?" one of the numerous multi-prefixed scientists asked.

"I feel fine," Cobalt replied. But he was growing increasingly agitated about being stuck, sitting in that damn chair—engineered, he was told, solely for that day's procedure. The man looked perplexed that he still felt fine.

"Would you say this is a normal state of mind for you, or do you feel different from when you're in the field?"

Definitely different, he thought. The orgiastic bliss he felt from seeing the exploding bits of blood and bone—the result of his handiwork—was incomparable to this tedious boredom. "Here, I'm useless. I need to do my job out there, not strapped into this chair." His voice climbed an octave as he tugged at the straps. That brought a guard to his side with weapon raised and an authoritative voice telling him to calm the fuck down. Some of the lab coats stepped back. The little one named Lundquist remained, meeting his gaze with scholarly interest. Did she know everything he had done, everything he could do to her and those around her?

* * *

"What happened just now?" Dorothy asked the man behind the imager, ignoring the agitated patient.

"Signal spike in the right amygdala," he said. "Interesting."

"Are you afraid?" she asked Cobalt. He didn't answer, only smiled. She had trouble looking away from those deranged eyes. Something active, malevolent behind them sought to hide. She went to see what was drawing her colleague's interest. "He's not being very cooperative," she whispered.

"Look here." He pointed at the brain region in question. "This area was somewhat hypertrophied, either through unusual neurogenesis during childhood or from an abnormal mutation that might have contributed to it."

She examined the chart and then nodded. "It was noticed before, but I believe it has shrunk fifteen, maybe twenty percent."

"But the patterns of activity are wrong."

"Well, we altered it," she said. "Not enough evidence to know for sure what that could mean in this case. It's not unheard of to have slight density variations following shunt adjustments. Most, if not all, subjects don't have any irreversible effects." She thought a moment, then walked over to the soldier. "Do you experience any hyper-sexuality, desires toward objects that might seem unusual since the operation?" she asked without a hint of modesty. "This might or might not include tumescence—uh, getting a hard-on at odd times—or any increase in compulsions to taste things."

The general in the background sat up straight, clearing his throat. "Jesus," he whispered.

She saw that her question cut Cobalt too deeply, and he struggled more, causing the military guard to kick his leg, yelling at him to calm the F down again. Cobalt relaxed somewhat. "I'll get real hard when I eat your heart."

He tried to sound contemptuous, but Dorothy knew he was telling the truth. The maniacal intent was as clear as day in his wide-open eyes. She knew she should go to the shunt controls and initiate an overload, make it look like an accident. It could seem like a normal procedure but would electrocute his entire CNS. The DOD would suspect her. They might never know for sure, but Keneth would, and whether forgiving or not, she would irrevocably wound his trust in the process, and that she could never do. Their friendship and love went way back. They knew each other better than most couples ever could. She had told Keneth she would help them, but seeing the monstrosity that they had helped create—the killing machine that became military gold—she knew she couldn't let this abomination live.

The military report they read had been significantly edited and censored. But even if they reported only Heggard's most benign tactical behavior, it was already too difficult to accept. Killing rates and arms expenditures weren't ethically appropriate therapeutic milestones for his psychological health. But his health wasn't the military's highest priority. In their records, he was dead already. The DOD wanted to improve upon the one weapon that wasn't locked in a standstill by the Paris convention for warfare sustainability: the human mind.

She motioned her post-doc aside from the computer while she opened the window for the shunt controls. Slightly confused, he watched her, having full confidence that it was a necessary function to check, albeit completely superfluous, for he had verified the power couplings already. But then he saw her change the input voltage, and his face went deathly pale. He couldn't speak, his mouth agape. She brought the current high enough to fry every synapse in Heggard's brain. Her finger hovered above the engage button. Beside her, he shook his head subtly, looking like he was going to faint at any moment.

Manne had told her that she should do exactly what they wanted. What did Manne know that Dorothy had missed? Her own knowledge of neuroanatomy was supposedly far superior to Manne's. She knew that nothing good could come out of this . . . man. But what if that had nothing to do with it? Manne hadn't wished to speak of her plan further—furtive as always—if she even had one to begin with. So, Dorothy had to rely on faith alone. And being there in that military research hospital gave her little faith to rely upon. She sighed, then choked down a whimper and hoped her tears wouldn't begin to swell.

She exited the shunt's input function, her lethal settings not saved. "We're done here," she told the general who was overseeing the process. "We can begin implanting the others."

* * *

Operation Medusa went online at 0400 the next day. No acclimatization period necessary, Cobalt ordered. Over an ocean and back, his new team, composed of eight additional men and two women, was sky-dropped over the Oskil River. Barely knowing them, Cobalt was already swelling with pride. They had been instilled with a patriotism they never knew they could have; every one of them eager to send as many Easterners as possible to meet Jesus's extended family. And they believed in Cobalt; he was the first. Their messiah, they had said. At sunset they were crossing the border.

Did he feel different from having his signal divided? At first, he thought it would be diluted, that he would lose his precious spark, but he felt just as great as before. It had been some type of experimental neuro-ident balancing match, the reps had told him, or something of the sort. He had stopped listening to their gibberish quickly enough. The only thing he had asked was that he wouldn't lose any of his signal feed. "That's the whole point of this sordid affair," the blond lady scientist had replied.

If these ten super soldiers did well, he would request—no, he would demand—they produce a hundred . . . nay, a thousand more. This was the time to see if they were just as useful as he was.

* * *

Thompson had received a letter from PrimaCore. Generally cordial, it declared there might be an additional transition period where his shunt's efficacy could vary. They were about to switch his current surrogate for a slightly more compatible user profile. It wasn't the first such letter he had received, so he wouldn't have cared, but this one seemed more personalized, possessing a greater need to assure him everything was alright—which made it sound worse. The letter also requested that he notify the closest facility if his satisfaction wavered, and they would immediately remedy the situation. User satisfaction was paramount, after all. But he already felt great. Why change a thing? He'd experienced so much pleasant human exchange that he hoped he wouldn't lose any of it. To have such rich feelings toward his fellow men was God's blessing. So, he took extra time that evening to pray for the shunt's success.

When the new transition period began, he didn't feel any different. He thought about his church, the people who worshipped there, and thought he still generally liked them all, even the fat, stupid ones. Actually, he thought he had grown a soft spot for the lazy and corpulent. God bless their gross, blatantly obvious imperfections. The dark demons inside never tried to take over, so he relaxed and went about his day.

Then his pants felt tight. Looking down, he saw the bulge. It was rather surprising, seeing as he hadn't had any impure thoughts or seen any women who should be shamed. He thought that maybe the demons were acting behind the scenes, pushing his body to do things his mind no longer consciously considered. Was this a wavering of satisfaction? Not something he would declare forthwith, obviously, as improper, humiliating, and vulgar as that would be. No, he thought, I can't talk to the reps about this. He couldn't even mention it to Dr. Bennings, who was no longer his psychiatrist in any event. He surmised his good health had something to do with it. Wasn't it normal to have periodic events of the sort? In the mornings, sure, he had learned, or while reading, hidden away, the physiology textbooks with indecent images. These occurred without impure thoughts or desires, a vestigial reminder of how powerful sexual compulsions could become if not properly controlled. Cold showers, flagellation, and prayer had worked then. Feeling cumbersome, he wondered whether he could still rely on those alternatives if the situation continued.

He was relieved to be alone and out of sight. This wouldn't be appropriate in the least if he were in front of the pulpit or inside the nun's abbey. He recalled the particularly difficult birthday he had had when he turned twenty-two—he and his jock friend visiting the brothel and all the humiliation that had ensued. Never again, he thought, shaking his head.

He returned to praying, this time for God to watch over the powerful demons that lived inside his unmentionables. Those two were particularly nasty, he remembered.

* * *

They had been sold out, or enemy intel was more advanced than Cobalt thought, but he was also happy to have so many Easterners waiting there. The general himself must have held a vested interest in their performance and set up this little test. So be it, Cobalt thought, zeal dripping out of his mouth.

This is what he had been born to do: scythe the world of the impure. His freshly oiled barrel's blast overrode the chaotic explosions his ears struggled to discern. The rhythmic pulsing of the war zone echoed between high-pitched tinnitus and the beating of his heart. Leaves and dirt flew about, exploding trees and balls of fire appearing to and fro amidst the lamentations of wounded Easterners. What a wonderful night, he thought with a smile. Cobalt yelled with joy, then ordered his platoon to advance.

Still cognizant of their training, they circled, dispersed, and leapfrogged their way toward the source of the gunfire. Cobalt saw the enemy was concentrated mostly along the mountain-side, keeping their position elevated while forcing Cobalt and his troops into a horseshoe to advance. "Predictable Easterners," he spat.

The enemy's gunfire tapered after they split into the trees. He could still see a few of his soldiers, but from their position, the enemy wouldn't. *Good.* His platoon had guts, but they still had brains.

One of his men, about twenty meters away, gestured toward the enemy camp. Cobalt caught his gaze and, with quick hand signals, ordered him to go left and draw their fire. The man nodded and then complied. While moving into the open, he shot incendiary phosphorous bullets that called forth attention like Independence Day fireworks while covering his movement in a thick wall of smoke.

Cobalt fired a quick round, taking out a sniper hidden under fake foliage. The dead Easterner, caught in his own camouflage mesh, dragged down the overhang as he fell. Two more soldiers who had been hiding under it scrambled to find a new position, but Cobalt executed them with shots to the spine and heart, respectively. Then he lobbed a napalm grenade, smoking out a handful of hiding Easterners. He did it all before any fire returned his way.

He leaned out of sight as wooden splinters sprinkled the air next to him. But his team was on the ball. As soon as the Easterners focused their fire on him, someone else took out those gunners.

A few minutes later—perhaps seconds, for it was difficult to tell time under fire—the scene quieted down. Sporadic, single methodical shots—not in fearful desperation and aimlessly like the enemy did—told his ringing ears that only his soldiers remained standing.

"Alright, maggots," he told his platoon. "Get me a survivor. I want intel. And find out how they knew we were coming."

He heard grunts of confirmation. Some of them, still holding formation, infiltrated the mount. Cobalt approached tentatively and listened. He heard footfalls in the distance that sounded like a retreat. Beside him, the younger woman approached, caught his glance, and nodded. More gunfire came from inside: two volleys of machine gunfire followed by a single shot. Then another.

"Clear," his man yelled.

Cobalt motioned to the woman to circle around and get on top of the hillside by the south and approach from their blind side. She nodded, but he heard more fire echoing from underground, then saw her fall. She hadn't been hit, but she grabbed her head and screamed like a panicked child.

"Bite your tongue," he said while scouting for enemy fire that he was certain wasn't there. He pinned her down to muffle her, but she convulsed with tremendous force, bucking him off while she tore at her hair.

"Man down," one of his men transmitted from deeper in the hole. So, one miserable Easterner had gotten lucky after all. But this one, advertising their position with a wail so loud it caused him to grind his teeth, wasn't the one who had been shot.

"The hell," Cobalt said. Then, unsure what was happening, he quieted her head against a rock. She groaned on impact, but then the spasms stopped.

* * *

Father Thompson stood aghast behind the podium. Something was wrong. Out of all the God-given times his spine shunt could have glitched, it had to be during his morning sermon. He cleared his throat and apologized for the hiccup, for that's all he hoped it looked like.

Quiet murmurs started, so he quickly recommenced before they grew distracted. The minds, especially those of the lethargic members, easily wandered unless he held their attention at all times. But today, they were the ones who eyed him the most meticulously, noticing something had gone astray when he lost his cadence again.

"Jesus wept when—" His tongue, like it had a mind of its own, darted in and out, guttural ululations sounding through the church's sound system. His hands darted to cover his mouth until his lips were back under his control. "Mother of Christ," he whispered. "What was that?" The churchgoers stared at him in bewilderment. "Hum, the Mother of Christ, had been with him, following the crucifixion and . . ."

Thompson was sweating, worried, and humiliated, but he knew if he held his composure and stuck to it, they might not notice his affliction. Most people had relaxed. But one, seated in the second row, stared at him. It was the latent pedophile from the week before, that wretched man who should be imprisoned and castrated. But needn't he, above all else, be forgiven? Thompson surely didn't think so at the moment.

* * *

She was only twenty-five, Cobalt remembered from her personnel file, but that detail had been trivial earlier. Now he felt ashamed for having let her die, for having crushed her skull himself. But he had had to do it, didn't he? There were bodies, Easterners at least, all around them who they had dispatched before losing only two. That was a success, wasn't it?

It hardly felt like it. Being as proficient as they were, they shouldn't have lost anyone—not a single one. He let her body slump face first into the foliage. Time to get back to work, he told himself, but he felt a nauseating reluctance. He sighed. Something was off with the implant. Those unreliable PrimaCore doctors with their shoddy technology. If he ever got back to North America, he would find that Lundquist and tear her a new—but no, not that. *That wouldn't be very nice.*

A refreshing coldness crept over him again. Just the adrenaline, he told himself. They would clear the place of vermin but first get one of the rats to spill his info. He felt better suddenly; he had never lost anyone under his command—never had anyone to command. Especially those he cherished, like these soldiers. That must be it, he thought. They definitely were valuable to him.

The soldier who carried a dead comrade—the man who must have been her subsurrogate (hadn't those scientists called it something of the sort?)—out of the mount appraised Cobalt of the situation below.

"We'll smoke them out," Cobalt said, slightly disappointed that the thought hadn't come naturally to his subordinate. "Occlude all but one vent, then scope the only exit."

They chucked down napalm grenades and then watched flames spew out of the hillside like a volcano. "They can't stay in there," he told his men. "I want one Easterner incapacitated, but not exterminated. Got that, you trigger-happy maggots?"

They resounded the aye-ayes.

Gunfire came from the south, and he was about to curse the woman he sent to cover their flank but then recalled she never went. He had killed her himself. He cursed at the fuck-up-prone logistics of having a ten-person team and wished he was still rogue. He had little time to think. One of his patrols farther west went down, as did one officer safe behind him too.

Then Cobalt realized how truly vulnerable his team was. The man behind him, whose subsurrogate must have been the one headed west, went into grand mal as well. The soldier wasn't screaming, but his mouth, dripping blood, told James that he had actually bitten his tongue. At least this one had the common decency to keep his voice down. The man's legs twitched uncontrollably, like he was trying to run in a nightmare from which he couldn't wake, but Cobalt knew the nightmares today were in the wide-awake world.

If the enemy got one of his people, they took out the sub-surrogate simultaneously. This was more than FUBAR; it was suicide. The plan had failed, and they had to retreat, or at least his team did. He could reap their vengeance upon the Easterners himself later.

* * *

Father Thompson kicked his podium with surprising force. It reverberated into his microphone, sounding off an odd echo. Again, he apologized and shook his leg away from view, feigning normalcy. Another hiccup, he told himself, hoping they wouldn't lose confidence in him. But an uncontrollable muscle contraction signal was sent to his leg, and it jolted again.

He swallowed and returned to his sermon. He needed to talk with someone from PrimaCore soon. Such disturbances were highly improper, especially for someone of his stature.

Father Thompson had never felt such uncontrollable compulsions before. Something outside him had animated his leg. Could the demons make his limbs flinch as easily as they had compelled him with evil words? The thought frightened him, but he forced himself to appear like nothing toiled within—a skill he had polished all his life. But he couldn't dominate his vocal cords like the charismatic figure of usual.

A few more sporadic murmurs broke out, and he worried he would lose their attention once again. So, he swallowed and continued with a controlled voice. Just get through this, he urged himself.

Instead he discovered what demonic possession truly felt like. There was no other way to describe it. His head shook from side to side as words that weren't words flowed through his larynx without any volition of his own. Arms flailing, his jostling legs sent him into a sprawl as he jerked and tried to steady himself on the gold-plated tabernacle.

An old lady shrieked in terror. Everyone else leaned forward to see what would happen next.

"I-I'm sorry. I don't feel well," he said but then fell into another bout of violent spasms. This was PrimaCore's fault. But some flicker dawned on him that blame wasn't the answer. He was the one who had sinned. When his problems had seemed too difficult to handle, he had paid for godless ways to alleviate his suffering. But this was not how it should have been. He had had to endure it all for God. It had been his trial, and he had failed. Now the demons had entered his mind—probably directly through the shunt's antenna—and taken hold of his body.

Everyone was staring at him. He could see it in their eyes; the high esteem in which they held him had been slandered by some malfunctioning subroutine in the spine shunt. The old lady who had screamed, Miss Smith, held her trembling hands in front of her mouth, praying. She was among his most faithful parishioners, but could she still hold him in such high esteem knowing he had just displayed such demonic activity? This was the end of it all, Thompson knew.

He caught a glimpse of the pedophile again. The man wasn't shocked; he was almost laughing, leering at him, at his plight, with indifferent amusement, like Thompson was a NetV show character.

"You," the priest said, pointing at him. "How dare you judge me?" The man's eyes shifted from left to right, but his nervous smile never wavered. "Me?" Thompson yelled, eliciting frightened gasps from some.

Thompson's body went slack, his vigor left him, and, slouching, he went into the antechamber from where he had first emerged, walking briskly away.

The patrons heard another door close. Whispering in confusion, they wondered if Mass could finish without the proper amen and "see you later." They simply sat there waiting, unwilling to be the first to challenge the unbendable etiquette.

But Thompson returned quickly, holding something behind him, his face twisted in painful consternation. He said nothing, just went straight to the man who was perspiring abundantly and still giggling uncontrollably, awkward as always at the center of attention.

Thompson assumed the man was assuring himself that no one else knew what he had confessed. The pedophile was relying on the fact that everyone thought the priest was going out of his mind. The entire parish around him, the man couldn't bear being singled out.

Thompson had repeatedly commanded that the kitchen staff maintain the cutlery in pristine condition. He would accept no sloppiness there. The knives were to be polished and honed regularly, and he had been pleased when he found the large meat cleaver perfectly smooth and razor sharp.

"Let God be the judge of you," he said, leaping the first row with ease, his right arm raised. The man screamed during this unorthodox turnabout, but had nowhere to flee for the faithful barred him on both sides. The blur of flashing metal was hardly noticed, but the smack was deafening.

Two fingers plopped to the ground, rolling over once or twice, leaving a trail of blood behind. The tremendous force with which Thompson had channeled God's will jammed the blade deep into the man's skull. His pathetic whimpering stopped the instant the blade stuck.

Then, following a silence so complete it would have made Mohammed proud, the screaming started. Everyone rushed for the doors, cries of the accursed all around him. But this wasn't over yet; today was the reckoning. And these people, he knew, were just as guilty as the pedophile had been. Righteousness was flowing through him. These sensations weren't demons inside. He realized then, after all this time, he had finally permitted God to act through him, and it was holy and pure.

He planted his foot on the man's ribcage and yanked the blade free. "I should have done this long ago," he said, pointing the bloody cleaver around him like the great decider. The churchgoers hurriedly retreated from him, stumbling, panicked, and disorganized, creating a bottleneck before the doors. "Repent your sins, children, for God is waiting."

* * *

Gunfire encroached, drawing closer every second. "What have I done?" Cobalt asked. He realized the shunt was offline; a catastrophic failure. One after another, the subsurrogates had fallen. It didn't make any sense. With the high number of surrogate profiles active on the mega-computer, there had to be deaths from time to time, but to his knowledge, no one had seen anything like this before. The subsurrogates must have been configured differently, configured in such a way that they could freeze or seize. He should have known better than to trust in PrimaCore, but worst of all, he still held all the memories of what he had done. How he had killed and mutilated people—people who felt pain and pleasure, had families and loved ones, who believed in the necessity to fight for their country, however imperfect their commonwealth may be.

Offline, he felt like he had been before the operation: weak and unable to kill. He was James again. He didn't feel so fortunate to still be alive, given how he felt now; it was irreconcilable for him to live with the guilt he bore.

The tree protecting him was slowly disintegrating. Why didn't they come? He wasn't firing back. But he knew why: they were frightened, the result of his slow, methodical, psychological attacks meant to destabilize their very psyches, damage that penetrated far deeper than bullet wounds. But James was afraid too, afraid of what they would do to him when they captured him. Afraid of the pain they would enact in retribution, a retribution he knew he severely deserved. That burden was far greater knowing he had excelled at his job, excelled magnificently. He merited death and deserved nothing less.

He couldn't wait any longer. He brought his gun to his mouth, seeking a peace in death that he knew he would never find in life.

CHAPTER 13

—

As simply as that, I found myself in Sam's employment. There were no contracts or formal agreements; I simply came, like the others, into her favor. A favor that, with trust, she promised would be blissful for us both. Well, Samantha could "facilitate" all she wanted, but I would still request, if this relationship continued, to get paid officially with monetary funds, MedAid benefits, and a decent pension plan. There was something inherently distrustful in the way Sam managed her so-called business. I still couldn't properly define what that was, but for the moment I pushed those ideas aside. Sam had proposed something immediate that suited me quite well.

Given what had happened to Francis, she wanted me away from Boston as soon as possible, and we both agreed we needed to investigate "Korea's" real identity. Here in the West, that couldn't be searched any further than what they already knew, and that had gotten France killed. But I had my hard copy, that shiny plastic-fiber paper with the curious font that he had printed out.

Sam told me the font was called Atbash, from an ancient Hebrew cipher. However, the letters were Latin, not Kabbalah, and the language was English. According to her, the message was impossible to read by visual software recognition alone. Something fundamentally imperfect and askew with the letters made them mash up and come out like gibberish through the deciphering algorithms. But the eye could easily compensate, and after a few lines, the oddness of it was barely noticeable. Sam explained it prevented anyone from scanning it from afar with keyword searches. It would take an actual human eye to read it for anyone to discover it was a confidential document, red-flagged information. But, apparently, no one did that anymore. It must have been why Francis had made it a point of giving it to me in person. And, like Sam had argued—a twisted logic, to say the least—the mighty *They* already knew that I knew about my surrogate, so there was no further danger in holding on to it. However, I did notice that no one read any part of that text aloud and no one had touched it with their bare hands but me.

The long flight over the Pacific provided more than ample time to think things through. Yet the more I dwelled on it, the less it made any sense: the dreams, the importance of my surrogate account, and the unknowing role I had played in the recent chaos. Indeed, there was nothing more for me to do in Boston but hide. So, instead, I wanted to know why this Mr. Korea was so important. That was better than waiting patiently for cloak-and-dagger operatives to come knocking at my door.

Working for Sam had its perks. I now possessed, or so I was told, a functionally unlimited amount of funds at my disposal to find this man. I certainly appreciated flying business class as I peered at the sardine-canned passengers in the back. The warm draft and sweaty foot smell that came forth constantly reassured me that I had made the right choice. Another business exec had complained about that earlier, and I laughed when the steward-ess only closed the blinds and boosted the air-conditioning in the front. This permitted fresher air for first-class passengers but didn't make it any more bearable for those sitting astern. Again, a solution for the elite that ignored the root of the problem. I would be quite surprised if anyone back there hadn't already complained their mouths off, to no avail. But there weren't any alternative routes between commonwealths. So, the flight was exorbitantly priced and as uncomfortable as possible—a perfect sadist-masochist relationship if ever I saw one.

Before leaving Boston, I received some hands-on training from Blood-Red herself in the use of odd-looking hardware and a new poly-tech (the old had surely been compromised). We were never formally introduced, but I think Blood-Red preferred it that way. Sam's tech-savvy tool girl—and probable assassin—behaved like a legit spy operative. The name "Megan" hardly suited the badassness she emanated. But she knew her hardware. My new poly-tech did everything my old model could, but also had tracking devices, a satellite uplink (which would enable me to call and receive calls from any zone on Earth, minus highly ionized battlefields, perhaps), out-of-commercial-spectrum radio frequencies (some of which I had been told never to use), and even its own electrode-firing Taser function.

"I'll just stick to the call button," I had joked with Blood-Red, quickly realizing she had no discernible sense of humor whatsoever. I asked her and Sam how the phone could possibly make it across security checks, but they assured me it would. I palmed the surface where the supposed electrode shots ejected, but they too were expertly concealed by the transgressive-style mold that was adored by the younger generations. I was also given a pair of comfortable-looking underwear (too gerontological to appeal to my sense of fashion). They contained micro transceivers in the lace fabric, which permitted them to track me no matter where I went on the globe. Another small device looked like an egg made from the same plastic that enveloped my implant. Apparently, it was so valuable as to need immediate destruction in the "unlikely" event of my capture. The self-destruct mechanism was activated by pressing firmly on both poles simultaneously.

"You're not serious," I said, wondering if indeed Blood-Red actually had a latent, albeit highly esoteric, sense of humor.

"No bang. Short-circuits the software. No one can discover what it does."

The . . . egg was in fact some type of homing device. If the address on the sheet had been fake—which Sam speculated to a high degree of certainty—the device would tell me if the signal received from Mr. Korea to the mega-computer was cognate to mine. "Proximity activates vibration."

"Then if you know this file's a decoy, why are you sending me to Asia?" I asked.

Sam smiled. "The region of origin is most likely correct." Apparently, signal sources and transmitter-satellite orientations required a geostationary contact, meaning they knew my surrogate's signal was at least close enough to where their hacked data proclaimed it to be. "If it was a complete fabrication, we would know the signal feed wasn't headed to the right place."

"Looks like a sex toy," I said, examining the egg.

"These days, everything does," Sam replied. "But feel free to use it however you see fit," she added with a smile.

"I don't know. The self-destruct mechanism kinda ruins the mood."

After everything had been packed, I didn't know how to feel about this spontaneous secret agent job I had gotten myself into. "I don't think I'm built for this shit," I said while glancing at Blood-Red, who looked very much as if she had been built for this kind of shit. "I don't even know what authority I'm trying to avoid or what bad guys to stay away from."

"That's the beauty of it," Sam said. "Get caught, and you're believably naive, so you won't have much to tell."

"Gee, thanks," I replied. "Caught by whom?"

Sam shrugged. "Either way you're safer away from here, and that device only works through your signal feed. No one else can use it to find your ident. Just don't worry, and don't go looking for trouble. Think of it as a vacation with an auxiliary agenda. Korea is apparently very nice this time of year." After a pause, she added a disclosure statement. "But if you do get into a problematic judiciary fiasco, I'll have my legal team there within hours, and Eastern Pol will be begging to let you go before my lawyers're finished with them."

And that was that. Now I was landing in a foreign continent in the politically adversarial commonwealth with high-tech spy gear and lethally confidential printouts. "Just a vacation," I whispered. Increasingly, everything seemed like a very bad idea.

The Seoul airport was located on a separate landmass outside the metropolis, where construction had overtaken the entire surface area, most of which had been dedicated to the airport, and the transit to and from. After the plane landed, I followed the other passengers but purposefully lagged, merging into the crowd to appear as inconspicuous as possible. Signs clearly displayed in many languages made it difficult to get lost. Then I arrived at the border checks.

The Western passport I held was my own, but Sam had made a special modification to the online databanks. How she managed such a feat was beyond me, but I started to believe there was little that was beyond her reach. My account had been de-flagged, Sam had said. Potentially confidential government annotations associated with my file, freely shared between commonwealths, could have caused me to be asked to step aside into the room devoid of human rights. This "de-flagging" never had been a certainty—they weren't even certain I had made it onto any secret wanted list—but would instead appear as normal as could be.

The lines were lengthy, but they moved efficiently, and before I felt I was ready, an armed security officer called me over. Looking at his no-nonsense frown and heavy build, I would have preferred someone less intimidating to greet me on my first spy mission.

"Name?" he asked, opening my passport. Obviously, he knew my name, but this was no time to be a smartass, so I told him. "Reason for visit?" he asked with a strong accent.

"Sightseeing."

"Where?"

Fuck. That caught me off guard. I couldn't possibly say the city where my surrogate lived, could I? It could be a total shit-hole, and he might know. I had to think of something fast. "Jirusan," I mumbled. Wasn't that a popular site? My mind couldn't remember.

"Oh, Jirisan," he said slowly, pronouncing at length for my wanting education. "T'was nicer before condo development. I would go to Jeju Island. Much better, much bigger."

"I might just do that," I lied.

He swiped my passport along the mag reader. It beeped, and by the look on his face, it didn't seem normal. Unable to see his screen, I couldn't tell what kind of warning he was getting. Criminal dissident wanted dead or alive? My heart started to race. I tried to keep a stupid smile on my face while silently cursing Sam's people for having fouled up my passport. The man shook his head, then tried it again. He looked at me sternly, then folded the document and slid it across. "Have a nice stay, Miss Hilt."

I sighed, hopefully not too overtly, and made my way into the main airport area. Apart from the overly curved architectures, which rendered the ceiling nauseatingly wavy, the place looked like any high-scale American mall, casino included. Curious, I thought. I had expected things to be much different, but perhaps that's how the media—mostly owned by Propaganda Industries—liked it to be portrayed.

My poly-tech rang. Had it turned itself on?

"Any hitches?" Sam asked, evidently aware I had landed and passed through security.

"No, just stupid Hilts," I said. "Should have studied the province a bit more, but it's okay. You sure it's fine to talk here?"

"Probably. The line is, but I can't tell who's around you. Avoid any naughty words in the open. And don't worry; there's a lag time before the judicial machines can coordinate to know you're flagged, which you aren't, at least according to official records here."

That last part didn't inspire much confidence. I didn't want to speculate on which kind of shadow organization Sam might be inferring—the ever-undefinable, faceless *They* who made people disappear.

"But the reason I called is because something big is going on. There's a lot of chatter regarding a certain high-end military contractor."

"Western military?"

"Shhh, bad words."

"Oh, sorry." I looked around to see if anyone had caught that. Although no one near me stared directly, anyone, I supposed, could be an agent of the mighty *They*.

"The contractor is PrimaCore. It isn't official yet, but it's going to break."

"Oh," I said, not knowing where this could possibly lead. Sam did sound enthusiastic about it. At least for Sam, such chatter was potentially profitable.

"Not certain how this fits with you yet, but I can guarantee somehow it does. What I can tell you for sure, through sources of mine that you'd best remain ignorant about—"

"Gladly." I already felt I knew too much, and Sam's omniscient powers of information gathering made her shady grapevine stretch all the way around the world.

Sam groaned. "Publicly, they're fine and dandy, but they're arming themselves against each other. Whatever deal they had, it went sour, and each is prepping their legal teams for the worst. But this is more than simply a judicial matter. Their contacts deep within the underworld are being quickened."

"Fuck, sounds demoniacal."

"Appropriate analogy," Sam said. "To sum it up, they have bigger problems on their hands right now than ident hackers."

"Are you the one who's going to break the news?" I asked when she paused from her monologue.

Sam laughed, then sighed. "I'd love to. Unfortunately, and I hate to say it, but this is out of our league."

"PC's pretty big, isn't it?" I said, using the abbreviation in case PrimaCore was a naughty word as well. Given what she had just told me, combining the word "military" with PrimaCore could have sounded off all the alarms, if they were listening.

"It doesn't get any bigger than that. The Army works like a business too, no matter what anyone says, and they aren't anywhere near as well funded as PrimaCore, considering all their unofficial subsidiaries and Eastern infrastructure. Barely anyone can tell with certainty how deep PrimaCore goes."

"Not even you?"

"Like I said, this is out of our league. But I'd rather they think us an insignificant moiety than a mosquito that stings."

"They already killed Francis?"

"He was a little guy. Meaning they still don't know about us, or we would have known through our own alarm systems. And we still aren't certain it was PC that sent someone to eliminate him in the first place."

Her logic didn't fully convince me, but I didn't want to argue with Sam now. Couldn't *They* have simply been sending Sam, through killing Francis, an "or else" ultimatum? Sam seemed to jump from A to B then directly to Z but was perfectly assured that she was on the right track. In fact, the more I thought about it, the more it seemed things weren't connected. Francis might have gotten himself killed trying to buy drugs in an alleyway for all Sam knew, some pickpocket junkie sticking him in the liver for his loose change. Yet Sam was ready to connect my surrogate to PrimaCore's military association due to some vague tip she got through shadowy dark nets, links that only paranoid deviants used. I wanted to tell her to get thicker tinfoil to cover her head, for the mighty *They* would surely read her mind soon.

"Alright," I said conclusively. Bad idea or not, I had gotten that far. Might as well go find out who this Korea was. The dreams were what I wanted explained, despite whatever else Sam wanted to discover. I still thought this man, who lived in a small rural city about two hundred kilometers away, would yield an important clue as to why I had been afflicted with those highly visceral images somehow. Let the Army and PC fight their battles on their own.

CHAPTER 14

—

Keneth looked like he hadn't slept in ages. His eyes were bloodshot, his clothes disheveled, and he hadn't bothered to put on cologne.

"Shorted-out shunts cause the same discomfort as any cold-turkey withdrawal," Dorothy said, trying to explain why the government-coined "Medusa" project had failed. "The neuronal plasticity from the connections we modulate normalizes during the acclimatization period, but like any chronically used drug, the side effects can be . . . somewhat difficult to bear."

"Who were these two, and why were they implanted?"

"Frederick Thompson. File says he desired to feel more compassion toward his fellow men. Doesn't sound too bad at first, but he should have been diagnosed for sociopathic tendencies as a child. It seems he slipped through the cracks—isolated in a conservative quadrant." She cleared her throat, then shifted through the files on her poly-tech. "The second is our friendly military's great success story, James Heggard, who requested the implant to better function at his job—of killing people. Our algorithms matched them to a high ninetieth percentile."

"Couldn't we have better identified this Mr. Thompson as problematic?"

"Pardon my French, Keneth, but we simply didn't know how truly fucked he was in the head. No one comes in saying they're a psychopath—and those who are, appear quite normal. We couldn't have known."

"He's still at large."

"Jesus," she replied.

"Heggard's been reported MIA, but my intel says he's been captured, or his body recuperated by Eastern infantry. So you can be sure they've analyzed the shunt and know about our contract with the Army." He sighed. "We should have known better than to go ahead with this."

Dorothy wouldn't argue with that, but she still felt she had to appease his dismal mood. "The symptoms from which they sought to escape came back tenfold when their configuration collapsed. They were simply overwhelmed. It was too much for both of them."

"And the seizures?"

"We're not certain about that, but it seems the imbalance in the auxiliary surrogates produced some unusual feedback. We told them it was still experimental. They pushed us to go ahead anyway. But we know the feedback was what disrupted the primary surrogate feeds."

"Then twelve people were slaughtered in Kansas, and an entire platoon was lost in Ukraine. We should have known better. Should have anticipated this."

Dorothy hadn't foreseen anything like this, but she knew who had. "Manne knew."

Like she had been summoned, Manne entered his main office just then.

"Is this true?" Keneth asked her.

"In war, people die," she replied flatly. "Our models showed that surrogate configuration was precariously dependent on a steady homeostasis. This is no surprise to either of you."

"You could have warned us more directly," Dorothy said, but she knew she should have known better.

Keneth sighed. "Makes no difference now." He scratched the stubble that was growing along his normally immaculate jawline. "Officially, they want us to know they're covering this, but unofficially, I'm worried. This won't end so easily." He thought for a moment. "I want both of you to stay in the institute for your own safety."

Both were about to protest but then decided against it. Keneth couldn't keep them there, Dorothy knew, but she felt it better to let him think they were considering it. She could stand it for a day or two, but she didn't think Manne would stay inside for long either. Manne wasn't someone who anyone could hold.

* * *

General McStevens told his staff to replay the footage once again. It showed the shunt installation that PrimaCore had done on their soldiers. Near the center of the large room, which housed a dozen other imaging-capable hospital beds, the volunteers were waiting face down for their turn. In the center sat Private Heggard, strapped down with security personnel ready to respond in case his proclivities kicked in. Around him, a number of scientists and medical professionals walked in and out of view.

"There has to be something," the general said. "Keep looking." The surgical precision with which they had been fucked over couldn't be a coincidence.

On the screen, Heggard said something and tried to jostle out of his restraints. The guard kicked Heggard's strapped leg, raising his rifle like he was about to clock him. Then the head scientist walked to the imager behind him.

"There," McStevens said, pointing at the male scientist. "Replay. Look at his face."

"Magnifying the footage, sir," another officer said.

"There's fear in his eyes," McStevens said with professional certainty.

"He's whispering to her not to do something," the officer said. "Shaking his head. Look."

"Do we have a view of the imager?"

"Unfortunately not, sir. It was their equipment."

McStevens sighed. "Mathews was worried she wasn't fully onboard. She sabotaged something." He shook his head. "We have to know what."

* * *

Dorothy had been at the institute for three days—two of those days prior to Keneth's indefinite curfew. But her commitment to follow his directive was already drawing thin. She had to check on her fish, after all. A large hundred-gallon tank held a cornucopia of exotic blue-red loaches, bright-red swordtails, and an assortment of rainbow fish. Manne had sent someone to feed them and check the pH and the filters as per Dorothy's instructions, but that also left her tiny Japanese Chin puppy, Odin, to be fed, walked, petted, and told he was a good boy, per her instructions. Odin's automatic door flap and food dispenser were no substitute for real human hugs. Poor Odin wouldn't have his mommy there to make him happy. She was comforted in part by the realization that their staff would give her pets the best care possible; no one would dare upset Manne. But she couldn't keep away from her pets forever, and this marked the longest absence she had endured away from them. Even the fish would be happy to see her, she imagined.

Dorothy told her staff that she was stepping out. She announced it matter-of-factly, without volunteering that she had been asked to remain sequestered there for the time being. But it was ridiculous to think anyone who wanted them harmed would be vigilant enough to get her on such a random outing. Throughout the past few days, she had immersed herself with even more work than usual. Either way, she would be back within a few hours to see the results of the new model that they had programmed earlier. This essentially was spare loading time, and she didn't want to spend it there or on her office couch.

Inside the primary mega-structure parking lot, she called for her vehicle as she waited by the automated valet system, checking her poly-tech for messages. Her car rolled by, and its door opened. She stepped inside without taking her eyes off her device's digital display.

"Home," she said, and the computerized driving algorithm plotted the fastest route for that time of day. She folded her device and looked out the rear passenger-side window as long arrays of columns flew past, revealing swaths of city lights in between. Her car veered toward the main highway and accelerated to cruising speed.

She noticed nothing unusual until her car exited far too early. After going down three streets that she didn't recognize, Dorothy looked at the map on the screen and realized she was no longer heading toward the Home icon.

"Crap," she whispered as she realized her vehicle had been hacked. She unbuckled, scooted between the front seats, and tried to commandeer the car manually. She hardly knew how to drive, but she knew better than to let whoever had reoriented her car bring her somewhere else. But the vehicle stopped before she could deactivate the driving subroutine. The doors unlocked, and a man she didn't know got in the passenger seat beside her.

He eyed her with overt irritation, then took a black object from his pocket and hit her across the face. Her consciousness wavered as her head hit the dashboard. She tried to yell, but no words came, and she slumped groggily forward.

Another man opened the back door and climbed in. In the flashes between the times she blacked out, she realized the man who was attempting to manually drive her vehicle was the same man who, years earlier, had accosted her about the prototype shunt models at the Berlin neuroscience conference—the assailant Manne had wanted her to try to identify. The one in the back she had met more recently in Keneth's office: the military intelligence officer named Petterson. Helpless, she tried to reach the controls, but the man in front inserted a mag strip into the computer, and it accepted no more input. Then the car sped off, its new programming enabling it to circumvent municipal driving laws.

"Imbecile. You hit her too hard," Petterson said. "We need her fully cognizant."

"She'll be fine," the other man replied without sympathy.

Petterson shook her back into consciousness. "How did you sabotage the Medusa array?"

Dorothy tried to tell how much time had passed when she felt the car lurch forwards, then upwards. She heard the tires rev without contacting the pavement and the man beside her cursing in bafflement. She tried to look out, saw the buildings at odd angles, and realized she probably had a concussion.

An acute hiss hurt her ears. Bright lights, too bright to stare directly into, flared at each corner of the vehicle's roof. Then the entire metal frame was ripped off. The man beside her, increasingly bewildered at the incredible turn of events, ducked. Then blinding light blanketed everything.

Something fell into the back seat, causing the vehicle to wobble like a boat on water. The black object moved in a blur, and the man in front was stricken hard enough to hurl him against the dashboard. He hit the solid computer surface with a thud far louder than the sound Dorothy's head had made. Petterson groaned, then went deadly silent. The goon in front scrambled to his feet, only to be sent sprawling again.

Dorothy thought she was fading into a dream when she saw Manne's face in front of hers. Manne strapped a harness around her waist, then tugged a rope, and Dorothy was propelled with sudden force up and above the car into a helicopter filled with half-familiar faces waiting to help her on board. Below her, her car, floating impossibly high above the advertisement-polluted

Boston streets, was clamped at both ends by the giant helicopter's retractable jaws. The roof was gone, and Manne, clothed in tight black Lycra, sent out a blinding barrage of strikes to the man in front, who quickly realized he was disastrously overwhelmed. Without giving him a chance to try anything more, she struck him in the throat, and he fell face-first into the driver's seat, unconscious.

The man was strapped into a harness and yanked into the helicopter as well. Then the car dropped directly into Squantum Channel with a splash that was seen but not heard through the sound of spinning blades.

"Are you alright?" Manne asked. Dorothy lunged forward, apologetic, and hugged her. "Keneth would have been devastated if anything happened to you."

Petterson, limp and unconscious, was already seated between two larger security personnel whom Manne had hired to work outside the main PC institute. Partly emasculated, they had hardly done more than watch Manne do her thing. Most likely they had been waiting for such a ludicrous rescue mission that Dorothy had half-wittedly gotten herself into. But Keneth had been correct to warrant caution. Those people had been waiting for her specifically. The moment she stepped outside the institute, they had been ready.

Just before she blacked out again, Dorothy heard Manne yell to the pilot to hurry.

CHAPTER 15

—

K arl rested his dirty sneakers on the dashboard beside Stacey's computer. She told him not to scuff up her car, but then he made her not care. She said it was inappropriate for him to accompany her on duty, but he was bored and felt he needed to get some fresh air. Moose had been cramping his flat that morning, and Karl had decided that if Moose wasn't leaving, he would. Worried Moose would start to leech off his stash, Karl had locked the rest of his pills inside his new desk, which his sugar mommy had bought him the day before.

When Stacey arrived, she appeared antsier than usual, looking for some action. But when she saw Moose half passed out on the couch, Karl was relieved that she was willing to forestall the inevitable. Then—cursing—she had gotten a call at the crepuscule of dawn: a car accident toward the end of Victory Road.

When Stacey pulled into the wharf, Karl leaned forward to get a good look at the carnage that was supposed to be but saw nothing out of place there. Just two people standing on the edge of the wharf looking down at the surf.

"Might be a crank," Stacey said. She verified with her dispatch, and they confirmed: witnesses reported a car driven into the channel.

"Maybe we aren't at the right place," Karl said.

"Wait here," Stacey replied. He watched as she stepped out to investigate. A few vehicles were parked at the marina, some in front of the lakeshore apartment, but the chilly, cloudy weather made most New Englanders seek alternate indoor settings. Stacey buttoned her oversized coat, noticing she seemed to have more freedom of movement within it than before.

Karl watched her walk to the edge, where a meter-high barricade protected pedestrians and vehicles from falling into the channel. He tried to see what she might be looking at. Then he saw her flinch, grab her poly-tech, and dash back toward the car. She had definitely found something.

Stacey plugged her poly into her CB radio as she entered. Karl overheard her requesting paramedics, a crane, and a water rescue unit, ASAP. He wanted to know what she found. It seemed ludicrous. Looking at her, he pointed toward the pier. She shushed him as she spoke to her dispatch.

He shrugged, waiting for an answer until her poly-tech was folded. She told him there was a car in the water; two rear blinkers were visible through the shallow surf. An oil slick was spreading slowly above the surface.

"That's crazy," he said. She waited. "The barricade's still there," he added.

She looked ahead. "Huh," she said. That it was. There was no sign of an incline that could have been used, no skid marks, no structural damage of any kind. But the fact remained: a car had recently fallen into the water.

A few minute later, they heard sirens approaching. Stacey rushed out of the car, then opened his door. "You can't be in front like this," she said, shoving him into the back seat quicker than Karl could shunt any compulsive argument to her.

He groaned, sighed, then burped. She took a step away, turned to catch his glance, and sighed loudly.

The bouts of stomach pain came so suddenly these days. Not that he didn't like eating tons of food, but it was a bitch when he didn't have anything to eat. Then again, wasn't he responsible for these whole shunt/re-shunt shenanigans? It was getting overly complicated.

Dejected, Karl sat low, looking at the process. She was arguing about the fence with one officer. Then he nodded and called someone else. Stacey was talking to another officer when they both looked toward her police car. He wondered whether they were talking about him. In fact, he worried suddenly that he had been arrested. Shit, had she found out? His anxiety reached heart-thumping intensity.

Karl saw his sudden jolt of paranoia cause her legs to jitter. She began to rub her arms vigorously as she spoke with the officer. He saw them nod, then she walked toward him, opened the door, and leaned in. "I want your cock inside me so bad."

"What? Now?" Karl said, feeling as spooked as ever. She ground her teeth. Again, he saw that wild look in her eyes.

"I have to find and question witnesses," she said. "But after I'm through here, you're mine."

He gulped. He had rarely seen her so intense. Karl knew she wouldn't hurt him—not too badly, but it was frightening nonetheless, like a ravenous animal staring at its prey. But after she walked off, he relaxed, and so did she. Thrown into a tangent, he had sent his mind into a state of paranoia, and hers had responded in sync. Yet, upon checking the doors, he noted he was still locked inside the back of her police car.

* * *

Wearing her sombrero indoors, the old lady said, "It was a *you'pho*."

UFO perhaps. "You couldn't make out what it was?" Stacey asked.

"The aliens brought them back," the old woman said, nodding like it was a certainty.

Stacey sighed but noted it on her poly-tech. "What did it look like?"

"It was dark black with a bunch of lights. Then it threw the car into the bay. They brought them up there," she pointed toward the ceiling, "then dropped them back."

"Into Squantum Channel," Stacey finished. The lady nodded enthusiastically.

The next witness she found was one of the people who had called in the incident. He worked at the marina as either the janitor, the bartender, or both. His overalls were stained, so Stacey hoped the former, but considering how the tourism economy was going, soon he would probably hold neither. "A jet-copter dropped the car into the water," he said.

"You saw it happen?"

"Yeah. Heard it coming. I was outside, looked up, the car was already diving, and then the thing turned, heading that way."

"It headed east?"

"Yeah."

"But you couldn't tell if it was a jet or a helicopter?"

"No, I saw it flying off."

She waited, one eyebrow raised.

"It had a propeller and wing jets. It was a jet-copter."

"Huh. Why didn't you report it the way you told me now?"

"You kidding? They would've thought I saw a U.F.O."

When Stacey stepped outside, she saw Karl sleeping against the rear passenger-side door. Across the bay, east from her vantage point, stood the giant structure that was the PrimaCore mega complex. No aircraft of any sort were in the sky, let alone jet-powered helicopters. The description sounded military, but the military weren't allowed to operate within civilian zones. PC, on the other hand, surely had the funds to build such fancy toys. But that wasn't the problem. If PrimaCore was involved in this minor traffic incident, it was rather unlikely—assuredly impossible—that the legal investigation would proceed much further. The warrant would go from Stacey's hand to her CO's, then to his recycling bin faster than he could castigate her for wasting his time.

She turned to see the crane deposit what was left of the dripping car onto the wharf. Had the jet-copter dropped the car a few meters farther out, it might have stayed at the bottom. But the low tide and the surf-breaking rocks near the shore had kept it barely below the surface.

"Where's the roof?" she yelled at the crane operator.

He shrugged. "Not my job." He pointed toward the divers.

Stacey approached the barrier and leaned over it. "Anything else down there?"

Snorkel in mouth, the diver shook his head. They hadn't found any bodies either. Well, she could at least run the plate. She was doubtful anything would come of it though.

She got inside her cruiser. Karl groggily slapped the metal grid to be let out. "Just a sec, hon," she said as she keyed the plate number in her computer.

Karl sat back and sighed, but when he saw the picture of the beautiful blond woman appear on her screen, he sat up. "Who's that?"

"PrimaCore," Stacey replied. "Senior researcher, R and D." Well that certainly gave her a reason to visit that place again. Without a warrant, she couldn't do more than ask a few questions. But if anyone could get those answers, it was her. And Stacey McGee would certainly solve this mystery—if the justice system permitted.

"I'm hungry," he said, sounding cranky and annoyed. He seemed to be hungry all the time. How someone so slim could have such an appetite was beyond her.

"Be patient. I'm on duty. You knew that before coming."

He sighed again. "What's that?" he asked as she loaded a USB into the dashboard computer.

"Let's see what we can see."

The video surveillance images appeared, the screen divided into four time-synced sequences from different vantage points, which she had downloaded from neighboring security systems.

Unfortunately, the cameras weren't oriented to hunt for UFOs, but she had to check, nonetheless. She rewound to the approximate time of the incident, less than an hour earlier. Then all four cameras displayed static.

"Did you see that?" Karl asked.

She stopped and replayed it. A man, her key witness, walked past lackadaisically, but then he stopped to crane his neck. When he did, the screens faded into pulsing noise, snow covering the signal.

"That's not good," Stacy said. "They must have jammed it somehow."

"There," Karl jerked forward, slamming his palm on the grid.

The car, tumbling in midair, flew past the video as some of the snow dissipated from a camera that must have been positioned on the south end. Stacey replayed the video frame by frame and magnified it to full screen. She flicked through the image frames until she could see it clearly. The car's roof was gone before it hit the water, and no one was inside. "No missing bodies at least."

"Huh," Karl said. Then he leaned aside to look up. There was nothing the car could have driven off of.

"It might have been a U.F.O."

"Right," he said, coming to the same conclusion that something had been flying and remained unidentified. "Let me out. I'm hungry."

"PrimaCore's R and D might have developed a few more toys than brain plugs."

"PrimaCore's developing U.F.O.'s?"

She stepped out without elaborating further. Then she opened the rear door. Karl, looking relieved to be set free from his temporary bondage, instead felt her pounce. She left the door ajar without a care in the world. She was hungrier than he was.

CHAPTER 16

—

In Seoul Central, I purchased a one-way coach ticket heading directly away from the Jirisan Mountains. The Atbash-laden text pointed me north, toward a region called Ch'orwon. There I would need to procure transport to a small village named Azalea-ri and find the Korean named Dae-Won Duri.

When I asked for a bus ticket, the polite yet exasperated teller had no idea where such a place was. Unsure of pronunciation, I opened my poly-tech and keyed in the location. Beginning to feel exasperated myself, I slapped the device against the woman's fortified plastic screen.

She sighed, looked at me like I was stupid, then addressed me in broken English. "Bus travel only to Ch'orwon-up. Then you get car or driver with car. No fancy Western NavCom there, *babo*."

So, now I was looking for a place the locals didn't even know existed. The town was apparently somewhat recent; older maps didn't list it at all. Either way, I was glad to leave the metropolis. The heavy smog seriously hampered my sightseeing visibility.

Seoul was different in some ways but was still comparable to most metropolises I had visited. They were all agglomerative mashups of consumerism-driven infrastructure. Gap and the Bay stood next to an express PC pain surrogate implantation hub. Metro strip clubs in the basements of organic food markets. The streets were clogged with vendors and panhandlers and honking drivers who needed to be elsewhere ten minutes ago, angered into rage by dysfunctional streetlights and confusing sirens. A different culture in a different region, but it was all the same.

I recognized the way some women wore their hair, twisted awkwardly around to cover the base of their skull, hiding the small dildo that they weren't configured to be confident about. With so many pain surrogate members, I seriously wondered when our demographic would supersede non-users.

When the air cleared, and the concrete-occluded scenery changed to smaller houses and sporadic trees, my mood livened. Since the operation, I had become more and more of a hermit. This was the first time I was entering a more rural area, and I was pleasantly appeased by it. It was like losing a stressor I never knew I had.

Years ago, during a wilderness excursion with my mother, I had wanted to return to the metropolis as soon as possible. In undeveloped nature, my poly-tech barely had a signal, and my big-screen computer was miles away. But now I promised myself that when I got back to Boston, I would return to the ever-shrinking White Mountain Natural Reserve. I wanted that much more than to be around people, especially packed tightly together in dense cities.

I had never cared much about questioning my reality prior to implantation. Now curiosity drove me to delve deeper with objective dispassion. But it was more than that. I felt compelled to push beyond the threshold—to press the mysterious, forbidden button to discover what it actually did, like Sam's putative panic button. I knew my curiosity, so driven, would lead to my destruction, but I had already come this far, so I felt compelled to dive deeper.

As I looked through the bus window, the natural scenery changed to industrial areas where residential housing was increasingly sporadic and dilapidated. The northern regions—where a formerly well-armed border had been transformed into a restricted demilitarized zone, then an industrial sector—hadn't recuperated well following reunification.

In fact, the farther north the bus went, the more of a shithole the country became. I had been right to avoid mentioning the place to the border agent at the airport. I hoped the province north of the old DMZ had fared much better than this region.

As the rust-covered warehouses and petrochemical storage bins dominated the landscape, I leaned back and tried to sleep. My antenna was slightly cumbersome, so I turned to the side. I wanted to recuperate some energy following the ten-hour jet lag, but when sleep came, I found myself in Waymount again. That wasn't where I wanted to be, but dreams have a way of ensnaring the dreamer, making us believe that where we are is how things should be. But this body wasn't mine. I was smoking cigarettes, and, judging by the pressure in my pants, I was a man. The body was alien, but the mind was mine. This can't be a dream, I told myself as I watched the world through someone else's eyes. I realized I had no control over any of this as I took another long drag of what tasted like this man's hundredth cigarette of the day—dirty and vile, like an ashtray. I/he chucked it. The red amber fell near many others. Then he gripped the steering wheel sternly. Leather squeaked as knuckles cracked. We were in the mall parking lot. I had seen this all before.

Soon little Bill would come along, bright green shirt and tiny baseball cap. Why couldn't I have been with him that day? Not many other children walked that path daily. Sporadic shoppers headed toward the rail station. The man controlling my body took out another cigarette, sparking it greedily with a golden lighter. Then he looked in the rearview mirror. His nose was bent slightly out of shape, and he his face was pockmarked, the result of bad acne or something like chickenpox. Then he looked at me—looked directly at the dreamer. I gasped as the man did too. I had seen him/me for what he was. Anger flared at the contempt I felt for his pathetic backbone, the wretchedness that was this being, but the man hated himself as much as I did. Couldn't he help himself? It didn't matter anymore. I would find him; I knew that now.

He realized it too.

Spooked at the sight of alien eyes inside his own skull, the man took a deep, anxious breath of pinching tobacco, burning through almost the entire stick.

This dream was all too clear; I knew it was real. My anger flushed out of me until I felt nothing at all. Then my rage tapered, and my sorrows turned into analysis again. But this was my chance. Time to gather as much evidence as I could, commit it all to memory, into my very purpose. The shirt he wore, the type of gloves wrapped around his small yet powerful hands, the empty pill bottle on the dashboard, and the vile sticks of dark tobacco he couldn't help but imbibe. This was my chance. Don't be afraid, I told myself. Hold onto the anger, but remember, remember everything of importance here.

His eyes tentatively searched the mirror again. They darted around, afraid of whatever they had seen. But I saw that too. The eyes that gazed back into mine were my eyes, blue irises fading to gray.

It's all your fault, Jade, you bitch.

Bill arrived then, walking past while kicking loose pieces of concrete. Anger flared as I tried to scream, to stop this man from doing what he was about do. But the shunt worked just as well when I slept, and the fury transposed into alien apathy. I shook myself out of that serenity. I wasn't finished with this rage. It was my rage. I tried to scream. *Bill! Bill!* Then my brother turned toward me. My little Bill stopped in his tracks and looked directly at me, at the cigarette-smoking man inside the car.

I straightened with a start to see the woman beside me aghast and the bus driver standing over us, trying to rouse me from my nightmare. The coach was stopped. My heartrate dropped back to normal as quickly as a jolt of lightning. Then the anger, pain, and sorrow were no more. Everyone was looking at me. I feigned indifference and made my way out as quickly as possible, whether I was at my destination or not. So much for being inconspicuous.

Ch'orwon-up looked like an out-of-place American town. I strained to identify any remnants of Korean culture while scanning the streets for transportation to Azalea-ri. I saw a taxi, but my vestigial impulse wondered about the fare, not knowing how far the village was. But then I discarded that consideration. Sam had said I had an unlimited amount of funds to learn everything I could. So, I walked over to the sleeping man in the yellow car and knocked on the window. He bolted upright and straightened his hair, looking surprised that anyone would need his services. He quickly unlocked the back door. "Uhdigaseyo?"

Unsure of what he had just asked, I told him in English where I wanted to go. He didn't recognize the name either, and his comprehension of my language looked even more doubtful. I opened the translator app on my new poly-tech. "Azalea-ri euro gajuseyo," it said. The driver nodded, obviously understanding, but he also looked at me like I was insane.

"What's wrong?" I asked. "Are you going to take me or not?" My poly-tech started to translate that too, but I muted it.

He said something else I didn't understand. I fumbled with my poly-tech, changed the settings, and asked him to please repeat the question. The device chimed in error when I spoke. "Why the hell would you want to go there?" my poly-tech then said, translating his words.

I shrugged. "Secret spy stuff," I whispered.

The man laughed. "I'm teasing. I know English. But man, those phones are slick."

"Jesus fuck," I said, then sat back. "Well, are we going or what?"

"Sure, sure. I've passed through a few times," he said as he swerved aggressively through traffic. "Not much there except warehouses." He obviously didn't want to waste my time, but the worry I would have felt from his reckless driving was uploaded immediately away.

* * *

Not much indeed, I thought while looking around after settling the hefty fee, along with a ridiculously high tip, with Sam's account. Should have hired a team of personal assistants, I thought. They could have driven me directly there, given me an on-road massage while I feasted on real grapes and endangered lobsters—which were great, I had heard. But no, I didn't want to antagonize Sam no matter how enjoyable that prospect might seem. All I wanted—even more than Sam did—was to discover who Dae-Won Duri was. I would have to deal with the whole Samantha "Cojone" Burgess situation another time.

Azalea-ri wouldn't even be considered a village except for the fact that whatever was happening there needed workers. There were warehouses and depots, none of which seemed open to consumers, to and from which moved different trucks and equipment. I also saw construction trailers and portable toilets but no houses or apartment buildings. I had told the driver that he needn't wait, that if I didn't find what I was looking for—secret spy stuff, he had reminded me—I would call him and wait for his return from Ch'orwon-up. With the two workdays' worth of a tip I had given him, I was disappointed he hadn't offered to wait and polish my shoes in the meantime, but I knew I had come to the right place.

The egg that Blood-Red had given me had started to do its job. Judging by the slow vibrations it was giving off, I was now certain it was a sex toy as well.

A man wearing overalls walked out of the long, gray building to my right, looked at me, then carried on. A tractor pulled away and headed west. Maybe I should ask someone, I thought. Farther north I saw a structure that looked more guarded than the rest. It was surrounded by a barbed-wire fence, and two men were standing at the door monitoring it. I didn't think they had seen me yet, but I had to get closer. I had a strong feeling that as soon as I reached that building, the egg would signal my X-marked spot.

I needed a better vantage point, one that was slightly more spy worthy, so I made my way around the large structure to my left. The huge garage doors had no way to be shut. Inside it was dark and somber, filled with nothing but rusting metal beams. No one was around. I crossed through, keeping an eye out for rats or worse, and exited out the other side. From there I could see the two men standing outside. One was smoking while the other paced dolefully, a rifle slung over his shoulder. *Guns, Fuck.* I sighed but decided to wait and see.

But my egg was less patient. The intensity was growing in pitch, and if it continued, it would soon become audible as well. But the fortified area hadn't moved. Dae-Won had to be elsewhere, I realized, the device about to tear a hole right through my pants pocket.

I turned.

Walking toward me was an older man with a shaved head carrying coiled wires slung on his shoulders. Scars on his cranium revealed past surgeries more invasive than shunt implantation. When he saw me looking at him, he dropped the coils and sprinted down a dirt incline.

"Wait," I yelled as I felt the egg tapering. "Dae-won!"

He glanced back but didn't stop, running like a frightened animal. I sighed. At least I had chosen shoes comfortable enough for a chase.

I let my momentum slide me down the short hill while gray pebbles tumbled down beside me. When I reached the bottom, I raced after him.

He entered another shoddy warehouse, and I yelled for him to wait. Upon feeling a strange inhuman apathy crawling over my intuition, I slowed before entering. The egg jostled faster than ever before, meaning he was close. There were no more sounds of footfall. He must be hiding, I thought. *Or waiting for me.*

I withdrew my poly-tech and found the secret button that Sam's potential number-one hitgirl had told me about. Now I really felt like a secret agent, my heart racing from the adrenaline rush that my shunt tried to prevent. But adrenaline affects the body, not just the mind. I was tense and ready to respond, not completely an automaton yet.

Silently counting an arbitrary few seconds, I rushed in. A metal pole hit the doorframe with a resounding thud as I ducked in anticipation. Had I foreseen this? The situation demanded much more urgency than lengthy contemplation, so I pressed the trigger as I tumbled to the dirt.

Two pulsing bolts of lightning, a current so strong it illuminated the darkness around me, arced to the man's chest. He convulsed, then fell unconscious. The clip ejected automatically from the poly-tech, and I realized that had been my one and only shot. "Fucking great," I whispered.

That wretched egg was still going. Since I no longer had any doubt who Korea was, I withdrew the egg from my pocket and clicked its self-destruct button. The vibrations stopped, and I smelled acrid smoke. Leaning back against a pile of metal beams, I tossed the least attractive of sex toys over my head. It echoed off something hard. Birds flew away, wings flapping rapidly.

What now? I looked down at my surrogate, feeling the worry and fear that I should have felt earlier. The shunt wasn't working anymore. Had I inadvertently killed him?

I started to cry.

* * *

No one came or went through all the time we sat there. My feed had normalized, and I regained some objective curiosity. It must have been more than an hour, but during that time, Dae-Won's breathing had become visible, strenuous but noticeable. He was a small man but had grown in musculature from what must have been intensive manual labor, his forearms powerful enough to have taken my head off with that pipe earlier. The scars on *his* head were numerous, some perhaps due to blows or serious misfortunes he had suffered. Others were directly orthogonal to known medical meridians. They weren't acquired by accident, but they certainly looked unfortunate.

As I stared at him, oddly, I wasn't worried about what would happen when he awoke. Granted, I hardly felt fear at all anymore, but I felt that our earlier meeting had been more of a misunderstanding than anything.

As I appraised him with intuition mistaken for logic and logic mistaken for intuition, Dae-Won groaned, grabbed his head, and sat up. After taking a moment to rediscover where he was, he saw me sitting there, my poly-tech pointed directly at him.

If I was mistaken, and he was dangerous, my only remaining option was to bluff, with serene certainty flowing through me that I could pull it off. But this man definitely wasn't serene. He was terrified.

"I just want to talk," I said quietly.

Dae-Won tried to stand, obviously wanting to dash, but I raised the harmless poly-tech and told him to sit.

"Who are you?" he asked with a rugged accent.

"I'm a super-dangerous secret agent," I said. "Now sit down."

He did.

"They said they would not come here anymore."

"Who said? Them, they, or a real *they*?"

He looked at me like I was crazy. So, I pointed my phone again, and he recoiled slightly. I shook my head and repeated the question.

Dae-Won turned and pointed to the antenna.

"PrimaCore people," I said. "Why would they come to you? You can't go to them?" Again, he stared at me, as if wondering how I couldn't possibly know. "What's going on here?"

"We build the pods," he said finally.

"Pods?" I asked, my poly-tech urging him to answer.

"Who are you?" he asked.

I sighed. "My name's Jade, Jade Hilt. I think I'm your surrogate."

His eyes widened, and his mouth went agape with marvel. "You mean . . . these wondrous sensations are yours?"

"'Wonder' isn't the word I would've used." I went through my purse and took out the pristinely folded pair of bugged grandma underwear. Undoubtedly, he might have misconstrued my intent, but having destroyed my tracking device, the underwear was my only alternative. I held them out to him. "You'll have to put these on."

He tilted his head. I was tired of people looking at me like I was an extraterrestrial and shook my poly-tech at him again. "There, behind the steel beams."

He complied readily enough, putting them under his pants and over his own briefs. "When you chased me, the signal was intense," he said.

"You looked frightened, but I'm not here to hurt you." I regretted saying that because I had already jolted him into unconsciousness using Blood-Red's high-tech mod. Although if he did become belligerent, I couldn't do that anymore.

"It was wondrous," he said, rejoining me with his pants back on. I didn't understand. How could he have enjoyed it? He had been afraid for his life. "The others," he added, "are not able to stimulate in peaks. They are stabilized."

"The others?" I asked. "You have other surrogates? But that's not how it works. The links are one-to-one. Everyone knows that."

"Only one out there. That is you. I am sure of it now. I am happy to know."

He wasn't making any sense. But I already had a long list of questions, and they were piling up faster than I was receiving answers. "Have you had the dreams as well? Dreams of my little brother—my brother, Bill, who was killed?"

He looked like he didn't know what I was talking about. "Maybe one of the others." His lower lip started to tremble. He looked very sad again.

"What others?" I asked, then sighed. "What's wrong?" But then I knew. He was getting my emotions. The sadness and the sorrow were being uploaded from me, bouncing off satellites, being transformed inside the mega-computer, then downloaded back into Dae-Won's brain every few milliseconds. He was sad because I was supposed to be, and that brought a strange melancholy knowing I was responsible for his sadness too. I needed to control my outputs.

"No, please do not," he said, as if knowing what I was thinking. "The pain you felt, it is necessary."

"My suffering, you wanted this?"

"Your emotions," he replied. "The love and the joy are so strong. The darkness is necessary to feel the warming brightness of the light. Jade, before your gift, I was not able to feel anything at all. I was a machine."

"You're a cyborg?"

He laughed so exuberantly that I worried—only momentarily before it flushed away—that someone would come to investigate. "No, a metaphor, you silly girl. But I suppose, with these in our heads, we are all part machine." He paused for a moment. "When I was a child, I was diagnosed with a severe form of Asperger's syndrome. I was unable to interrelate with my parents or make friends. That did not seem like a problem at the time, but as I grew older, I was estranged. I could not associate myself with others in any meaningful way. I lived in isolation. In fact, I preferred isolation, taking the time to learn what I could from society without being a part of it, like learning your language. But I knew from books and videos the concepts of love and hatred. First, I thought them a burden, but when my parents died, and I did not care, I knew there was something about being human that I would never have. Doctors tried to operate, to inhibit the troublesome zones, but it never worked. Only caused . . . new problems."

Great, now I made him feel pity.

"So, you went to PrimaCore?"

He nodded.

"But it didn't stop there?"

He shook his head. "My condition was, they said, unique. They said I could help much more than a single person. Years ago I was paired with surrogates who, they said, were unsuitable for me. They required someone with a feed so powerful that it would . . . counterbalance mine to the highest percentile."

"Mine."

"Yes, it has to be," he said and smiled.

"What I was feeling, I couldn't tolerate."

"But it was what finally made me touch the fabric of the heavens."

I sighed, growing uneasy about the topic. "So, it seems we were a good match." I lowered my poly-tech and placed it inside my purse. He didn't try to escape. "But it didn't stop there, did it?"

"No. They said the hydra was able to take many more."

"They call you a hydra? Like the mythological monster—"

"—with many heads." He looked at the dark ceiling, where some pigeon-like birds had returned to roost and paint the walls white. "Then they brought new people here and added them to my feed. At first it was very difficult for me. Every time they added someone new, they took away some of what I received. It was never as good as now, with you, but it became diluted each time someone new was added. At first it worked for them, but . . ." His eyes swelled with tears as he forced himself to recount. "Then I killed them all."

"Killed?"

"PrimaCore did not know how I did it, but something in my brain," he said, fingering his scarred cranium, "something in there made them do it, made them take their own lives."

Being his surrogate, it wasn't the kind of news I wanted to hear, but any fear generated by that was sent back to him. Indeed, he seemed genuinely worried.

"How did they . . . commit suicide?"

He sighed and searched the dark ceiling for answers. "Pills, jumped off a skyscraper, shotgun, pills, car accident—that one also took another family with him. Another hung to asphyxiation, one bled to exsanguination—"

"Okay, okay, I get the picture. But couldn't they stop it?"

"It all happened within hours."

"All of a sudden? Just like that?"

"I could not explain to them what it was, but I knew what changed inside of me." Tears rained down his face.

"What was it?"

"Despite the feed dilution, I was still happy. My human sociability finally was becoming normal. And for the first time in my life—I had never been able to justify it before—I knew, in my heart, that God exists."

"God . . . God killed them?" I asked, incredulous. Since I was a child, I had accepted that God might exist, but I had never thought about it too much until I received the shunt. Then my introspection increased, pushing my agnosticism toward full-blown atheism. Belief in God was an emotional response toward one's inability to fully accept the universe, the escapism that one latched onto due to their unwillingness to fathom, or to contemplate, what crude inconsequentiality lay beyond the threshold of life.

"When I felt the true love of God embracing me, I took that feeling from each one of them," Dae-Won said, "tenfold more potent than what I received, and left them with the crippling certainty that everything was for naught." He paused for a moment.

"I did not want to be responsible for any more harm. I told them I no longer wished to take part, but they gave me little choice."

"Jesus," I whispered. I couldn't be sure that wouldn't happen to me too, but despite my new mechanical objectivity, I was still driven by a consuming curiosity that gave me a purpose—one that God's absence couldn't take away. I couldn't end up like them; it seemed impossible now, post-op.

Once again, it was like he knew what I was thinking. "Since then, they have reconfigured the hydra surrogates to have certain precautions," he said. "The pods hold these fail safes."

"They keep saying that neuro-ident profile matches are always configured one-to-one. Why the pretense? What difference would it make?"

He stood, then reached for my hand. "Come, my precious Jade Hilt, and I will show you."

CHAPTER 17

—

Father Thompson pondered what he had done and what remained of his future while sitting atop a large pine tree near the training ground he had carved out for himself. Despite it all, the sun shone brightly, and he felt wonderful. What happened had to happen—he knew that now. The new love he felt for them still permeated his thoughts, but he also knew they didn't deserve to live. If only he could have finished them all. If the stronger ones whom he couldn't transubstantiate to hell hadn't intervened, he might have done just that.

They had disarmed him, but they weren't able to keep him pinned. The rest of the congregation fled, screaming in panic, cursing the demons that had taken control of him. The church closed, strapped with yellow police tape. The convent was in disarray, and the entire parish would likely be disbanded. But perhaps it was better that way. He presumed he was now ex-Father Thompson. Never had a priest taken such an active role in saving souls, but he was certain head office would not approve of his initiative.

For two days he had been hiding within the twelve-acre forest near the convent. Since he knew the land better than anyone, it was difficult for the authorities to get the upper hand on him, even with IR-capacity helicopters and genetically enhanced, super-olfactory canines. The two officers who had come close to his first trap were already dead. Now he simply waited.

He pondered his options. He could always try to acquire a new identity from lowlifes in the metropoles. Alter his facial structure and reintegrate into a new convent, perhaps not as head bishop but at least as a brother in the continual service of the Lord. It had always seemed like his purpose, but he knew he would never feel fulfilled unless he was at the head of the podium. But fanciful thinking only went so far. His career was irreparable, and he knew the cause; he knew what had pushed him over the edge. It all stemmed from PrimaCore. First his psychiatrist, Dr. Bennings, who couldn't have helped him in any event, had written the prescription for his visit to the pain surrogate facility. She would have to die. He hadn't decided how yet, but he would lovingly improvise something. She was the closest, so she would go first. Then, in Topeka Central, the receptionist and the MD who had implanted his shunt. After that, in Boston was the head scientist whom he had seen on television, Dr. Lundquist. Finally, the man who started it all, the man who was constantly overdressed and overtly atheistic: Keneth Mansfield.

Thompson's shunt still worked, but it wasn't the same. Except for the incident when he went off the edge, so to speak, he still felt compassion for his fellow people, but his mind was jumbled. The demons who were always at the subsurface of his mind were now intermingled with his shunted psyche. It was an interesting feeling, to say the least. Like he had, for the first time, truly accepted the demons as part of himself. And it felt wonderful. He was glad to be alive, breathing, and believing—truly believing—in the altruistic potential of humankind but knowing for a certainty that he still had much fat to carve before humanity could become how it should be. If anything, he was truly at peace now, for he finally knew his purpose in the world. It was his duty to make it a better place, a place where God would be proud of his children. At the podium, there was only so much he could do; words only sank so deep. His people's convictions had to be their own, not his. But now there was a more poignant way, he had joyfully discovered. Blades could be driven deeper than words. Much deeper. Even better, they couldn't be ignored. These people would repent or be cut down. He would be the righteous scythe clearing the fields for a new crop to take their place.

He heard rustling leaves and dogs barking. Thompson perched himself steadily, waiting like a trapdoor spider. They're so one-dimensional, he thought as he looked at the officer trying to restrain his overeager dog. The man stopped beside the piece of robe that Thompson had placed there. Pathetically typical; the officer was bent over right where he needed to be.

The officer's neck broke Thompson's landing. The dog barked, wailed, then became silent too. Thompson disposed of the policeman's body, then chucked his dead dog in the pit beside him.

Thompson decided he had contemplated long enough. It was time to move on to the next stage of his grand design.

* * *

When James awoke, the pain sent him howling, but the sorrow he felt drilled down to his soul. Lying in a dark room in a strange hospital bed, he wailed that he should be dead. His jaw was clamped shut, but the sound of his grief cut through the frigid air. He was strapped down, and trying to move sent sharp pains throughout his body. He realized his jaw wasn't completely intact, and judging from the intensity of his headache, his skull had not fared too well either.

The last memories returned full force: the team he had lost, all the people he had killed, and finally, taking his rifle into his mouth. But he had failed at that too. Without the shunt's feed, he had always been useless. When it failed him, he didn't even have the capacity to finish himself off. Such a pitiful soldier, he thought as a new wave of self-hate surged through him. At the back of his neck, the shunt was still there. He felt it pressing against the sweat- and blood-stained pillow. But it was different. He was still Cobalt, but he was also Flinch, feeling the worst of each. He must have damaged the shunt tendrils somehow, but—not knowing much about brain anatomy—he wasn't sure how he could have injured his brain without killing himself either.

Evidently, he was still alive, but that was wrong; he needed to die more than anything. He did not deserve to be in this world. James "Cobalt/Flinch" Heggard struggled in his bed, but all he managed to do was trigger alarms. Wherever he was, he knew he wasn't in the friendliest of hands. He had no doubt he had been captured by Easterners, but they possessed enough humanity—despite all he had done—to take care of him. Even so, he also knew they all had to die. "God," he cursed in confusion. His neurons were a mess.

A man and a woman clad in white rushed in and held him in place, telling him not to move. *English, eastern European accent.* The lady, wearing a protective mask, pinned him down while the man brought a vial and a comically large syringe. James struggled and tried to speak, to ask where he was, but the man pumped the vial's solution into James's IV, downstream of a clear bag of saline. Then they argued in a language James hardly recognized in his current state of mind. All he could do was remember what he had done, and that pained him more than anything. Through the pain, he worried how his counterpart was faring now that their connection had been somehow . . . altered. Then he faded back into comfortable oblivion.

* * *

Thompson found a nice vehicle to borrow. The owner no longer needed it after Frederick showed him the ways of righteousness. The older man had tried to argue that he wouldn't confess to the roaming arm of the law, but Thompson knew that was a lie. So, even after repenting, the old man still hadn't truly done so in his heart. No one knew the vehicle was missing, but Thompson would trade it in for a new one soon, just to stay one step ahead. Evidently, the police couldn't give up on him; they would pursue him until the end, but Thompson was certain he would be granted the opportunity to finish his work before they did. Only then would he consider whether it was time to meet God in a blaze of glory; not before.

Dr. Bennings had tried to argue that this was all a mistake, that showing her who God was wouldn't undo any of the hardship that Frederick had undergone. At first, she seemed eager to accept the Lord within her atheistic heart. When he decided to give her a chance, she seemed adamant that she would change but then tried to blindside him with a marble bookend. She almost made him the fool with all her lies, but Thompson made certain she would never tell another. He cursed himself for being so gullible. Sweet words might trick him, but if he remained vigilant, he would never fall prey to such womanly wiles again. He had given her a chance because he knew it was the right thing to do despite all the godless atrocities she had performed on so many innocent minds. Everyone should have the chance to repent, but she had chosen to be ravaged by Satan for eternity instead.

This wasn't the first time he had been on the run, and not simply for exercise. At twenty-three years of age—before he found God—he had the idea of stimulating his fire insurance business with a little arson. In the small town of Viola near Wichita, with relatively no fire-suppression service available, he had started selling such insurance. A few purchased it, but the first time an uninsured house burned down, twelve more people called him urgently. When the first signs of foul play arose at an unfortunate man's burnt house, he increasingly sold the most profitable of sales packages. And so it went for four years, the police unable to identify the serial arsonist, and he, "Jorge Carlow," a shy hermit, had collected the profits. He argued that with such a prolific arsonist still at large, it was foolhardy for him to sell insurance at such a low rate. "He could strike anywhere, anytime," he said nervously. "With such a payout, I would be out of a job." But surprisingly, not a single insured house went up in flames. His clientele paid six times their starting fee before he had to disappear.

One uninsured homeowner was waiting with his shotgun in the night, guarding his place with a sly suspicion on the off chance that the arsonist would strike. He was right. After the warning shot that Thompson felt graze his bicep, he fled, but he knew he had been identified. So, he quickly left the place, fake name and all. Realizing the error of his ways, he knew he had to change. Thus shortly thereafter, he joined the order and found himself—like anything he really applied himself to—better at it than everyone else. So, he climbed the ranks of the devout until he earned the parish priesthood of the Fellowship of the Ardent Faith. But now that racket was done too. No matter into whose basket the patrons paid, God would sort them out in the end.

Driving to the metropolis was a long straight line through nowhere. Fields to feed the masses and cow pastures to fertilize those fields. All that time to remember how he had received his chance to repent. In his mind, he knew he had done wrong in the past, but through the Lord he had found salvation and, more recently, his true purpose. Long and hard was the road out of hell, but paved with his deeds, it would shine brightly with the words of God lighting the way for all sinners to see.

* * *

James was jolted awake the minute his physician proclaimed him fit enough to speak. He came to on the cold hospital bed with stern faces surrounding him. But these weren't simply doctors and nurses; they wore uniforms dressed to Eastern codes of etiquette.

"Do you know where you are, chap?" By the look of his insignia, the man was a colonel. His calm, patronizing tone and accent were about to send James into a fury, but he felt disarmed by the unanticipated atmosphere, nonetheless.

"P.O.W.," he ventured, barely able to get the letters out.

The colonel laughed as the others frowned nervously. "I'm afraid it's not as simple as that," he said, then looked at the doctor. "You don't really exist, chap. Your citizenship, your military records, heck, even your birth certificate doesn't exist anymore. We couldn't even repatriate you if we tried."

"Rrivate Hames Heggar . . . MIN eighty-four . . ." he mumbled through the jaw clamps. He realized his lips had been scorched off.

"We know, chap. You've told us already." The colonel sighed. "We know everything." Vaguely, clouded like a half-forgotten dream, James remembered telling them. Screws on his jaw slackened, so he could articulate more clearly. He remembered the pain that had entailed. Drugged with thiopental or some derivative, he had recounted the same information over and over again. Or had that all been a dream?

"There's no point in denying any of it," the man in the colonel's uniform said.

Or was he drugged now? Trying to trick him into confession, could they have implanted that memory? Could they do such things now? Ease him into telling them what they wanted? His dazed paranoia couldn't make heads or tails of real and digital. He tried to shake his head, but the brace made it impossible. His eyes darted sideways, and a nurse brought an arresting hand over his shoulder.

"You see, chap, you're a victim in all this," the colonel said. "You aren't responsible for any of it. This was done *to* you. An experiment gone horribly wrong." He paused, shook his head at one of the physicians. Whatever the doctor was urging the colonel to do, James had no clue. He wanted to tell them he had volunteered, that he was guilty, but it was so difficult to get the message across.

"There'll be a great deal of legal fiasco from this whole shit pile," the colonel said. "And if the international courts—if they can even help to clear anything up—must address the hornet's nest your government trampled on, warfare will never be the same again."

"Waff do hoo want wif me?" James asked, painfully trying to free his jaw.

"You're evidence, chap, proof that we need a whole goddamn rewrite of the Paris Convention." The doctor noted something on a pad and showed it to the colonel. He nodded, then turned back to James. "We need to keep you alive, chap. You might just be the most important man in the world right now."

"Ohhhhh . . ." James tried to scream a negation.

"Give him the best-possible care, doctor," the colonel said. "This man's health is your personal responsibility. I hope I make myself clear."

James shook in his bed, feeling sores he hadn't discovered yet. His IV pumped full, oblivion crept over him again. "I hust want to dhyeeee . . ."

* * *

Through the forest, across the mountains, over the ocean, and inside the PrimaCore institute complex, MI Specialist Petterson awoke, realizing immediately who had captured him but without a guess as to where he was within the building. The PrimaCore mega-structure was so huge that their intel couldn't know the full extent of the restricted areas, external additions, interstitial floors, fake walls, and acutely positioned mirrors.

"I'm about to show you how to perform a real interrogation," a voice said in the dark.

"Why did you sabotage the Medusa array?" Petterson asked. Three armored figures stood watch, their flexible ballistic mesh glimmering despite the low light. He couldn't identify them, but the one walking toward him; he had already had the pleasure of making her acquaintance. She wasn't there to answer his questions. Manne had her own.

"I'll tell you nothing," he said, then realized he was bound to a medical chair, like the one they had used for Cobalt. Above his head he saw the edges of a brain imager. He knew he had to hold out. His subordinate might already have taken his own life, but a person of Petterson's rank and intellect had other proclivities. He was implanted with a sub-dermal tracking device that would alert the military to his position, and he had obtained the best psycho-imprinted anti-interrogation cognitive blocks available. They could fry his testicles under high voltage for days, and he still wouldn't break a sweat. Plus, his liver had been genetically enhanced to metabolize almost every known drug or poison. "Do your best," he dared them.

Manne took a glass vial from her pocket. "This one we removed," she said as Petterson's eyes darted to the bloodstain on his wrist. "And deactivated," she added. "A duplicate signal in the seabed has already transmitted confirmation that you are dead. At this moment, covert military divers are combing the toxic silt for your decomposing body. How long do you think they'll search for it?"

"They'll confirm your signal's a fake," he said.

"In time," she said, walking behind him. "But too late for you, I'm afraid."

He tried to move his head. "What are you going to do?"

"Tell me what progress you've made with the shunts."

"Suck my cock."

"Then I shall give you a taste of what is possible," she said. "As my scan indicates, you are already aware of some of the shunt's alternative modalities. We implanted you with one of our regular commercial models. It is quite sufficient for the task, I assure you."

"I'm uploaded?" he asked. "You made me a surrogate? To who? Why?"

"You see, Mr. Petterson, you and your military have always been asking the wrong questions." She looked at the imager and smiled. "I like monitoring the patterns. There's a sudden surge of fear rippling through your brain just now. Anyway, it's not about what you can get a person to do—that's limited by their physiology. It's about getting the mind to believe it's doing what's right."

He didn't know what to say. He was certain she was monitoring confusion in addition to fear.

"Like the animal you are," she said, then configured the shunt, "feel pain like you never imagined possible." And then he did. Like burning pinpricks of biting cold, his entire nervous system was stimulated by the signal downloaded through the shunt. Petterson jerked as much as his entrapped body would allow. To say it was the worst thing he had ever felt was an understatement. It was not a pain he could tolerate, control his mind to override, or get used to if it were maintained. The horror echoed through his entire peripheral nervous system, like a lesson learned of something hideously atrocious. He couldn't fathom ever feeling it again. He had been stripped of this reality and encased within an isolated shell of the most appalling pain possible. "That was zero point one seconds," she said, grinning. "Would you like to try one fifth of a second now?"

Startled by the screams, one of her armored guards straightened as Manne looked back. The man next to him leaned in close to the newer recruit. "Manne won't tolerate such lack of attention in the future," he whispered, "so redouble your concentration. Two things you have to learn quickly here: first, never let yourself believe she's any less capable than a man—that might lead to broken bones. Second, while this can be divided into separate subcategories of severity, never, ever fuck with her in any way whatsoever." It seems this military fellow has already broken both rules. "Now see what happens." The younger recruit gulped as he turned back to watch.

"Please," Petterson said, "I'll tell you everything. Just unplug me from this infernal device."

Manne shook her finger slowly. "Not yet, dear. As lead scientist at military R and D, I want you to tell me everything. And don't try to lie; this machine and I can read your brain better than you can."

At the prospect of what he had just felt, lying was the furthest thing from Petterson's mind.

When he was finished giving her information, she didn't look pleased. Perhaps she had expected as much and wasn't enlightened by their talk, or she was displeased by the extent of what they themselves had tried or tested. But he at least thought she believed him, and he was eternally grateful she hadn't jolted him with anything like he had felt earlier. Once was enough. He had cracked, been broken by the simple touch of this woman fiddling with the tendrils linked directly into his mind.

"Unstrap him," she ordered. Two men came, one on each side, and released him, his shunt easily unsnapping from the alcove groove.

"You're releasing me?" He was surprised, but given that she could wirelessly deal him such pain at will, he doubted he would do anything to cross her—at least until he got that vile thing out of his head.

"That was business," she said casually as she pushed up her sleeves. "Now this is personal."

"No, no, wait," he said, "I'm on your side now," he said as she loomed over him.

"You crossed the line. Whether the plan came from you or orders from your CO doesn't matter to me," she said, looking down at him. "When you went after one of my girls, you made it personal."

"Oh, man, he's really going to get it now," the rookie guard said from behind his face shield. His partner elbowed him to shut up. Manne laughed.

"Come at me," she said, gesturing to Petterson.

"No, I won't," he said, though he was well trained in self-defense.

Manne looked up as if the dark ceiling held the decision for which she searched. Then Petterson felt a horrendous swelling coming out of his pores. Infinitesimally smaller than the surge she had made him feel before, he realized she could control that directly through her own mind. That bitch, he thought. Then the anger swelled within him until he couldn't help himself. He swung at her with enough force to break her jaw. But he felt like he was stuck in molasses. His brain, like running from a dangerous animal within a dream, was unable to properly stimulate his muscle fibers to work at normal speed. But she moved like it was nothing at all.

His hefty punch swung languidly through the air, but she was beside him, hands folded behind her back. She struck him with movements faster than he could see. He was sent sprawling against one of the guards, who lifted him back to his feet—politely, apologetically. Manne stood in front of Petterson, urging him onwards. She was like a psychopathic cat playing with her food, a sadistic spoiled child relishing the sight of his pathetic-ness. If he stood defiant, she would give him a larger jolt. If he went at her, he would get his teeth kicked out. Petterson wasn't one to give up easily; he would at least try to give her a black eye. No matter how much she wounded him physically, he would choose a lengthy beating over a millisecond jolt of the pain she made him feel through the shunt.

Then he realized something else: there had never been a cloaking device. What this creature—he couldn't quite fathom her as a normal human anymore—had was speed. As much as he tried to push himself to claw at her, the more he seemed tied down by his own muscles. He didn't have to ask who his surrogate was; he knew. It was her. Not knowing quite how she had accomplished it, it was certainly something that his superiors would be interested to hear. She controlled not only his psychological feelings but also managed to grasp his neuromuscular system as well. She made him languid and slow while she, receiving sadistic pleasure through his suffering, was boosted to preternatural alacrity. These were aspects of spine shunts that they had never envisaged before. If only he could bring that intel back to his research team. But she had shown him much more than he could know, and he realized then that he wouldn't get the chance, no matter how subjugated, to leave that place of his own volition.

Manne threw Petterson to the ground once more. He'd been sure he had her that time. Feigned a left, then sent a right, but she was toying with him.

With maniacal glee, she towered above his beaten body until her mood went deadly calm. "Enough fun for today," she said. "Send him for installation."

CHAPTER 18

—

I let Dae-Won guide me toward whatever he wanted to show me. The armed guards outside knew him well. They didn't so much as raise an eyebrow when he told them that I was visiting—except to check me out, of course.

"They are local, you see," he told me once inside the gigantic elevator. "PrimaCore does not officially own property here. Subsidiaries and run-offs, accounts so intricate that perhaps the right hand does not know what the left is doing. Either way, these men are not here to guard the place with their lives; they are here to prevent illegal trespassing. Never have they been inside."

Dae-Won waved a keycard in front of the controls, and the grand elevator—so large it could fit more than one of those tractors outside—jostled online. As we descended, I wondered how much access he had. The only thing that came to mind was that I was being shown, secret agent that I was, another supervillain's high-tech lair. "Jesus," I whispered.

"What was that?"

"Nothing . . . I said nothing."

"Huh," he said, approaching me. "The people left down here are not the most fortunate, I must warn you." The elevator went ridiculously slow, clanging every few seconds to let us know we were still moving.

He looked sad. "I told them they should remove those people, that they should not be treated in such a way. But they said this was their sentence, that the government tribunals had proclaimed it so, that if I mind so much about these refuses, then I should care for them myself."

I was perplexed. "I don't think I understand."

"Pods keep them alive," he said, ignoring my statement, "but only just. It is not enough. They get sores, you see. Their brains, PrimaCore needs nothing more."

"PrimaCore's hiding people down here?"

Dae-Won smiled. "If hiding was so, then they could be discovered. But already, so many know they are here."

It didn't make any sense until the doors opened. Two rows of half a dozen medical stasis beds were installed against the far wall. Each was covered by a transparent yet lustrous plastic dome through which I saw bare skin.

"Yet nothing has been done," he continued. "And I have told many, but they hardly believe. Told our local news agency. That sent them laughing. 'Who would care about pederasts and muggers, murderers, dealers and whores?' they asked. 'So what if they are drugged into a coma instead?'"

"Instead?" I asked, half listening as I walked toward the blinking displays and exposed flesh of those *They* wished forgotten.

"Executed or exiled, institutionalized for life. Here they do not cost the state anything at all, but they generate revenue from the shunts they share."

Inside the nearest pod was a woman. She didn't look flash frozen like I imagined she might; she looked like she was sleeping. I saw the drug-abuse sag of the skin under her eyes, the rough texture of someone who took greater care of her veins than her appearance, and the sagging breasts of someone never fortunate enough to have had the proper support—social, financial, or otherwise. The naked Jane Doe wasn't identified on any folio, nametag, or brand; simply notarized as Pod-001. Numerous IVs and electrodes patched into their bodies to keep them alive, barely.

"They're all surrogates?"

"In essence, yes, but not exactly," Dae-Won said as he opened the pod farthest from me. I smelled sweat and desiccated urine. "The term they used was subsurrogate. Each of these people are connected to us, Jade Hilt."

"To us?"

"For each one of these, at least one person out there connects directly to one of them. But they require the feed either of us transmits—in our case, mostly mine." He lifted the older man's body and turned him onto his stomach. Dae-Won readjusted the man's tubes and wires, checked the monitors to see that they were all in the green, then closed the lid.

"But that's not how it works," I said. "Why would they repeat that one-to-one rhetoric all the time?"

He shrugged. "This is not the norm, but it answers the long-standing anisotropy dilemma."

"Anisotropy?" I asked, still confused. I was sure Dae-Won thought I was a dunce.

"The unequal distribution of probable neuro-idents, you see. You cannot possibly think there would always be a good match for everyone? Sure, everyone can have . . . issues, but most world problems begin by how society treats a person rather than that person being born with an innate incapacity to function properly as a human."

"Granted."

"That is something they would not want advertised, but it is not the only reason, I believe." He paused and took a deep breath. "You recall when I told you about the feedback that was amplified tenfold?" I nodded. "That is applicable to anything. Imagine if the feed from a madman could be duplicated and transmitted at will to whomever they wished. Like a broken man perfectly subjugated into doing whatever task was asked of him, the advanced PrimaCore computer would be able to download those subservient feelings to millions at once. Or, if one wished, they could send a good fraction of the population of the Western Commonwealth into a patriotic frenzy favoring—who is your president now?"

"Bouquets."

"Ah, yes. Trigger mass voting for Bouquets at the touch of a button. The implications are far more troublesome when you consider that any given feed is not restricted to a single surrogate couple. If that feed goes wrong, it might be unfortunate for the two, you see. But when you can trigger controlled emotional waves in more than one fifth of the human population, you have the capacity to control the mindset."

"Tinfoil hats," I whispered.

"What was that?"

"Since telecommunication in the early nineteen hundreds, there've been many who think that radio, NetV, and, well, really anything transmissible by poly-tech are already being carefully contorted by Propaganda Industries or their predecessors." I wasn't certain I actually believed that myself. Images and messages that were popular and enjoyed by many were just as easily propagated without eliciting conspiracy theories, but I couldn't help but feel that the entire image of society was framed inside an immaculate "there can be nothing better" illusion of the status quo.

Dae-Won giggled. "Then imagine how much easier it could be when the transmission is sent directly into the brain, bypassing the information-seeking and information-selecting gateways that are our eyes."

I was about to ask something else when he continued enthusiastically. He was happy to talk to someone. "Decidedly, it is difficult to connect more than two people together. They have not lied about that. But it is in their policy to keep the mono-link rhetoric popular. Even most neuroscientists believe it is ludicrous to try anything so crazy like Project Hydra. Have a look at scientific publication databanks; there has not been any serious publication or patent on anything but one-to-one surrogate connections." He slapped the pod known as 004.

"Safety infomercials say that since surrogate couples are linked together, there hasn't been a single adverse reaction—safer than Viagra," I said. "That implies they tried other configurations, but maybe it wasn't prudent. You said these pods had fail-safes." I walked to pod 002, where a much younger man lay without legal appeal. Naked from the electrodes down, I noticed he had been neutered, his small, flaccid prick commanding over a deflated sac.

He sighed. "They *are* the fail-safes, Jade." Dae-Won moved to another person, then skipped two of them. I couldn't tell what kind of schedule he had or if anyone else helped him. It seemed like a good deal of responsibility for one man. "When more than two neuro-ident surrogates share a field, there's an increased chance of destabilization—or so I'm told. When you add another brain to a stable duet, it can cause everything to collapse, creating erratic signal fluctuations in the other surrogates, which can be fatal. But it is also why we hold these. If, for some reason, the mega-computer, with its new advanced configurations, cannot prevent a destabilization from starting, then that signal is diverted here, like a floodgate, releasing a confused jumble of hate and anger, love and fear, apathy and libido, all in a sudden thunderstorm of unimaginable sensations."

I wondered what that felt like. I had been unable to live with such tremendous grief, but the feed wasn't keeping me alive either. Granted, it could affect my health—grief *had* been affecting my health—but the shunt's efficacy was limited to my psychology, not to the sustainability of my vital organs. Like a broken heart—a colorful analogy—but the heart wouldn't literally fail because of it. But it made a whole lot more sense thinking that the godlike mega-computer could strike down an unfortunate third wheel with a bolt of lightning to the brain.

When I went to the third pod and saw the man's face, Dae-Won gasped and fell back, holding a hand over his mouth, tears swelling around his wide, frightened eyes. But I ignored him, focused liked a laser beam, and analyzed every imperfection on the naked man's face. Pockmarked scars and a bent nose, lips yellow from excessive nicotine, eyes—which should have been my eyes—closed calmly. It was him, I was certain. I stared with cold calculation as Dae-Won screamed in agony and despair. He choked with cries of torture and grasped at his throat to find breath.

Like the workings of some hideous insectile mind, the man whom I thought wretched and inhuman had been processed, without our knowledge, by some malign machine mind—justice forsaken. Testicles removed, drugged into a coma, and sentenced to be a fail-safe for a computer that worked far less assuredly than everyone thought. It was so mechanical, alien to the ethical process that I had believed the law could be, like some artificial intelligence had found the most efficient way to dispose of society's undesirables. In retrospect, I had wanted far worse for this man, but seeing him like this, impotent and defenseless, I wondered what exactly I could have demanded in retribution. This wouldn't bring Bill back; nothing would. I didn't know what I should feel, but even that was robbed from me as the emotions that should have been mine sent Dae-Won screaming in torment.

After he found his breath, he started laughing, a laughter of irony. "Oh, Jade, how could I have known?" He wasn't laughing anymore. He looked sorry for me. So very sorry.

"You saw what this one did to me?" I asked. "What he took from me?"

"No, but I felt it. I felt what you should have felt."

"Does it bother you?"

He sighed. "No, Jade Hilt. If anything, I love him even more for what he has given me, through you. It is he who has made all this love possible. I do not crave hate inside my heart like you did in yours. I do not know what this man has done, neither do

I want to know, but that wondrous flowing essence of life makes all things beautiful. Born from its opposite, the beauty emerges from the horror of existence."

"You're crazy," I said. "There's no beauty in any of this." But I also felt little about the inhumane processes that had led the unwanted subsurrogates there. Should I be bothered by it? How should I feel that the man who took Bill from me was there? I didn't know, but Dae-Won was getting awfully preachy, and there was only so much philosophy I could handle in a single dose.

I knew what I had to do.

He seemed unfazed by my words. "You, Jade, wanted to feel nothing. Whether you decided consciously or not, your scans showed that, showed that you wanted to shy away from the passions of this universe. You chose to be blind to the beauty of this world. You—" Then, his head straightened seeing what I was doing, and I realized too late just how naive I really was.

When the shutters closed and the alarms blared, it was Dae-Won, despite having heard it before, who was sent into a panicked fright. He darted away, half propelled by fear, half knowing what he had to do. Dumbfounded, I watched him flee beneath the closing barricade, leaving me alone with the naked pod people.

* * *

"Jade, you should be surprised I can reach you. That poly-tech, it's truly wonderful. But I got an urgent ping when your phone moved away from you," Sam said from her end.

I sighed, then rubbed my nose. "The underwear moved away from me. I made Dae-Won Duri wear them."

"On Korea," Sam whispered. "I had no idea your relationship had matured so—"

"Cut the innuendo shit. I tripped an alarm somehow."

"When you tried to send a file. From the tech."

"To call you," I said. "I found him, the man who killed Bill."

"It *was* Duri?"

"No, but the guy's encased inside a pod. Drugged into a coma and . . . fucking neutered."

I heard Sam exhale as she thought about that. "Maybe he fled overseas, was arrested as an offender there for something else, and put away, undocumented. Disappearances happen rather too frequently, I do believe." A testament to Eastern judiciary efficiency. "But Jade, you have some more immediate concerns?"

"What can you do?"

"I'm having our favorite Red triangulate the infrastructure's security software by geo-positioning."

"Is that even possible?"

"We'll see. What about Duri?"

"He ran away. I don't know." I thought for a moment. "Please tell me they aren't going to come in shooting."

"Jade, I'm doing everything possible to make sure this situation doesn't escalate. But don't you remember the story I told you about how we found the intruder at Fr—at the party?"

She was right. The fact they were slack with their security personnel didn't mean they were slack with their security software. "The story where you had one man killed."

"Change of subject, please. For your sake if not mine."

I sighed. I sigh more than I breath it seemed. "Just tell me they aren't going to come in with weapons drawn."

"Jade, we aren't even sure who you pissed off yet. Time might be short, so give me the gist of what you've learned."

"Some PrimaCore subsidiary is housing comatose surrogates—subsurrogates of Duri's, or mine—mostly Duri's—inside the pods here. He said they're fail-safes for the hydra." I was yelling over the blaring speakers, ignoring the pulsing red light that bathed the entire structure in crimson red.

"Hydra," she whispered.

"Bad word?"

"Very bad word. Schoolchildren might get a visit from the spooks if they unwittingly use it in the wrong search engines.

But he said that? That you had subsurrogates also connected to your shunt's feed?"

"That's what I said. It's not all one to one."

"I see." Sam didn't sound surprised in the least, and I noted that for later. "He said you were connected to a hydra?"

"He said *he* was the hydra."

"Oh, how interesting."

"Sequitur?"

"Very sequitur."

"What about that alarm?" I asked, and like a sign from the great beyond, it stopped. The protective shutters fore and aft started withdrawing, and the lights steadied to a serene white glow. The elevator was still at my level so, by association, Dae-Won's anxiety tapered as I saw the cavalry wasn't coming for us. "Well, thanks."

"You're welcome," she said after conferring with someone else.

Dae-Won edged out of a narrow inlet between the far door and the shutter.

"Okay, I gotta go," I said.

"No, Jade, wait, it isn't as—" I flipped the retro-style flip-screen shut and double checked to verify it was indeed offline.

"I would have thought a young Westerner like you would know about digital security," Dae-Won said, looking more disappointed in himself than anything. "Good thing most employees are away during the weekend, or you would have angered quite a few more. But the alarm has already been reported."

"What's back there?" I asked, pointing in the direction from which he had just come. Where had he run off to during the alarm?

Before he could stop me, I edged inside, hearing him gasp behind me. He knew I had seen it all too. Shaking his head, not knowing what to do with this out-of-control child, Dae-Won pulled me back into the antechamber.

"So many," I whispered, my implant barely able to upload the full impact away from me.

Then he told me about that too as he ushered me out.

* * *

Just before the elevators emerged into the daylight, Dae-Won slapped me hard across one cheek, then back-handed me across the other. I reddened in shocked, but he knew what I had felt. He returned to the calm expression of a Zen monk he held most of the time when I wasn't thinking about anything horrible. But when the doors opened, and I saw more than the two lowly men standing there with weapons drawn, Dae-Won laughed exuberantly. Then he went to one of the guards and casually told him something I couldn't understand. They both relaxed.

He pointed at me and spoke with an accent much heavier than the one he had used earlier. "You so stupid, American girl." The guards laughed too. "So stupid, American girl," he repeated while they all joined in, except for an older non-Asian man, who eyed me seriously from atop a roofless jeep. I thought he looked northern European. Most of the guards dispersed after that. Something so ridiculous wasn't worth shooting, or so I imagined them thinking. Then Dae-Won went to the humorless man and whispered something at length. The man nodded, as did Dae-Won, and then they both turned toward me, my face glowing red.

The man got into the driver's seat and floored the accelerator, sending dust pebbles toward me. To show the extent of his disrespect, he spat at my feet as the jeep drove by. He missed. Maybe he didn't really want to hit me with his loogie. But, dejected, I hardly felt any fear or worry from the situation, a situation where I might easily have been killed—or harvested like those below and turned into a comatose surrogate. That robotic, apathetic sentiment worried me more than my corporeal safety.

Dae-Won had my real feelings painted on his face, and he definitely thought I wasn't safe there anymore.

"What did you tell them?" I asked.

He smiled as he gazed toward a quieter region of Azalea-ri. "I told them that you mistook the fire alarm for a light switch."

"That's pretty stupid."

"Yes, but they will not know what caused the alarm until PrimaCore coordinates with the people in place. And before then you, Jade Hilt, will be long gone from here."

"I've seen enough of your . . . city," I said. "I've no desire to linger here anyway. But why didn't they question or arrest me?"

"To be honest, I bluffed, I told the corporal—"

"Eastern military?"

"Yes. I told him you work for PrimaCore. He must have believed it."

Had they wanted to identify me, facial recognition software was built into our poly-techs, which could connect directly to the border agencies. Or he could have used the old-fashioned way: they could have looked at my IDs to corroborate. But they hadn't. They took what Dae-Won told them at face value. He had played a façade, had controlled himself marvelously, adopting the part that was required to get me out of the potentially deadly situation. His ability to change moods so suddenly and drastically was eerie, seeming unnatural even to my previous emotional context. He not only had the ability to feel but also displayed whichever social mimicry fit the situation. He seemed like a manipulative psychopath, yet a very trustworthy and sensitive one.

"But they'll know you lied to them," I said. "They'll know I tried to upload a photograph."

"Let me worry about such things."

"They'll kill you."

He tapped his head while leaning in close, as if to tell me a secret. "I am much more valuable alive." That didn't assure me he wouldn't become the next man inside a pod. "And awake," he added with a disturbingly coincidental wink.

* * *

After I reactivated my poly-tech, I only had time to send the taxi a request before it rang. Who else could it be? I wondered with a sigh.

"Hi Sam," I said.

"Jade, what happened?"

"Oh nothing. Got shot, raped, then shot some more."

"I see your sense of humor has returned."

"You were going to tell me how you managed to deactivate their security system?"

Sam took a deep breath. She wasn't going to be led in such ways. "We didn't have time. It was deactivated locally."

"I know. Dae-Won cut it, then bluffed our way out. But I'm glad you fessed up. I didn't think you would."

"This whole attitude's unbecoming, my dear. If you hadn't been so rude earlier, I might have told you. But forget about that. Where are you now?"

"On the outskirts of Azalea-ri, waiting for my chauffeur. Dae-Won thinks I should leave, that I might have pissed off the Army here with these shenanigans."

"I concur. But I'm afraid the people who might be looking for you now because of these shenanigans won't be deterred by borders. But I can at least assure you of one thing."

"What's that?"

"You will be safe inside my office."

I laughed. "What is it with you? What do you want with me? You want me to become another pawn in your childish spy games? You want to feel my titties or force me to plug your asshole?" The long slur of profanity came like a mindless wave once again. All the while I imagined Dae-Won shitting bricks, shaking his fist in rage at his newfound God in the sky.

"Jade, you're more valuable than you realize—to me and to the world."

"You say so, but I'm only me, a nobody. Dae-Won is the hydra. I'm just his lowly surrogate." I said it so empirically, feeling peace at the realization of it. Such humility was something I never would have accepted prior to my operation. "And you don't know what's going to happen."

"To the full extent, no one ever does."

"You didn't know what I would find here."

"No, but I speculated."

"And you were okay with sending me on a potentially danger-ous errand around the world for something you . . . speculated."

"The extent of your involvement was always yours to decide, Jade. I never forced you. And I didn't throw you inside that place either, if that's what you're intimating."

"You didn't know for sure that my passport would even grant me entry into this commonwealth."

"We had a high probability index that it would."

"So, you gambled someone more valuable to you than the world just to satisfy your curiosity."

"It's what I do, but saying it like that makes me sound like such an awful person. I do care, Jade, I assure you." She paused for a moment. "Your naivety is what got you so far. Had someone else tried to infiltrate the place, they would've been stopped at one of numerous checkpoints. They could've been identified trying to purchase or rent a car—you took the public bus. They could have tried to infiltrate the already more than bribed workforce of Azalea-ri, and certainly, they would have been discovered that way too, but you simply got there, harmlessly, by yourself. Sneaking into the facility unannounced would have been just as foolhardy because of the numerous hidden cameras. You, Miss Hilt, simply walked through the front door, escorted by a man you befriended a few moments before. It was so perfectly up front that anyone who noticed brushed you off as natural or inconsequential." She took another breath. "That's why my intuition knew you would succeed."

"You still put my life on the line," I replied, but I couldn't help but think Dae-Won was feeling a hint of pride.

"We all put our lives on the line," Samantha said. "Some more than you realize. But your refreshing innocence is what's worth most to me. And I want you back here as soon as possible. For your sake and mine."

"No."

"What?" She sounded truly shocked.

"Like you say, I might not truly understand the extent of what technology can do, but I've come to realize that you, Samantha Burgess, aren't as all-powerful and all-knowing as you claim to be."

"Ouch."

"At the same time, you hold an air of authority and use others with vague explanations, promises of this or that, but you're transparent to me now. You're just as lost and confused as I am." I said what I thought had to be said, but I knew that wasn't only true for me; it was true for everyone. Same with Bouquets. He acted like he always knew what had to be done, but he was just another confused pawn in the worldwide chess game played by the blind. It was all so clear now. Authority: those who feared perspectives without limits governing those with limited perspectives.

"You wish to stay in Korea then?" Her tone was jovial but threatening. Taking it in stride, she wouldn't let me get to her. I smiled, as I surely thought Sam would get upset but didn't. It concretized in my mind that Sam was made of sterner stuff than I first believed. The will compels the mind, I thought, and a properly focused will could be more powerful than any force on Earth.

"You knew about the industry's higher-order shunt configurations, didn't you?"

"I knew they tried, not that they got anything that was actually functional or of the likes you described," Sam said. "You believe me?"

"Yeah." I did. Had she wanted to make something up, it would have been overly convoluted. "Tell me how you know I'll be safe with you in Boston."

"I'm afraid I can't get into that."

"Then I'll have to take my chances in the DMZ."

"You're really not afraid, are you?" Sam said. "Jade, listen, it's not because I don't want to. It's because there're others at stake here."

"Tell me or I'm gone, and you'll never know what else I found down there. You won't know why I knew you were full of it. You'll never know why I realized this whole situation is way, way more serious than you or any of your goons realize. Because what I know now is so fucked that shit and fan will merge into an orgy so violent, the whole world will be submerged under a hurricane of scat."

Her silence was answer enough. Then I was glad that Sam was Sam. Info was gold to her, and I had just baited her with something way more tantalizing than accepting her sexual advances.

Sam sighed like it pained her to betray her source. "You'll be disappointed." She whispered something to someone, urging the person to leave the room.

"What, Brent made a dirty bomb?"

"No, nothing so crude, but something surgically precise and right to the heart."

"So, what is it?"

"Not what, who. But answer this. Doesn't Brent look like someone else you might have seen? A public figure who also enjoys being constantly overdressed?" I shook my head, but Sam couldn't see that, of course. "Think big—all the way up there."

I tried a guess. "The owner of PrimaCore . . . Keneth Mansfield?"

"Oh, what a bright girl you are."

"Brent is Keneth Mansfield's son?"

"I didn't tell you that. You guessed."

"Yes, that's what you're all about, I know. Who's his mother?"

"She died when he was five."

I thought about it. "Is he estranged from his father or what? And how does this make anything safer?"

"It's a bit more intricate than that. A good deal of our own start-up funding came through Brent's investments. My business was funded by that, and, in essence, we're a PrimaCore subsidiary. I doubt they have us clearly laid out in their books though. Besides, I never picked a fight with them; that is, until today perhaps. But we'll see what happens. Maybe it all can be explained as a misunderstanding."

I thought not, and I had a sudden urge to giggle, but I suppressed it. Dae-Won had told the military man the truth then. I did work for PrimaCore.

Just then I saw my taxi approaching in the distance. "But I don't understand. You told me just a few days ago that Brent was hiding too."

"Brent isn't hiding from PC. He's hiding from Bouquets' minions, the Department of Defense or worse. The military and pharma are having it out under the table, discreetly. They look nice and friendly in public, but the two're ready to carve a chunk right out of Boston if need be. The kettle's cooking under pressure, but it hasn't boiled over yet from what I can tell. Brent got enough information through his father's channels—who surely tried to convince him to go to the institute instead, but Brent, that prideful prick, wouldn't accept that handout, and he knew he was safer elsewhere. He's gone rogue before. He knows how to stay out of trouble."

"And me?"

"Well, as of earlier, you still weren't flagged by either commonwealth, but if what you say is true, a few people within PrimaCore will be very eager to talk to you, and I can promise there're people working for PC who make military tactics look like child's play. I don't think you would be able to hide if you were red-flagged—you'd have no idea how to go rogue. But to be on the safe side, like your new friend told you, I think it's best if you get back here as fast as fucking possible. We'll try to clear any border complications on the fly."

"Alright, okay, as soon as I can," I said as I waved at the wandering taxicab. I couldn't speak openly with the English-practicing driver in earshot, so I hardly had time to tell Sam about my big secret. I gave her a blurted version instead. "The room I told you about contained pods for our subsurrogates. There was a total of twelve. Dae-Won said they were ours. But in the next room, there were hundreds, perhaps thousands, all the same, all hooked to surrogates inside."

"Thousands," she whispered, trying to grasp the implications.

"Dae-Won said that project's called 'Tapping the Main.' A preliminary study on population psychology."

"The main? Like the province? He said that?"

"Yeah, north fucking New England, Maine. Why, what?"

"I . . . I'm not sure."

"Okay, got to go. Bye."

CHAPTER 19

—

Brent tossed his empty energy drink beside the overflowing waste receptacle at the off-road pit stop in southern New York. He had always liked the big province. Since he was on the run, he chose to spend much of that time driving around there. Through his dummy accounts, he had purchased a late-model BMW that still ran on fossils. He preferred to feel the motor when he drove, but it obviously wasn't the best way to avoid attention: loud motor and blue smoke trailing the car that out-muscled all the rest. "It's a good way to avoid looking like you're trying to hide," Sam had said. But that didn't really matter. The feel of power beneath his feet was pure joy, and that was worth more to him than drugs or money. Driving the car was a whole different game than being driven by it. One had to experience it firsthand to know.

His dad had paid out the money; he just didn't know it yet. Not that he would have refused. Keneth was always trying to give Brent more, but Brent never used those accounts. Somehow skimming some off the company accounts without being dis-covered was a better incentive—made him feel he deserved it. Besides, he preferred they lost their money and time looking for Armand B. Crupps, who had existed only on paper but no longer. His next dummy account became active in a few hours.

Inside the BMW he opened his ghost computer and checked his messages. Rapid triage with his deft fingers left only a few remaining items. Sam had sent him a nice picture. By the angle he couldn't even tell if it was her or not, which made it all the more enticing. He sent his love through a verbally agreed-upon cipher account. Next, one of his contacts in Boston had more serious news about XP. He had indeed been gunned down like the autopsy noted. Ballistics confirmed the gun to be a model used by the infantry. Could they be that stupid? They were dumb or sloppy—either of which certainly could be true—but if they had arranged it, Brent was certain they wouldn't have used a patented, restricted gun model. His colleague thought likewise. *Doesn't this remind you of a carefully planted passport at a crime scene?* It did, and he forwarded that without added comment or opinion to Sam too.

It didn't sit right with Brent that XP had been killed so blatantly. Had they truly crossed the line with some less-than-paternal authority within PrimaCore? That bitch, head of PC security, was crazy enough, but she was crazier for his father and their vision than to hunt surrogate hackers. She knew Brent, surely what he did, and had always looked away. There certainly were others inside who had qualms about his father, and it wouldn't be unheard of if they went after him, but XP had hardly been connected at all. A friend, sure, but business ran deeper than that. XP had been good at what he did, and that had worked out well over the years for them both. But XP hadn't been as off-limits as Brent.

He sighed, not knowing what to think of everything. Brent couldn't say he was shocked or saddened with any real conviction about XP's death. Turning the key in his old-model car, feeling the pleasant motor rumble under his seat, he wondered whether *he* was someone who needed a shunt.

The passenger door opened—a mistake surely—and someone wearing a long, dark trench coat with a clerical collar sat where his computer had been. "The fuck, old man," Brent said, "Do I look like a taxi or what?"

"Oh, I just wanted a peek inside," he said, smiling. "I used to have one like this back in the day, before they turned all generic. These were real cars." He closed the door.

Brent shook his head but didn't know what to say. "Look, I've got to—" The long knife the man withdrew from his lapels silenced Brent then and there.

"Drive," the man said, his eyes alight with fire and folly.

Brent tried to bolt, but a hand much stronger than he would have expected pulled him back like he was a child. He couldn't help but recoil in pain. The man was unfazed, and Brent saw from the pink hue and muscular tone around his neck that the old man was quite fit.

"Buckle up and drive," he said, his tone serious. "We're heading east."

Shaking, never having been in any real danger before that moment, Brent bit his lip and pushed the car into first gear, then into second as he went up the ramp. "Boy, this car really is something," the man said, smiling amicably. "It must have cost a doozy. Where'd you get it?"

"What are you going to do with me?"

The old man sighed. It wasn't the answer to the question he had asked. "That's not for me to decide."

* * *

James knew something was happening through his surrogate. At times his mind was calm and serene, but then, like an ocean, it picked up calamitous waves, capsizing wayward boats and pounding the unlucky sailor onto jagged rocks. His signal squirts felt like that now. Violent surges of hate and contempt followed by valleys of steady, stress-free peace. But maybe the latter was the morphine.

James knew he was unlikely to be freed from this bed no matter how much his condition improved. He started feeling better physically, but that wasn't any consolation. The doctors and nurses, in some strange hospital deep within Eastern territory, took care of his physical wellbeing, but they hated him. They feared him, and they performed their duties, but that was the extent of it.

When he asked the nurse where he was, she ignored him. But after he kept repeating the question, she sprayed him with a long slur of Eastern curse words that couldn't be mistaken in translation. He had to be in Russia, he thought. The doctors were the same. Silently, they checked his ECG, EEG, and his blood metabolites, changed his bandages, and readjusted his drug regime as necessary. Indeed, he was getting more hands-on care than he would ever have received under MedAid.

His surrogate connection had changed. While Cobalt would have felt those urges to kill, Flinch returned and made him question all that. Then he fell down the deep, dark pits of despair until he was drugged to sleep or a new tidal wave arrived. Would his surrogate be getting these ON and OFF signals too? What would happen when James was given a stronger dose of opiates? Surely that affected the brain's neurochemical properties.

As the urge to kill them all grew, James called his nurse and complained of intense pain. She checked the timetable for his chart, then administered what she thought was appropriate. If only he were free, he could tear out her jugular and drink the torrent of blood; surely that would get him executed. Then, when the warm sensations of senselessness returned, and his desire for her blood tapered to wanting to kiss her neck, he would tell her how much he loved her. This woman who hated him, doing the least she could, looked like the most wondrous of angels now. But maybe that was the morphine too. He exhaled at length with relief.

He knew with a certainty deeper than intuition—as deep as the central nucleus of his amygdala—that his surrogate was up to something. James knew better than anyone what type of feed he got from that person: the vile hatred, the righteous antipathy for his fellow brethren. All of that hadn't been born inside him but had come through the mega-computer into his deadly hands. If James couldn't die, he wondered if he could attain any kind of atonement. But what came to mind was only *Paradise Lost* by Milton, a book force fed to him in school. At the time he could only qualify it as being long and hard as hell, and now it was lost from memory through time and explosive trauma to the brain. But, without purpose, he had to do something more than wish he were dead because the people around him made that nearly impossible.

* * *

The old man wasn't gov; Brent knew that from the start. Neither West nor East, he served a whole other political ideology. But he was twitchy as hell. From smiling happily to gritting his teeth while praying, he seemed to jump from one state of mind to the next like nothing. He told Brent to keep it steady. Well, he was keeping it as steady as fucking possible, but this old freak was the one who had to keep it cool.

The knife was still on the man's lap, his hands clasped ascetically above it. They had been driving for almost an hour. The old man hadn't said where they were heading, but he had told Brent to take the exit toward Albany. Now the lunatic, who went from serene to devoutly praising the Lord, yelling loudly, red-faced about how God shouldn't tolerate this extent of human sloth, was dozing off. His head bobbed, readjusted, then bobbed again. All the while, Brent eyed the blade resting on his lap.

The priest kept nodding off, but all Brent could remember was the sharp pain he had felt in his shoulder when the man grabbed him with uncanny strength. Scenarios toiled in Brent's mind, how he could slam on the brakes and get the knife before the old man awoke. Or how he could "expose" himself, as they say, and get the authorities to find him. But this man, intentionally or not, had guided him away from all the photographic toll roads.

The thought of being caught by the spooks didn't worry Brent much anymore. And he truly wondered if that was what he'd have to do. Afterward, his father might—and it was a doubtful might, knowing the extent of the shitstorm starting with PC and the DOD—through the right channels get him released once again (it wasn't the first time the law had come a-knocking for Mr. Mansfield Junior). Brent bit his lip harder.

The man's head was tilted strongly but didn't jolt upright. If Brent had any chance, it was now. But he couldn't. Something about the man was far worse than gov operatives. Brent was unable to summon any courage.

"Are you a sinner, Brent?" the man asked, his head lifting slowly to look outside. The shunt showed clearly behind his neck.

Brent's heart raced as he remembered he had given him his first name, the real one, because, being stared at by those eyes, he couldn't have said anything other than the truth. But the old man hadn't pressed further.

"I . . . would hope not."

"One would know."

"What do you want me to say?"

"Tell me why your soul deserves to be redeemed."

"Can't I be innocent now?"

"No." His voice was flat, and he swiped his knife across Brent's exposed belly below his fishnet shirt. The car swerved, but he steadied it. The cut wasn't deep; the priest hadn't meant to injure, just chastise, but Brent's skin reddened, and a thick line of blood appeared, trickling onto his black pants and the seat. "Do not stray from the path, Brent." Brent thought about his driving, but the man hadn't meant that. "I can tell you suffer from overabundance. You have too much wealth for your own good. You wear clothing that a woman would, and you smell of far-too-rich cologne."

"I love someone," Brent said, then regretted how corny that sounded.

"Love is indeed something to be cherished, but the love of God supersedes all. Are you saying this for your own sake or for the sake of another?"

"My woman would be quite sad if I were to . . . disappear."

"Woman," the man repeated, surprised.

"Yeah, I'm het," Brent replied too quickly. He didn't think explaining to the old conservative that what he had chosen to wear today meant little about his sexual orientation.

The old man thought for a moment. "Tell me how you sinned, Brent."

"I sell neuro-ident profiles to whoever can pay." It came out before he could stop himself. "I took drugs and pilfered money from my dad." He couldn't think of anything else to say. Or rather, he was so frightened that he couldn't think clearly at all. This God-loving lunatic controlled him in deeper ways than he thought possible. Like a struggle of dominance between animals, the age-old code of jungle survival, the elder priest had made him submissive. Biting his lip, Brent choked down the urge to cry as the priest contemplated his fate. "No, I'm not innocent, but others have done far worse than me."

The old man nodded silently, accepting the forced confession like he always did in church. "In this world, no one's innocent. But that is not the point. Everyone can be made to see the light. Everyone should have the chance to redeem themselves. Don't you think?"

"Oh, absolutely."

"Do you see the light, Brent?"

What did he want him to say? "I—no, not yet, but I want to. Oh, I very much want to see that light."

The old man smiled and nodded. "So would I, Brent. So would I." Then he became silent again for a long period. "The profiles you sold. PrimaCore, weren't they?"

Brent nodded, then confirmed more definitively.

"You aren't a member?"

"Nope. Didn't want them in my head." It was true. Besides, Brent's father, the owner, first inventor, and major patent holder, didn't even have one (although, for publicity reasons, he sometimes proclaimed he did or pasted a fake one onto his neck). Keneth had never brought up that topic to Brent either, and that in itself was reason enough to stay away.

"Smart boy," he said, smiling like they were good friends. "I was at a point where I had little alternative, and in some rare cases, maybe it is necessary. But it's not used to help people anymore. They give easy solutions that prevent users from struggling and finding the true answers to their life's crises."

Brent agreed with most of that, but the true answers to life were a bit subjective. The whole pain surrogate craze was a travesty, the commodification of a device meant to heal and ease suffering transformed into a way to escape one's self, to leave one's troubles and angst behind. "Yeah," he said finally.

The old man appraised him, as if to see whether he was purposefully being sycophantic or if he actually agreed. "There must be a reckoning. The time of righteousness will soon fall upon them."

"Them?"

"Those who made all this possible."

He meant his father, Dorothy, and perhaps a thousand others. "What are you going to do?"

The priest smiled. "What God wills."

Brent's heart jumped a noticeable frequency as he realized how incredibly worrisome his situation was. Did this man know his familial connection? He couldn't. Hardly anyone knew; it was kept secret for good reasons. This man who had abducted him, as unbelievable as that was, was hell-bent on destroying Brent's very father. He was doubly glad the old man hadn't continued his initial line of questioning regarding the specifics.

"You're a hacker?"

"Programmer," Brent corrected. Both were true, but one sounded much less sinful.

"Who is able to infiltrate PrimaCore's computers?"

He gulped. "Yeah." His heart raced again as the interrogation continued. The worst for Brent was that he was certain he would tell him anything if the man asked the right questions.

"Then perhaps it was God's design that I found you, my dear boy."

"I . . . I don't understand."

"You're going to get me inside."

"That's—that's unwise. You'll never get in." He couldn't call him stupid.

"Why not?"

"Security's better than Fort Knox." He looked at the man between glances at the road. The priest didn't seem bothered by any of it. "There's this crazy chick inside, some special-ops mercenary," Brent continued. "She'd kill you before you got to any of them." Why was he telling him this? Wouldn't it be better to get him there first, then let Manne do her thing? But he was afraid for her too. Did this old but athletic man have some capability or power that she wouldn't be able to handle? It seemed impossible, knowing everything he had heard from his father and what Samantha had dug up. But this man was something wholly different. Brent simply couldn't, in good conscience, bring him there directly.

"God doesn't roll dice," the man said. "That's why he brought me to you. I saw your car, and by the looks of you, I knew you needed to be shown the ways of the Lord. This is no coincidence, my boy. It is part of our destiny. The path I follow will be revealed to me. I shall be shown what to do when we arrive, I assure you."

Brent shook his head. He looked out, trying to find some way to pop up on the government grids, a way to dis-rogue his status without making the man aware of it. But he knew he couldn't. His will had been shattered by some eerie and unfathomable force. Even if he saw a facial-recognition camera, he wouldn't have the backbone to raise his subservient head and make eye contact with it. How could the man control him so deeply?

"Take this exit," the priest said. Again, he directed Brent away from heavy surveillance zones. Whether the man knew gov security better than anyone or if it was all a coincidence, Brent still wasn't sure. But his divine path plotter—the guiding hand pointing the way for him—sure had a competent GPS. They were heading back to Boston, back into the sprawl.

Not enough time had passed for Sam to become worried about his lack of reply and send operatives and hackers looking for him, nor would it have been easy for her if Sam tried. He cursed himself doubly for having made this car nearly digitally untraceable as well.

* * *

That son of a bitch is certainly up to something, James thought morosely. His willpower was shot, and he knew why: all that cerebral energy was being uploaded back into the man filled with horror and pain. That was why he felt so depleted despite it all. The atrocities he had committed haunted him, but his desire to die wasn't just his; the other was shunting it to him. What remained in his surrogate, concomitantly depleted within him, was a purpose so fiery it could consume the world. All he could do as he lay in bed was ponder how his shunt worked.

James knew he couldn't give up. That would give the other even more force of will. He had to stand up to the situation and rid himself of this despair. But being strapped down like a mental patient more dangerous to himself than to anyone else, there was little he could do. The last time the nurse pumped him full of morphine, he had felt wonderful. Maybe that was the way out—to pump himself so full of happy juice that his counterpart would be dulled by it too. Nothing broke determination like opiates. But he would be the one who suffered the secondary physiological effects and the withdrawal it entailed. He couldn't be certain it would work either, but he remembered the calm seas he had felt through the shunt, that it had been calmest when he was sedated. But the doctors decided when, and if, he received any more analgesic, and, coming into sync with their daily schedules, he wasn't due for another shot for a couple of hours. The downside was that if he kept asking, they would instead taper his dose, afraid he was developing a taste for it. But his surrogate was active now; James felt the jolts of hate and rage, the antipathy for life reaching its fulcrum. It felt like it had no maximum, no crux from which to recede.

Cobalt/Flinch tossed and turned and tried to get the nurses back. He needed another dose, and he needed it now.

* * *

"Stop the car," the man demanded. Brent, the psycho's personal chauffer, was about to argue, but he held his tongue.

He pulled into the parking lot of an abandoned farmer's market, local organic food producers long since put out of business by Big Agro. Grass was pushing through the upheaved cement. No one had been there in years.

"Why are we stopping?" Brent asked, suddenly worried. He had almost started believing he was safe since their last talk, but the man's eyes were on fire once again.

"Tell me, what are you trying to hide from me, Brent?" the old man asked, his words piercing Brent's very soul. "I can smell the shame coming from you. The secret shame you can't bear."

"I . . . I haven't lied to you."

The rapid motion was almost too quick to see as Brent felt jarring pain in his chest. This cut was deeper and bled profusely. "Tell me."

"I didn't lie," he cried.

"I know you didn't, Brent, but a lie of omission is still a lie. There *is* something you don't want me to know. You've stolen more than money. You've hurt the innocent in despicable ways, or you fancy men in bed, don't you? Tell me, Brent."

"Yes, all of it," he lied, mostly. He certainly wasn't innocent. No one was perfect, no matter how devout. But he still thought of himself a good person. Maybe he wasn't completely het either—who really was? But that wasn't anything to be ashamed of. This man claimed to be holy but killed people who didn't fit inside his episcopal mold. How could that be innocence in any shape or form?

The man cut him again. "This time, you lied. What are you hiding, Brent? Tell me now, or you shall die."

Was he bluffing? Didn't he need Brent to get into PrimaCore? Either way, Brent wasn't even sure if he could manage it at all, given what he knew about Manne's local security seals. The old man didn't know that yet, but he sure didn't look like he was bluffing.

The priest brought the knife back toward Brent's flesh, slowly this time, letting Brent savor the anticipation, forestalling the pain that would come.

"Mansfield . . . Keneth Mansfield," Brent blurted against his better judgment. "He's my father."

The priest sat back with a widening grin and raised his hands toward the heavens. "Thank you, Lord. Once again you have shown me the way." Then his hideous eyes turned to Brent. "It was not by chance that I came to you, Brent. I knew when I saw you that you would be important to our divine purpose. But now I know you have a big role to play within the reckoning too. Whether you believe it or not, God has chosen you to be a witness by my side, a servant to the Lord's blade."

Brent wanted to tell him he was fucked in the head, that he needed his shunt readjusted, but not more than a whisper came out of his mouth. He fumbled with the buckle, tried to flee, but the knife slashed his hand. Then the priest's heavy, insanely powerful hands clamped over Brent's face. The priest pulled him close. Then Brent felt his neck being constricted, and his vision faded.

* * *

James pulled at the restraints with all the strength that remained in his battered body, to no avail. He tried to yell, but no one came. He tried to tear his head loose from the clamps, but he only managed to flare the agony once again. James felt blood trickling down his forehead. A few arduous breaths later, he tried to free himself again.

He strained till his body couldn't take it anymore, and then he fell back, tired, in more pain than ever, letting out a moan so filled with despair that it chilled his own skin. But no one came. His increasing pleas for morphine, they had been ordered to ignore.

CHAPTER 20

—

D orothy's head still hurt despite receiving adequate care by her own team of physicians and scientists. She knew her nociceptors—the neurons sending pain impulses to her brain—weren't being stimulated, but she was in pain, nonetheless. Some sub-somatic injury not caused by physical damage, an existential pain that cut much deeper, was throbbing inside.

As she watched the surrogate feed that shouldn't exist anymore, some of her own angst seemed inconsequential. How could her pain matter now, knowing that such an abomination had been loosed upon the world? She wanted to shut it down more than just for the simple fact that it was erratic. But given that the recipient there on the mainland had gone on a killing frenzy during the brief period when the feedback overloads collapsed the stream, it didn't seem like a good idea to give Frederick Thompson the full extent of his own mind. And since his military counterpart was acknowledged as captured by the East, there was little danger from that end. But all this would blow up in their faces sooner or later. There was only so much that PC and the DOD could deny.

The police hadn't yet connected the fact that their wanted priest was a pain surrogate member, but like for any police warrant, their client's privacy agreement overrode the Access to Information Act. Notwithstanding, the pertinent authorities didn't know they could pinpoint his location to within a few clicks. The signal was much harder to trace than poly-techs, but it wasn't impossible. So, PrimaCore already knew the man was heading toward Boston. But Keneth had told them they wouldn't turn this information over to the police, who were supposedly coordinating with the Department of Defense, but the DOD didn't seem to want to find Thompson either. In fact, they were pretending he didn't exist, like he was just some random perp who wasn't their problem anymore. But when the legal authorities do find him and see that classic protrusion behind his neck, they would wonder why this couldn't all have been averted—and rightly so. Everything was going to blow up in their faces. Now she knew what she had to do.

"I don't think this is the best time for you to resign," Keneth told her in his office.

"I never wanted any of this," she said, "and I warned you against it. But no one listened."

"I need you," he said, standing beside her. She knew he meant it. She shook her head and stepped back when he tried to hug her.

"It's all getting out of control. The more we try to fix it, the more it spirals out of control."

Manne, as if she had manifested out of the ether, placed her hand on Dorothy's shoulder. Dorothy brushed it off. "We can't even speak without her in earshot."

Manne's lip pursed but she didn't say anything. Keneth nodded to her, and she excused herself. Dorothy watched her exit Keneth's office, still believing Manne would overhear somehow. Almost every room in the behemoth complex was equipped with recording devices, for security, of course. "She's sick," Keneth looked like he couldn't tell if she meant of the body or head. Dorothy said, "And she's responsible for much of this."

"She saved your life more than once," Keneth said. "I trust her, and so do you."

"Maybe we shouldn't."

"Why? What do you know?"

She exhaled at length. "Ask her what she's doing in Korea." Dorothy knew there were things Keneth simply didn't want to hear about. "Ask her why her feed's been boosted. Ask her why she has migraines."

"Migraines?"

"She doesn't show it when you're around, but I know she isn't well. The configuration she's linked into has been pushed to its limits, and it's going to kill her if it continues. And I fear it'll get much worse before it gets better."

Dorothy left him to dwell upon that.

Outside atop the catwalk, towering above a hundred stories, she saw Manne staring across the chasm. She liked to overview the entire facility from above, her eagle vision making out the tiny pedestrians below. But her attention was focused on Dorothy at the moment. A sly smile crossed her lips, and her piercing eyes seemed to know more than they should. Dorothy cocked her chin away from Manne and took the elevator down to her lab area. She didn't care what Manne knew or didn't know anymore. She had had enough of all this.

* * *

After the doors closed, Manne's radio chimed. "Yes, boss," she said, looking across the way into Keneth's transparent office.

"Come here, please," he said through her earpiece.

"You've received a great deal of leeway from me in the past," Keneth said as soon as she walked in.

"And I very much appreciate that."

"I've turned my back to certain hearsay, and I've ignored reports that perhaps I shouldn't have. But above all that, Dorothy is very worried about you."

"Oh," she said, appearing genuinely concerned.

"Tell me what's happening in Korea."

Manne smiled, walking slowly toward him. "A few side projects we're looking into, nothing more."

"I don't believe that."

"Nothing dangerous, I assure you."

"I'd like to believe that," he said, holding her back as he looked into her eyes.

She was silent for a moment, her mind churning. "Configurations that permit an extension of Project Hydra."

He pondered that while Manne caressed his arm. He told her he should have been informed. She looked apologetic, but her dexterous body began intertwining with his. He bent down and kissed her forehead. "You should have told me," he repeated.

"I know," she said like a remorseful child. Then she craned her neck to kiss his lips. He didn't push her away. She felt his manhood flaring despite his worries, and he kissed her again. Then she withdrew and looked at him with stern eyes full of a much deeper wisdom.

He tried to bring her back and kiss her even more passionately, but she resisted, still analyzing every facial twitch. Then his eyelids started to lower. He looked tired suddenly—so very, uncontrollably fatigued as he leaned against her.

"What . . . what have you done?" he asked as his body went limp, his awareness drooping. He had no idea she had coated her lips with a sedative to which she was resistant. Her perfect lips, her kiss of death.

"When you awaken, the whole world will be yours."

"I loved . . ." he whispered as she caught him.

"And so do I."

Her enhanced physique easily allowed her to lift his much heavier frame. She hauled his limp body to his personal elevator, used his hand to bypass security, and soon hefted him onto his penthouse bed.

* * *

Far below, the natural workings of the massive institute continued unperturbed. Officer Stacey McGee came to the front desk and asked to speak to Mr. Mansfield. The receptionist laughed and told her that Mr. Mansfield was a very busy man, that he rarely received visitors, and given that Stacey had no appointment, it was entirely impossible for her to speak to him or Dr. Lundquist directly. If she wanted to convey a message, the receptionist assured her that they would receive it.

"Told you there was no way in hell you would get up there without a warrant," Karl said when Stacey returned. She knew that getting that warrant would be impossible in any event.

"Wait over there," she told him, pointing to a seating area. "Be patient. I'm working now." Looking at him as he walked away dejectedly, she thought he was getting fat. She turned to the blond secretary. "Look here, you. This is a police investigation. We found the car of one of your employees in Squantum Channel, and we have reason to believe that some type of helicopter implicated in a felony is located within your hangers. Now, either you let me do my job, or I'll come back with a warrant and more media than you'd think possible." She hoped the lady wouldn't call her bluff.

"Look, Officer McGee," the woman began, then paused and looked up as if for some divine answer. "I can put you in contact with one of our legal representatives, who'll assist you in any way he can. But I'm afraid that, without a proper warrant, we aren't legally obliged to grant you access upstairs."

Stacey wanted to wring her pretty little neck, but instead told her to contact the lawyer and that she would be waiting right here until he showed. "Please have a seat, Officer McGee." Stacey looked back. Three more people were waiting behind her. The receptionist dismissed her by leaning aside to talk to the next person in line.

Karl looked tired and, when she sat, he told her he was hungry again. "Damn, you sure eat a lot." Her appetite was barely evident. Looking at his protruding belly and the growing fat around his cheeks, she realized he had probably gained as much weight as she had lost in the past few weeks—he was at least fifteen to twenty pounds heavier than when they met. She needed to get him on a diet.

"Can't we go?" Karl argued. "They aren't going to let you go upstairs."

And just like that, she felt her pants chafing her. She wanted to jump on him right then. Certainly, she was the horniest cop on the block. How would PrimaCore security react if an officer started doing anything of the sort in their lobby? She wanted so badly to find out. "Not now," she told Karl, who was dying of boredom.

When the legal representative came—she was surprised he actually did—Karl was sleeping in his chair. Like a broken record, the man told her word for word what the receptionist had said.

"So, PrimaCore is above the law?" she asked.

The man shook his head, smiling. "We serve the law as much as possible, but we need to uphold our clients' privacy above all else. That is legally binding too. Do you know how many requests—official requests—we receive from the feds asking us to disclose what little information we have about our clients? Do you know how many people wish to speak to Mr. Mansfield? I understand your dilemma, but I'm afraid that without a warrant, we can go no further." He laughed. "They don't even let *me* up there, unless I'm invited."

* * *

Manne stood alone in her boss's office looking outside onto the bay. She saw three helicopters approaching. "Like clockwork, boys," she whispered. Opening the security panel, of which she was the penultimate user, she activated the institute's defense systems. After she had reactivated Petterson's implant, it didn't take them long to try to retrieve him from there. But no one had bothered to tell them that Petterson's comatose body was currently flying somewhere over the Pacific Ocean.

This was the first step in her plan—to expose their black operations within the mainland. To publicly discredit the DOD and Bouquets' regime. Her security system had more surprises than their covert operatives knew about—she being one of them if the first line failed.

Missile turrets emerged from the roof and launched a volley of sublethal anti-aircraft missiles. "Sublethal" referred only to the fact that the EM pulses were harmless to humans, but that wouldn't be any consolation to the passengers in the aircraft half a click above the ground. Numerous cameras arrayed onto the building's structure captured the unfolding events from multiple vantage points. The helicopters, military by design, were as black as the night sky and contained no identification numbers or insignias of any kind. As deniable as any black ops could paint them.

As expected—when information is commoditized and worth more than currency, any confidential datum became obtainable—the helicopters' automated antimissile laser systems targeted the approaching volley. But these weren't simple missiles. Equipped with an ultra-reflective outer shell, the polarized light bounced off the surface in wild spectral hues. Seeing this, the gunners started firing at the flying missiles with gunpowder weapons in a last-ditch effort. They hit a few, but it wasn't enough. Stray bullets flew directly onto PrimaCore's north face, but all the windows above level fifty were shielded by transparent high-grade ballistic-resistant polymers.

The exploding missiles did little damage with shrapnel, to each soldier's fortune. But Manne knew that as their systems went on the fritz, they would wish they had died in the explosion. Two copters crashed in a ball of flames onto the multi-level parking lot. The other less-afflicted craft glided uncontrollably toward the main entrance. Despite the high-g springy cribs, no passenger ever enjoyed crash-landing firsthand.

Manne looked down at the carnage that had begun as anticipated and decided the time was ripe for the next part of her
plan. Walking slowly outside the office, she tied her suit harness
onto the railing and propelled down the hundred-story chasm
at breakneck speed. She had done the maneuver multiple times
before and had frightened many. "Like base jumping," she ratio-
nalized. Her cable, made from high-capacity re-engineered spider
silk, was just long enough to take her to the ground floor. As she
slowed her descent, she saw the craft crashing through the lobby.

* * *

Stacey swore to, or at, Jesus when she turned and saw the helicopter going way too fast and already way too close to the main
atrium. It didn't fit the profile of her jet-copter, but it didn't
worry her any less. From her perspective, the gigantic nature
of the atrium easily betrayed the real size of the multi-person
craft; almost looked like a child's toy, but such toys don't propel
lethal blades.

Still spinning, the twisted helices crashed into the walls
beside her. Karl awoke, confused, cowering from the flying glass,
marble, and dust. He, in turn, also cursed the first deity or religious figure that popped into his mind.

Glass still falling from higher up, Stacey saw the craft's main
carriage skid until it rammed into the fountain, which was
so massive that it was hardly jostled at all. The front desk was
demolished; the people who had been there certainly dead.

The craft's doors opened. "Go, go, go," someone yelled as
numerous men clad in black emerged holding military-grade
assault rifles.

"What the hell?" she whispered, then shoved Karl back behind
the large sofa. He tripped, fell, and then ducked behind it.

It wasn't the most elegant of entrances, but the men were
armed and undoubtedly intent on illicit activities. Despite the

reasons for her visit, she was still a cop. Stacey drew her sidearm and called for assistance on her collar mic.

Wearing full-face shields with visual amplification systems, the men formed a V, each one at the flank covering their rear. They were professional, and their mission was specific.

"Police! Stand down," she yelled in her high-pitched voice. The five burly men were less than friendly with their loud, arrogant, rapid-fire replies. Whatever their mission, apparently, it didn't matter who stood in their way.

Stacey ducked behind a pillar and heard Karl chanting a long ode dedicated to fucks. "Quiet there, baby. Mommy's going to protect you."

"Jesus Christ," he replied. "What the fuck?"

When Stacey looked back, one man's head was gone. They had reconfigured their formation into a square. Another fired seemingly at nothing but was struck by something. The other three unloaded as fast and as wide as they could.

"What the fuck?" Stacey repeated as she saw the blur of a woman in tight Lycra, her forearm holding blades that moved just as fast. It almost looked like a distortion, but the woman moved beside the men, around them, faster than they could point and shoot. Then there were only two. They stood back to back. Stacey was about to urge them again to stand down, but a long blade emerged out of one man's torso, penetrating through the other. The woman pushed them both down the staircase like discarded rubbish. One weapon discharged aimlessly during the man's death thralls. The woman wiped her brow, then exhaled.

"You, stop!" She stood a good twenty meters away, looking back. But the woman didn't stop. She walked directly toward Stacey. So close she couldn't miss. Stacey ordered the woman to drop her weapons. Surprisingly, the woman did. "You're under arrest," Stacey said.

"It's not time yet," the blond-haired woman replied.

Stacey pulled back the hammer on her gun. "I'm afraid it's not a choice."

* * *

Karl flinched when he heard Stacey's gun go off, but he gasped when he heard her scream. Then he peeked, saw her right arm bent at an impossible angle, and saw that the strange woman held his much shorter but wider girlfriend. Then the Lycra-clad blond clamped her other hand onto Stacey's esophagus.

"No," Karl yelled as he tackled the incredibly beautiful woman in an act of rare bravura.

She seemed surprised as Karl sent her sprawling back, but only for a moment. She quickly caught him, spun, and flung him down. Then she looked at him, her expression puzzled. He must have felt like a flaccid child to her.

"And who might you be?" she asked him. Stacey fumbled to reach her gun using her left hand. "Touch the weapon, and he dies," the hard-as-steel woman said to Stacey. "I can kill him long before you get a clear shot."

"Don't you hurt him," Stacey said from behind the cracked marble column, holding her injured elbow.

"I'm Karl," he mumbled through a physical pressure far greater than Stacey's weight, but she wasn't focused on him anymore. The woman then shook her head, realizing something. "You're too early. But it doesn't matter anymore." She looked right and left. "Officer, I have much more pressing matters to attend. I'm sorry, but I must leave. Report what you've seen today. And both of you: hope with your dear lives that you never see me again." She stood and yanked Karl to his feet with such speed that his blood pressure hardly compensated, and, lightheaded, he stumbled to find his balance. He tried to follow as she pulled him backwards rapidly as a shield. Then she grabbed something behind him on the ground. "Farewell."

Karl gulped. He waited a moment before doing anything after he heard the pulley whoosh. He didn't dare look up despite feeling a few droplets of blood, flung off during her ascent, falling onto his head. Then, shaking, he quickly made his way back to Stacey. "What the fuck?" he said for the nth time, then asked if she was alright.

"I'll be fine," said the much-sturdier-than-appearances-would-dictate Stacey McGee. Sirens were coming from the highway. Police followed by firefighters and paramedics—the whole caboose was here. "What's going on? I didn't call this many," she said.

The reports had probably piled up, Karl thought. The place wasn't hidden, and with two bonfires going over the parkade, it must have gathered a fair share of attention. But he had to admit they all coordinated rather efficiently—a little too efficiently.

"She couldn't be so strong or so fast," Stacey whispered to Karl as she rubbed her throat, nail prints still visible. "It's impossible."

"She tore those men to shreds," he whispered back. The pool of blood at the center of the atrium was spreading, not fully recognizable body parts strewn about it.

Stacey grabbed him and kissed him. "You might very well have saved my life, but don't you ever do anything so stupid again. Do you hear me?"

"I . . . I really don't know what came over me," he said truthfully. He had risked his safety for someone else, but throughout his life his own pleasure and corporeal security had always been paramount. Maybe it was the shunt, he tried to assure himself. But looking at the carnage that the woman had left behind, something bothered him more. "Hey," he said, suddenly realizing something, "she took one of their heads."

CHAPTER 21

—

Videos of military helicopters firing at the PrimaCore institute in Boston became a breaking bulletin. A nicely packaged and pre-narrated video was anonymously donated to the two largest news outlets. Despite the context, the rather politically sensitive matter wasn't barred from the air. It seemed that the mainstream Eagle newscaster's supervisor, tugged at the heartstrings, had received the apparently brilliant idea that this would be fantastic NetV—despite his professional judgment. Today was a day to take risks, he thought as he rubbed the back of his neck, itchy below the shunt.

Curious as that coverage was, at the same moment, his counterpart at DNN felt oddly compelled to show the same footage.

The offices of Propaganda Industries were aghast that the story was shown describing the full implications of the DOD's activity on the mainland. Their CEO knew this was an emergency that needed to be resolved rather forthwith. Contacting their favorite senators and governors, the Propaganda Industry CEO told them that if they didn't immediately censor both Eagle and DNN, their political careers would end precisely today.

These senators and governors pulled their staffs together for an emergency session of unparalleled haste, telling their cabinet that the full extent of the law was required to close both multi-medium news agencies immediately. And that they did. Within twenty-five minutes of the first broadcast, the police in New

York stormed the DNN complex in Times Square, ordering the arrest of their director. Six minutes later, the Eagle building in Los Angeles received a similar platoon of re-diverted police. Their freshly printed warrants atypically charged two rich men with sedition and high treason and called for their broadcasting systems to be interrupted until such a time when trustworthy individuals could take the helm.

Alan Elsmutt Bouquets, the president of slightly more than half the free world (by surface area), had had a growing headache for the past half hour—for obvious reasons. His staff of carefully selected individuals assured the situation under control, he tried to convince himself, but when every single one of their asses was also on the line, he thought it rather problematic that one pair of antsy buttocks might suddenly jump ship and rat out the others, with him at its helm. The second meeting they had in the last twenty minutes assured him that the video had been successfully suppressed. He knew PrimaCore had sent the footage—who else could have?—but why in the world had those two idiots decided to air it? Didn't they know better? This was not election time, not a proper occasion for smear campaigns of any kind, especially any that humiliated *him*. Perhaps nothing linked the black ops to his bureau. At least he hoped nothing did.

But trying to hide such information was tantamount to screaming for attention. Thus, it was then that the lesser-known but still prolific news agencies—GMA, Sunset, and Western-Times—also uploaded the censored footage on their websites. But now there was more. The full-length content showed not only the black helicopters firing at a civilian hospital complex but also MI Specialist Petterson recounting the full extent of the Army's desire to militarize the supposedly only-for-pharmaceutical pain surrogate spine shunts.

The shot zoomed in on Petterson's clean face as he made his confession. "Bouquets himself was there at the meeting," he said to someone off camera. "He signed the freaking papers."

Another angle showed the back of a different soldier's head and the shunt in the back of his neck, but it revealed nothing beneath it because there was no body below to show.

Other footage, edited by an Oscar-worthy team, appeared of Keneth Mansfield talking directly to Petterson and two colleagues, but for the first time in the history of his public appearances, Mansfield looked angry as hell. He shook his fist. "You're talking about enhancing, weaponizing . . ." The military trio looked nonplussed and then departed—without a handshake.

Manne had told Keneth to avoid direct contact with any of them because they could have infiltrated some type of dermal toxin, despite her security team's best efforts to detect.

From what the viewers could see, obviously no deal had been bartered. Next, the footage showed the face of the carefully identified Corporal Mathews, looking quite worried as he exited PrimaCore's lobby. Billions of people watched on their NetVs, poly-techs, onboard seat monitors, tablets, dashboards, canoes, and computers.

Bouquets called frantically for another meeting to address this new issue. Those worthless sons a' bitches had told him that all this was under wraps. "Mansfield's out for my neck," he told the first pale-faced assistant who entered his office. She was followed by her team of attorneys, who did not look particularly eager despite their quintuple-digit hourly fees. "I know Paul from Sunset. He wouldn't fuck me in the ass like this. I was at his sister's wedding, for Christ's sake. That Mansfield, even with all the breaks I gave him, connived against me. He paid them off. He paid 'em all." He shoved the stack of simulated-paper documents onto the floor.

* * *

From an anonymous source, Samantha, to her fortune, had received a rather lucrative piece of full-length footage ten minutes before airtime. Her apps were ready and, as demand increased, so did her price. It was time to reap the rewards, for at that hour the following day, the video would have been copied and downloaded so many times it would be worthless. She sent her people into full upload mode as she watched her bank account crank up like videogame currency. But this was real; it was gold. And the more the powers-that-be and their bots tried to delete, suppress, close down, and bar access, the more requests she received. If only they had tried to brush it off as non sequitur, it might all have been averted. But how the hell did it get shown on the hour of misinformation, 6 p.m. primetime on DNN and Eagle?

* * *

Another curious coincidence was that certain neuro-idents, upon seeing the video montage, received a startling jolt of nationalistic pride. They normally wouldn't have cared in the least, but that day, knowing their very government—which existed to protect them—was instead targeting its own civilians, was just too much to bear. In the capital, a hundred or so pain surrogate members took to the streets and marched directly to the Capitol Building. Highly improbable as it was, those conglomerating individuals—soon to be mob—all lived within a few kilometers of the House of Representatives.

Bouquets was beyond embarrassed as his legal team, instead of suggesting a way out, opted to schedule a press conference where he would address the commonwealth to announce his resignation. "Better than being impeached," one of the lawyers, another pain surrogate member, had said. Bouquets swallowed his pride and, out of character, instead became calm and relaxed. Suddenly, he thought resignation wasn't such a bad idea. So, his staff began writing his heartfelt speech.

"But not before I get General McStevens' resignation letter— or arrest, whichever comes first," he said.

"The chain of command will be quite perturbed by that, sir," one of his military attachés replied.

"Ah, fuck it. The entire DOD is on standby till this thing blows over," Bouquets said. Then he felt curiously happy about that too. "Let my successor worry about it." Throughout his career, he had been an obstinate proponent of a stronger defense budget, but now he felt that had been his worst mistake. "Write this down, you bunch of quacks. My last order as president of this wonderful commonwealth is this: We surrender." Then he laughed uncontrollably and walked out of the office. Bouquets felt fantastic; the best he'd felt in years. The staff awkwardly looked at each other, not knowing what to do. There weren't any flowcharts for such an incident.

* * *

The Eastern military, amused by the embarrassing news articles that were appearing over their media outlets, asked their superiors whether they should attack. The standing order was to hold position, as it had been for decades, but this was their chance. So, their commander asked his commander, who discussed it at length with his superior, who said it wasn't his call. The generals were to discuss the situation with the Senate and the House of Representatives.

President Squattuso, Bouquets' doppelganger from Myanmar, happily received several high-ranking generals for an unscheduled meeting in St. Petersburg. They told him at length what their plan for attack would be and how the logistics of border expansion would be carried out. Squattuso nodded politely as he listened, then shook his head. "No."

The generals wondered how they had failed to show the imperative value of capitalizing on this crucial moment of political turmoil in the West. Didn't Squattuso see it too? Indeed, he had, but Squattuso, who had gained popularity for his zero-tolerance, zero-compromise against the West, felt peculiarly compassionate that day about the unfortunate circumstances that had been brought to light, disrupting the political stability of his neighbors on the other side of the world. He had always held a firm hand, but perhaps that had been a mistake.

"But they've violated the Paris Convention."

"Perhaps in spirit but not to the letter," President Squattuso replied. The highly over-decorated general stood silent, his jaw hanging. "Besides, gentlemen, we were also investigating the possibility of using the surrogate arrays to our benefit. They simply beat us to it—and lost their credibility by doing so. In fact, I don't think it's time to press forward. I think it's time to offer them a ceasefire." The military men were chilled to the core.

"This could be an opportune time to write the official armistice," one well-dressed assistant added. As coincidental as it may have seemed, he drew the very file from his briefcase. A representative from PrimaCore, a woman with the curious name of Manne, had helped him edit the text two weeks earlier during a surreptitious meeting while he was in Washington City. The lobbyist had always been a proponent of peace, but he was skeptical that their House of Representatives would even read such a bill. She had told him to be patient.

Squattuso amicably patted that lobbyist's back and told him he would be happy to read it, and he meant it. He felt so relaxed. Like a huge burden had been lifted from his shoulders, like that time he had rented the entire brothel to himself. Besides, the general's presentation had seemed so dull and dreary. But peace, that could be huge. In fact, if he pushed this further—and now he certainly felt like he could—he would be remembered in history as the man who spearheaded the unification, the one who formed the one-world nation where everyone lived in equality and peace. Right then and there, he was certain that was his destiny.

"The time is now," he whispered. He was certain, and he knew the populace would eternally remember his wisdom. Statues would be erected across the globe, and his name would be praised for centuries to come. He had to—it would be difficult, he had to admit—but he knew it was necessary. Such creative energy flowing through him. *My pain surrogate feed to boost my self-esteem is working great today,* he thought.

* * *

All this hustle and bustle made Sam forget her growing worry as to why Brent hadn't replied. He had to have seen all this. But one thing was clear to her as she zoomed in on a single four-second shot that interested her more than any other frames. XP had made the headlines too. The apparently outraged Corporal Mathews had killed an innocent young man named Francis Godin, or at least his gun had. Apparently, the unfortunate young man had inadvertently discovered the military's secret Medusa project. Thus, he had to die. The forensic ballistics were shown next to the crime scene of a blurred-face corpse riddled with bullets. It was definitely XP. Sam knew by the tattoo on his exposed shoulder. "That crazy bitch," she whispered, because finally, she knew. That paramilitary blond had used Sam's unofficial operation to disseminate her trigger information.

During the time Mathews and his scapegoated colleagues were palavering with Brent's dad, Manne must have X-ray scanned and digitally recorded every angle and groove of Corporal Mathews' sidearm and barrel. Then metallurgists and gunsmiths had painstakingly reproduced the piece to micrometer perfection, and they probably did so without question when paid adequately. Such money granted her more than enough capacity.

* * *

"Where's Keneth?" Dorothy asked Manne after using her personal ID codes to open his office. Manne stood by a large improvised computer terminal hooked up to loads of monitors that showed live news broadcasts from across the globe, security cameras in indiscernible locations, and several of what she recognized as neuro-ident profile graphs. When Manne turned, Dorothy saw that she looked gaunt, like she had aged tremendously.

"He's indisposed," she said after a long pause. She turned back to the computer, took a deep breath, and closed her eyes. "Didn't you resign?" Manne's voice was quiet, distant.

"Keneth never ratified it, and you'd only know if you were eavesdropping."

"I might have forgotten to turn off audio-captors."

Dorothy sighed as she walked to where Manne had inaugurated her control platform. "I never should have installed your shunt."

"But you did."

"Where's Keneth?"

"He's safe, but he can't talk right now."

"You took this too far. Do you know what you've done?"

"I know exactly what I've done," Manne said. "What had to be done."

"It's out of control. Bouquets is resigning, the Senate is in chaos, there're riots at the House of Representatives."

Manne shook her head, then turned toward her. "No, Dor, for the first time in the long history of humanity, things are finally being resolved. The war will end, and the world will finally be united."

Dorothy immediately recognized her population psychology algorithms running at high bandwidth on one of the monitors. "It was designed to predict, to understand, not to influence," she said. She stood and looked at the long stream of data with professional detachment, then shook her head. "But you modified it. The intelligence enhancements you received were perhaps the most dangerous of all. We should've known you would modify your own array."

"Theory, semantics," Manne whispered, almost out of breath. "They never really satisfied me."

"Intelligence applied onto intelligence. You must have grown exponentially more acute."

"With speed, strength, and highly synergized neuromuscular activation. Neurological activity approaching maximum capacity of the synapse. I calculate my CNS activity as fifteen times faster than following the first cognitive enhancement." Manne had never been a slouch to begin with, Dorothy remembered.

"Taking something from each person in those pods." Dorothy shook her head. "We should have stopped this experiment long ago."

"Pushing their counterparts took a toll on the subsurrogate systems. The feedback overloads were redirected back to the pods only, so not a single person on the mainland suffered."

Dorothy was surprised Manne had been able to accomplish that, but she had surpassed Dorothy in almost every way imaginable, exceeded the cognitive and physical capacity of perhaps every single human being on Earth.

She stopped her mind from wandering and grabbed Manne's arm. "You have to stop." When she turned, Dorothy thought she might have crossed the line and was about to be thrown across the room, but all Manne did was pull away.

"You should be proud. It performed like we thought. Besides, my work's almost finished," Manne said. She looked tired. Her skin was clammy, and her hair had lost its luster. "Look," she said, pointing to a screen in the lower-left corner.

Rioters were inside the House of Representatives. Spray paint covered the walls, art canvases had been destroyed, and tables overturned. Three dozen people had erected a barricade to block the doors and were trashing the place as much as possible. One person was trying to light the flag on fire, but the material seemed oddly flame resistant. Then, like a switch had been flicked, they all stopped, looking at one another in confusion. They knew what they had done, but suddenly, they had no more appetite for it. So, they made their way to their makeshift barrier and began dismantling it. Another pod went offline in Azalea-ri, two more in Chile, and another in their facility in South Africa.

"They felt what they had to feel when the time was right. I've been coordinating the process, subcategorizing the surrogates into mindset pools, which are stimulated in unison, in coordination with the media broadcast. Each of those thousands of carefully selected individuals." Manne's eyes were drooping. "Whenever key individuals became a surrogate member in our massive neuro-ident list, I had them conjugated to another pod inside one of our holding labs. Thus, at their other end, they became connected to me."

Dorothy saw the modulator, an app holding a large scroll-bar where Manne had selected whichever group needed to be stimulated or inhibited. Then she made them feel what they needed to feel. "But how can you maintain the feed, maintain the emotional flow? We never could reproduce any neuro-ident profile using AI. Can't start a circuit from nowhere. The uncertain nature of never knowing which neuron would fire made it impossible for a computer to duplicate."

"Stochastic neurosynaptic prediction algorithms."

"But that's imp—"

"The formula is over there. Basically, I locked them in a steady stream of whatever it is I first sent to them, whatever they needed to receive. Kept it activated until they were finished with their tasks. Their brains couldn't tell the difference. It works in practice, but it's not perfect. All those pods I lost . . ."

"Pods you lost? There were people in them."

"No one innocent."

Dorothy knew she couldn't argue with Manne. She hardly could before her procedure, and it was impossible now. But it paled in comparison to the hundreds of thousands who died every year through warfare, so she knew her own arguments were hardly valid. Looking over the controls, Dorothy couldn't even guess the function of the numerous other apps.

"So, you twisted my population psychology software to control the minds of thousands of people around the world."

"And through them, millions more."

"You have to stop."

"It's not finished. There's still a significant possibility that someone unfavorable will replace Bouquets."

"They'll stop us. The military already attacked, yet you continue with this . . . psycho-digital takeover of the world. Maybe they had reason to come here in armed helicopters. Did you ever think of that? They came here because of you. I know they did."

Manne turned to Dorothy and grabbed her by the shoulders. She brought her in and kissed her deeply, then pulled back and looked into her eyes. "Keneth is the most beloved man in the world right now. They saw him stand up to the military. He didn't want the system to be used nefariously, and he risked everything to defend his ideals. He will be nominated after the unification. It has already been set in motion. It's almost irrevocable now."

"That's never something he wanted."

"And that is why he deserves it most."

"He only wants to stop suffering, like I did. And so did you. Don't you see you've crossed the line?"

"This *is* about suffering. The world is suffering. Injustice, inequality, overpopulation. Ecosystems are dying, mass faunal extinction. Everything is falling apart. The planet is suffering more than anyone cares to admit. And this—this is my gift to the world."

"We all wanted to change things, and we all thought we could, but not like this," Dorothy said. "We wanted people to make the new world for themselves. But not this anthill psychology. You're no better than the military. You're using what we created to remake the world in your image, Manne, just like them. You're no better. No matter your intentions."

She turned quickly, and Dorothy thought she would finally receive the blow, but Manne toppled and then fell. Dorothy grabbed her, trying to ease her fall. She realized just how much weight Manne had already lost through overexertion. Dorothy eased her onto the marble floor and reached for a button on Keneth's desk.

"Yes, boss?" a voice answered.

"It's Dr. Lundquist. Send an EMT unit to Mansfield's office right now."

CHAPTER 22

——

The two in the car looked at the youthful, silver-haired girl walking toward the entrance of Sam's secluded offices. She pressed the code, waited, then was invited inside by security personnel.

"You know her?"

Brent sighed. "Yeah, I met her once. Think her name's Jade. Works for my girlfriend."

Thompson had been forced to change his plans. Due to the political maelstrom that seemed to originate from the PrimaCore Institute, he no longer thought that Brent could get him inside. More police units were there than anywhere else in the city, along with firetrucks, paramedics, and a range of construction crews. The place was locked down tighter now that the police knew the military might illegally attack again—or so they had been told. The entire main entrance was off limits, and the patient-care wing was closed to civilians indefinitely. The entire perimeter was crawling with newscasters and lines of PC reps with legal degrees to answer their questions.

Brent, his poly-tech and every other wireless device confiscated, hadn't seen the full-length footage yet, except vicariously through public displays. Without contact to the digital world, he felt more alone than ever. The man who held him never let him venture more than a few meters, and rarely that far. Brent couldn't tell exactly what was going on, and he worried for his

father. He worried for his own sake, and now, after he had reluctantly given the location of Samantha's office, he worried, above
all else, for her.

The last three days had been hell. He was tired—he couldn't
sleep under such duress—and he was tired of being afraid. The
man had cut him again, the large bandage he wore over his belly
now hidden under his black jean overalls. "Exposed navels are
for fags and whores," his captor had said, then ordered him
to change. Watching a guy strip was somewhat gay too, Brent
thought, but he didn't dare argue. He felt that some of the cuts
might be infected, but all the wretched man had done was buy
some bandages from a drive-through pharmacy.

He should have screamed from the back seat then, but he
could barely control the muscles around his mouth. His lips had
parted slightly, but he had not let out even a peep. Brent couldn't
respect himself anymore; he should have stood up to the man
earlier. It would have been better to have died trying to escape
than to help him endanger people he loved. But whatever this
psychopathic old man asked of him, he did it immediately. He
didn't have a will of his own anymore. Better to kill me now,
he thought.

Brent opened the door and hurled the soup—force-fed to
him an hour earlier—onto the wet pavement. The man yanked
him back into the BMW, slamming the door behind him.

"Disgusting. You're revolting."

Brent just stared back without saying how he felt about him.

"In two minutes, we go," the man added, handing him a
napkin left over from their breakfast. "So, hurry up and clean
your filth."

Brent wanted to vomit all over him, but he didn't have anything left. Nor would he have dared. He cursed his weak-ass self.

When the old man had told Brent there would be a change
of plans, Brent knew that no matter what that would be, he
wouldn't like it. Brent had tried to convince him otherwise, that

he still could get them inside the PrimaCore Institute, where Manne would deal with him, or so he hoped. If she couldn't— and Brent couldn't be certain of that either—no one could. The old man wouldn't even consider it after seeing the traffic around the bay. Thus, he had told Brent that if he couldn't get to Mansfield and his slut Lundquist, he would make them come to him. When the man asked Brent where the safest place to go would be, he couldn't think of a lie. The man had loomed his cold steel so sharp and deftly handled that Brent's tongue spoke of its own volition. He had told the man to go there, that Sam's offices were basically his hangout, where Sam ran the business in his stead. Hardly any legal authorities knew where it was located, but Keneth Mansfield did. It was an investment he had granted to his son.

* * *

James pushed his wheelchair up the icy ramp and into the pharmacy. They had evicted him so simply from the hospital. He had no idea what kind of political clusterfuck was taking place for that to have happened, but he had been unstrapped, lifted into a chair, then rolled out to continue with his own inertia, without passport or credits, to discover the true spirit of Eastern generosity.

He was almost certain he was in Russia, but since he couldn't read Cyrillic, he could be anywhere from Kamchatka to Stockholm. But he thought closer to Georgia for reasons he couldn't quite pinpoint. After spending the last twenty-four hours as a shell-shocked war veteran who couldn't speak, he found very little promise of advancement in such a career.

But now he was compelled with a new purpose. For the last two days, his counterpart had been quiet, pensive, waiting, but now he was back in action. James's dull, throbbing pain started to become sharp and acute, his rage spiking like lightning strikes. The dark pain came not only through his wounds but also from that dark heart across the world. And now, fresh out of pills, he had few alternatives.

After handing an old lady her laxatives, the pharmacist watched as James wheeled himself in. Head slumped to the side, unable to support the metallic cage fastening his jaw together, James knew he must look like he had been struck by a truck, then passed through a meat grinder, and dipped in a lava pit. When the pharmacist read the prescription slip, he didn't seem worried about whether James might be an addict. He seemed absolutely certain that James needed those pills. Even when James displayed anxious impatience and told the pharmacist, in English, that he needed those pills "right the fuck now," the pharmacist didn't procrastinate.

But the pharmacist did frown when James received the bottle. Pellets passing through missing teeth like coins in a slot machine, he immediately dry swallowed much more than the recommended daily dose.

James was in pain, true, but the pain he felt wasn't fully his own. He wanted to stop the hurting, prevent the rage and hate, cut the piercing poison directly at its source. Cobalt/Flinch turned the chair abruptly, then wheeled himself out with impressive momentum.

* * *

Sam smiled and spread her arms wide when the elevator opened. "It's our most lovable coprolaliac."

"Hi," I said, entering the leisure area. "So, my expertise is foul language now. Oh, I like it, don't get me wrong, but I think I'll focus on clothing design, thanks." I took another few steps into the central area and stared at the monitors. "You weren't kidding about big news coming."

"Jade, you have no idea," Sam said. "The provisional government ratified the armistice. And most of the turnaround seems to favor PrimaCore interest. Coincidental, very coincidental."

"They released the black ops video?" I asked, having followed the story as it had unfolded from the plane's first-class seatback monitor. My return had been mostly hitch-free, with only the overnight flight delayed. Otherwise, I had an easy trip; no visit into the room devoid of human rights with the many probing fingers of latex.

"Most definitely," she said. "But the transition has been smooth—too smooth. I'm not quite sure how they could have orchestrated it so precisely. The logistics of it all are uncanny."

"Tapping the Main," I speculated. "You remember what Duri told me?"

Sam stood, nodding, but she looked distracted.

"What is it?" I asked.

She shook her head. "I'm not sure, but you might be right, Jade. It's just that with this political salad toss, they'll have larger fish to fry, so Brent should be able to come back. But I haven't heard from him since before all this."

"Unusual?"

"Very. But it's not impossible he's found a new drug or some chick to binge upon. But with all this," she said, raising her arms, "he should have had some sardonic comment to add. It's just unlike him."

I shrugged while Blood-Red brought Cojone some data disks. Sam thanked her, then they both turned toward the opening elevator doors. The stainless steel parted, and, speak of the devil, Brent was standing there in the middle.

Sam gasped when she saw the two bodies sprawled on the floor with patterns of arterial spray behind them and a taller, much older person clad in black holding a long knife against her man. "Not under the best circumstances," she whispered.

"Everyone get out," Brent said.

"No, no, no," the man said, twisting the point of the knife into Brent's neck, a thick ripple of blood painted a red streak. "Everyone stay right where you are."

They shouldn't have gotten past the cameras, I realized. Unless Brent had, or someone had made him, deactivate the system—without Sam realizing it. The two guards had appeared to be well-trained goons, but they mustn't have fared well in close quarters against the knife-wielding elder with the clerical collar.

"Who are you?" Sam demanded.

"I am the harbinger of the reckoning," the man said.

More empty philosophy. I sighed. The old man looked at me but then turned to Sam.

"Tell them," he whispered into Brent's ear.

"He wants to get Mansfield and Lundquist here. Then he told me he would let you go." The knife twisted again. "Then he *will* let you go," Brent said, correcting himself.

"I wouldn't know how to reach him," Sam argued. I was willing to bet that if she didn't know offhand, she could find out in a hurry.

"Sign into my phone app," Brent said. "His personal office number is the Chronos profile."

Some of the half dozen employees looked at Brent, surprised he had the means to contact the owner of PrimaCore. I thought the profile was quite fitting. Sam looked into Brent's eyes and nodded slightly, then looked around. There were two men wearing suits. One, I vaguely recalled, was named Alex. The other I hadn't met. Blood-Red stood to Sam's left, and the smaller girl with the pink frills observed quietly from a few meters behind. They had all come out to investigate the commotion, then waited to hear what the old man wanted. No one looked like a hero.

The man holding the knife told Sam to call Mansfield from within that room. She did as he asked, first going into her boyfriend's profile—the passwords she apparently knew—and then dialing Chronos. The speakerphone system rang as everyone waited tensely, but no one answered. Then the line cut out. "No one's home," Sam said, her lips quivering.

The old man thought for a moment. "You," he said, pointing the bloody tip toward Blood-Red. "Disrobe."

"It's your tech," Brent said as she stood there, staring. "He wants you out of tech."

Blood-Red sighed, then dropped her well-equipped leather jacket, which clanged loudly to the floor. She unbuckled her belt, pulled her pants below her hips, then let them fall. She walked out of the denim and stood in front of him, wearing only her panties and a silk shirt, arms open invitingly.

"Over there," the man said, then turned to the suits. "Now you two." Wearing only their briefs, they joined Blood-Red in the timeout corner. Pink-Frills was next. She removed her shawl, rubbed her hands sensually on the silk surrounding her torso, then lifted her skirt to show her bare buttocks. The old man groaned like he had been stabbed in the testicles but then pointed her to join the rest.

Sam asked the old man what he wanted to do with them. "I do as God wills," he said. Cojone stripped to a classy bra-and-panty set, almost like she had planned to be seen in her underwear that day. That left only me.

"You," he said.

I simply stood there. The old man waved the knife like it was a wand, but it didn't compel me with magic.

"Jade," Sam whispered.

Instead, I walked toward the old man and his captive.

Like many before him, he looked at me like I was crazy, but he could see I wasn't afraid. He shoved Brent violently to the rest of the group, where he stumbled and was caught by Alex. Sam immediately took him, appraising his condition.

The man grabbed me by the wrist, pulled me to him, spun me around, and in less than a second, held me as he had held Brent. "Do what I say, and you won't get hurt," he whispered.

"You are nothing," I replied coolly.

"What?" he said with as much shock as surprise.

"I said, you are nothing. Worthless. You sack of shit." I said it calmly, whispering it like a secret that only he should hear.

He was taken aback and almost released his grip, but he steadied himself. As if he were determined to teach me respect, he passed the blade deftly around my neck, releasing a streak lined with crimson pearls. Many screamed. I groaned but didn't stiffen. I turned slowly, my slender neck dripping blood, while he hardly held me with any strength at all anymore. Face to face, I met his fiery eyes. "You don't need to make everyone feel as empty as you."

He grabbed my collar and raised the knife above his head. "You should learn some reverence, my dear."

"I'm not afraid of you," I whispered, my lips close to his. Indeed, I wasn't, but Dae-Won was probably trembling.

* * *

On the same continent as Dae-Won, a wheelchaired veteran wobbled, but the chair held him up. James felt the pulses of rage coming and going like the tide. But he was making the hurricane serene again with the opioid void. Limply, he raised his hand to swallow as many pills as he could. He could hardly feel his limbs anymore. The traffic flew past at speeds faster than he could perceive. Pedestrians avoided him like discarded rubbish.

* * *

Frederick wondered how he should feel about this girl. Jade was as strong-willed and determined as him. It was like God worked within her too, her purpose just as unflinching. He could only kill her, he realized, but like Jesus on the cross, he could not break her. How could he kill her, an innocent woman, who didn't even fight back? Thompson felt oddly impotent, and the steady hand with which he held the knife started to shake.

"I see through you," the silver-haired girl said.

"God acts through me," he said through clenched teeth.

"I met God. He's the same as nil. Brought out of insignificance by the mind of a small Korean man. The god within you is you, and even *it* has no real power here."

"Blasphemy," he said, raising the knife higher, tugging at her collar. But she only gazed, staring death in the eyes as she held her composure. She should obey, but why didn't she? The demons that had made themselves at home in his mind weren't urging him. In fact, they weren't there at all. All he could think of was his unfinished work, getting the revenge he wanted. "Where's Mansfield?" he yelled at Sam. It was apparent that she was Brent's girlfriend—and the one who seemed to be running the place. She nodded and tried the phone app once again.

But this one in front of him, ready to be killed without opening herself to God's love, was what perturbed him the most. Her courage—or foolishness—was awesome. No one had ever stood up to him like this. No one had ever withstood his will so stoically.

"The last person who hurt me got his balls chopped off. Now he lives the rest of his life as a vegetable inside a pod," the girl added.

She was nuts; she had to be. Wrong in the head. He had to kill her now before he lost power over the rest.

Repeating his girlfriend's advice, Brent tried to convince Jade to be quiet. Thompson looked from Brent to Jade and back to Brent's tall girlfriend. He gripped the knife tighter and knew what he had to do.

But his determination wavered, his certainty troubled. Why wasn't God's will as crystal clear as it used to be? She was standing right in front of him, but she still wasn't afraid. Her lips were almost touching his, and she wasn't pulling away. Lured by the flesh, he couldn't help but be distracted. It must be so, he told himself. He had to kill her now.

"Do it," she dared him, so close her breasts brushed against his chest.

He couldn't find the strength to push her back. No force, holy or otherwise, remained within him.

"I told you, you are nothing," she said, her voice even softer than before, like a mother teaching her child.

This girl, he realized, had more power than he did, had power over him. So beautiful, he thought. But her eyes looked right through him. She saw nothing holy, only disgust and contempt.

She kneed him in the groin while shooting her hands to his wrist, trying to pry the weapon loose. Compelled by urgency instead of purpose, he regained his wits and threw her to the floor. He was still much stronger, he realized as the paralyzing pain swelled between his legs. He had been wooed by a sly feminine mind. Rage found him once again. Thompson stumbled, then lunged at her.

* * *

Paying no attention to those he had stripped, his focus was only on me. And that's when the mad Pink-Frills decided to act. I noted that the woman's ballerina costume had veiled her core strength and abilities as she tackled the lunatic from behind. After her came Alex, then the other half-naked suit.

Certain that I was sending Dae-Won into stupefied panic, I pushed myself to a sitting position and watched as the three barely managed to wrestle the strong old man. I thought I should help too, but that also felt like nothing of consequence. But when I saw both men, each grabbing an arm, the next horrible imagery was for Duri to feel.

Pink-Frills, sitting atop his chest, had gotten ahold of the knife. With a banshee shrill that would have sent anyone running, she stabbed the old man with incessant repetition. Blood gushed over the rugs and onto the pool table. Jagged bone-crunching thuds repeated over and over until the two men pulled her away. They told her that was enough, that he was dead. When the knife clattered to the floor, there was no question about the priest's status. I stared at the spreading puddle of blood and bone.

Not far away from me, I saw the other three still huddled together: Sam, unable to hold back tears, was holding Brent while Blood-Red consoled her. One of the men shook his head, trembling slightly while keeping his balance against the wall. The one named Alex found his poly-tech and was undoubtedly calling the proper authorities. Pink-Frills went to change her crimson-stained tutu.

Deciding that this new career path wasn't really for me, I thought of a new turtleneck I would design that very evening— away from Sam and all this spy shit. A tad too much for my taste, I was forced to admit.

* * *

Like clearing a bowel movement, James felt the cancer within his mind fade to oblivion. The hate and malignancy that had perme-ated his life since his shunt had been installed stopped. Like a taut string finally broken, the tremendous pressure and burden that had afflicted him, which had permitted Cobalt to be born, was gone. Only Flinch remained. But no, he knew better than that. He had never been Flinch either. He was James, a sensitive, compassionate person who didn't want to kill. Flinch had only been a facade for him to hide behind.

James pushed his wheelchair toward the train terminal. Now he had a real purpose; rather, he'd found his innate purpose, which had been sapped from him to feed the other's will. He knew he had much to atone for, much work to do to help others heal. There had to be a line of work where he could convince those confused people how to love each other, how to under-stand beyond conflict, to look past the hatred that was so care-fully impregnated for generations into the mindset of each com-monwealth about the other. He knew it was time to go home.

CHAPTER 23

—

Karl sat on the couch with Moose, Stacey snug between them. She watched as he brushed off the scratch marks where Moose had undoubtedly tried to pry open the drawer in their absence.

"Don't you have anywhere else to go?" she asked Moose politely.

Moose shrugged as he rolled a marijuana cigarette.

"She means get lost, prick," Karl said.

"Fine, fine. I'll leave you two lovee-birds alone."

"Come visit on the weekend, but not for drugs, okay." Stacey said.

Moose looked at her like he couldn't understand English. "Yeah, sure." Karl knew that if it weren't for drugs, Moose might never visit—not that that would be such a horrible thing.

Trailing smoke on his way out, he closed the door. Then Stacey turned to Karl. "Crazy couple of days."

"Yeah, pretty crazy," he said, about to open the drawer to get his stash.

"You don't need that right now," she said.

He hesitated. "Yeah, maybe not right now." Karl looked at her from head to toe. Her arm was in a sling, but he noticed how loose her uniform was. She would need to get a smaller size once more. Her body was getting nicer, so he slid his hand under her shirt. She kissed him back but didn't get carried away just yet.

"I felt so mad I wanted to punch our president right on the nose," she said.

He nodded. She snuggled up to him.

"Officer Jeffries was arrested today," she then said. "It seems he was laundering drug money for Eye at the same bank I upped the protection fee. Jeffries had been tipping-off Eye, so that's why the detectives on the case never got anything on him. But you know what? Eye came in with a plea bargain, that he would 'Fess up his accomplices in trade for a lenient sentence.' After talking with Jeffries sometime after our visit, that Eye . . . somehow, believed there was a much bigger investigation going on than what Jeffries knew about, meaning that Jeffries was about to get caught too. Something or other pushed Eye's paranoia over the edge it seemed. So 'To get the spooks off his back' he gave himself to Boston Police."

He nodded in surprise, not too sure what to make of it. Karl then sat back and sighed. He couldn't go on like this. "Stacey, there's something I have to tell you." She waited with wide eyes. Then he did; he told her everything. How he had discovered her, compelled her, manipulated her to get what he wanted.

At first, her face was blank, and he thought she would get mad, dump him, beat him, shoot him, or all of the above. But when he was done, her lips twisted into a smile. "Of course I knew." He shook his head and waited for her to continue. "Since a few weeks ago, I knew we were perfect neuro-ident pairs," she said, "so I decided to test it. Every single time you reacted like I would have without the shunt. So, I realized you were my pain surrogate. Like winning the lottery, right? I knew I could get you to do whatever I wanted, and it worked." She smiled even wider, her eyes bright and happy.

He stared at her in shock. "No way."

"Yeah, it seemed too coincidental, so I realized you already knew. You had to know. Figured you paid hackers. But, being a woman—and if you had more experience with us, you might have realized this—we're much better at getting inside men's heads. To keep the upper hand, I knew I had to let you think you had control of it all."

"But the money, the drugs, the gun—"

"Bah. Every officer does that. Most do far worse, like Jeffries, and they distrust those who follow the rules to the letter. It was nothing, really. But I knew you would think you held me by the strings after that." She laughed. "I might have to answer some weird questions at my old partner's trial, but we'll see."

"And you got me to do . . .?"

"No one's ever been so attentive to my womanly needs, dear," she said, then kissed his forehead.

"Jesus," he whispered, then reached deeper in her uniform shirt. "What a pair," he said and cupped her breast.

* * *

Dorothy sat in her boss's chair, holding her drowsy head. She had lost track of time, but the control center was still buzzing with numerous activity reports that only Manne could have understood.

Keneth, still supposedly upstairs, was locked behind a door that only he or Manne could open. Dorothy had tried, to no avail. It wasn't a time to get workers up there to help her break in, not with everything going on outside. She sighed. She didn't know what to do. The phone rang once more, but it wasn't for her to answer.

She heard a faint rumbling, then turned to see the door to Keneth's private penthouse open. Keneth leaned groggily against the doorframe. His beard was many days old, and his suit was rumpled over his chest. He pulled at a long IV tube that came out of his rolled-up sleeve. "Where is she?" he asked.

"Manne's dead." Dorothy gave him the non-sugar-coated version of the news. "She knew the risks."

He nodded, looking both relieved and full of sorrow. "What's going on?" He looked through the window at the bustling activity below. "Tell me everything."

Dorothy recounted all she knew, as best as she understood it. The attack, the video, the politics, and what she thought this large machine, newly built inside his office, did. Sometime after she had answered his questions, he stood where Manne had and tried to understand the complex algorithms with their esoteric mega-computer data scrolls.

She had drugged him, he said, and placed him upstairs under a similar cocktail that she had devised for those in the pods, keeping him alive with intravenous nutrients. He had woken after he metabolized the last dose of sedatives.

"What was her turning point?" he asked. "The cognitive enhancements?"

"That initially permitted her to continually enhance herself, yes."

"And she tapped into thousands of people?"

"At least twenty-two thousand, as far as I can tell. But I still don't understand half of this. I'm afraid to touch anything, really." They stood in silence as they watched the system dish out loads of alphanumerical characters, displaying neuro-ident waves of various surrogates from around the world. "Before her breakdown, I believe from massive excitotoxicity, she sent her own feeds to those she desired to stimulate. But now, without her, I really don't know."

Keneth had heard enough. He started pulling out monitors and tearing away random cables attached in configurations that neither he nor Dorothy would ever remember. She tried to stop him, arguing that Manne could have advanced the field of neuroscience an entire decade with only this device, but he didn't care. Hardware cracked as he flung it to the marble floor.

"She wanted you to be president," Dorothy said, trying to calm him. "She said you would be adored by the entire world."

He laughed cynically. "It seems I am forever cursed with a positive public image. No matter what I do, I come out clean and more beloved than before."

"Come now," she said. "You're a good, honest person." Despite his reluctance, she knew he would be a great world leader if given the chance.

"I'm selfish and egotistical," he said when the device was sufficiently dismantled. "I do what serves my desires. It wasn't all about helping people."

"You still helped millions."

"Helped? We alleviated the debilitating illness of a few thousand, sure, but I don't think we helped the rest any. In fact, we enabled them to be the worst versions of themselves."

"That's not true."

"You said it yourself years ago. How did you put it? 'We lost perspective when desire overruled necessity.' That was what you said."

She shook her head. Maybe she had said that, but that wasn't important now.

"I'm not a good person, Dorothy," he continued, walking out of the office as she followed. "Didn't you resign?" he asked, looking back.

"You . . . you haven't ratified it yet."

"Well, after today, you won't need me to."

"What are you going to do?"

"After my son was born," he said, ignoring her question, "not long after I was starting to get the big money returns, I couldn't keep my dick in my pants."

She blushed and felt a tinge of regret, for she had known him intimately then.

"I was full of desires and so full of power that I thought I could get away with anything," he said while holding the glass door for her. "Women, drugs, orgies, doing drugs on women during orgies . . . whatever I wanted." They walked down a long, empty corridor. "But my wife . . ."

Dorothy remembered Eydis. Brent's mother had looked much like Dorothy. And Manne. And most of the other women working inside the high-security zones. "I loved her more than anything. But she wasn't the same after that. I pushed her over the edge." He paused, looking at his tech. "Brent texted that he's okay now. I wonder why? But I'm glad to hear it." Keneth resumed his path to the core.

She sighed. "It wasn't your fault she took her own life. Manne's death isn't your fault either."

He turned suddenly. "It was. And it is." Keneth stood in front of a large metallic door and pressed his hand on an indiscernible panel built into it. After he was scanned and identified, the door slid open like an ancient tomb that hadn't been visited in eons. The sterile atmosphere within the cyclopean chamber that housed the mega-computer smelled of warm ozone, making it hard to breathe. Save for half a handful of highly qualified technicians, the room was off limits. Dorothy herself had never stepped inside. Dim red lights painted the rows of stacked processors as far as she could see.

"You couldn't have known," she argued.

"There was a time when our technology could've helped her, but I didn't. I had the power to save her, but instead I chased fleeting highs. I ignored her difficulties, her problems with intimacy when she was depressed, her lack of libido, and her thoughts of suicide. I could've helped by giving her a shunt. But I couldn't see beyond my dick. When she was too tired or wasn't in the mood, I went out and fucked someone else—you maybe. I don't remember."

She stopped in shock, shook her head, then followed. It wasn't about her or even them. Dorothy's relationship with Keneth had matured to what it was. They weren't a "couple," but they hadn't wanted anything more. She pressed onwards; she had to tell him that things had turned out for the best, but she didn't really believe that either.

"Don't you see the vicious cycle I put her through?" he asked. She realized that he also hadn't bathed since Manne had taken over the world. She felt greasy and disheveled herself. "I destroyed her life, Dor."

She didn't know what to say. She always thought that maybe she had contributed to Eydis's suicide. But that was a pain she had learned to live with over the years. It had made her a stronger, better person, or so she tried to convince herself. "And even if you did?" she asked, changing the subject.

Surprised, Keneth turned to her, but he had arrived at his destination. "I don't have the right to be adored." He looked over the mega-computer controls and found the lever.

"You can't do this," she said, finally realizing what he had in mind. "Think of all the suffering that will ensue."

"This farce has gone on long enough," he said. "Everyone running away from their real problems, no one addressing their issues. They just call in for an adjustment. No one works to better themselves anymore."

Manne did. Dorothy thought sardonically.

"This has to stop," he continued. "People have to face their own minds. They need to improve their lives to feel right, so the world can become a better place, not change their brains to contort their lives, letting this insane, broken world tell them how they should behave. After today, there'll be no question about my public image because there'll no longer be any surrogate program at PrimaCore. Most will despise me, and that's truly what I deserve. But—and you might disagree with me, Dor—giving them back all their pain, joy, fear, insecurities, obsessions, and orientations is probably the best thing that'll ever happen to them."

Dorothy didn't know what to say, but she couldn't help thinking that maybe Manne had wanted everything to happen exactly like it was currently unfolding. Maybe Manne knew Keneth would behave exactly as he was right now. Dorothy hardly understood what had happened, not to mention what would happen next, but Manne did. She had played the world like a video game, and the repercussions would endure for decades to come, for better or worse.

"It's time for us to learn how to handle our own problems," Keneth said. With that, he flung the power control lever to zero. One by one, the rows of motherboard circuitry went black, static tension easing.

Meanwhile outside, all around the world, people fell back into the agonizing sobriety that had once made them who they were.

CPSIA information can be obtained
at www.ICGtesting.com
Printed in the USA
LVHW012053090820
662765LV00001B/83

9 781525 575112